figure; and flying in mortal terror, spread the news. The next night, several agreed to watch. They, too, saw it; and the rumour getting over the country—the many giving courage to the few—every night the vicinity of the pit's mouth was thronged.

"Pshaw!" I managed to exclaim, contemptuously, though my eyes turned timidly to the figure ever by my side. "What country clods, to believe such absurdities!"

In the dining-room I found Susie. She was seated, sewing busily; but looked up on hearing my step. I expected, as usual, to meet her ever welcome smile; but this time, in its place, an expression of unspeakable horror and alarm spread over her features. Trembling violently, she arose and retreated from me; her lips pallid, her soft eyes dilated, her finger extended, as she exclaimed, "Merciful heaven, Sydney, look there!—there, beside you! Who is he? What—what does he want?"

"He! What, Susie?" I articulated, hoarsely. "Girl, are you mad? What do you mean?"

"He standing by you, Sydney, his hand on your shoulder, is Squire Orton, risen from the dead!"

I opened my lips to deny it; I could not—my tongue was paralyzed. She, Susie, then, was the other to whom my uncle was to make himself visible. I felt the guilty, accusing blood rush to my face. My eyes dropped before the clear, inquiring ones of my gentle companion. I stood a criminal confessed. My crime was discovered, and *to her.* I had no power to refute it.

Swiftly Susie moved forward, caught my hand, and gasped, "Sydney!"

It was a simple word, but the tone in which it was uttered was all eloquent of horror, of interrogation. I made an effort; I lifted my eyes; but rapidly averting them, covered my quivering face from sight.

"Oh, my God!" I heard her ejaculate, as she fell prostrate on the floor.

In an instant I was kneeling by her.

"This—this," I c____ _____ed, addressing the spirit, "is *your* work, and you said

It smiled, and fi;  ned away, and, summoning a No sooner had I done so, than an awful fear took possession of me. Supposing, in the moment of recovery, words should escape her lips which would proclaim my guilt to others? The idea had come too late. I could not prevent it now. What did it matter? I began to feel the end must come; what difference, then, if soon or late?

In a dull, lethargic stupor, I waited news of Susie. Each step approaching shook me like a reed.

At last, the door opened, and Susie's own maid entered. As indifferently as I could, I took the note the girl brought, and, dismissing her, eagerly tore off the envelope. The contents ran:—

"Sydney Orton, your secret is safe with me. Heaven forgive you! I hope—I *believe* you must have had some great cause for what you have done; or, rather, that it was occasioned by maddened anger, or accident, for which repentance may atone; but we two must never meet again. By *his* desire, expressed in his will, the Hall is to be my home till I marry. I would fulfil this desire. Heaven knows, I would not fail to do so *now* for worlds! Hence, as no longer I can mix with the household, may I ask permission to keep my present suite of rooms? Illness will be a real excuse, for the blow I have received I shall never recover. Farewell!"

I seized a pen, and, with dim eyes and grateful heart, wrote:—

"Heaven bless you, Susie Mayfield! Each wish of yours shall be complied with. Bless you a thousand times for not quitting this ill-fated house, which your sweet presence alone can purify. Pray for me—save me! One day you shall know all."

After this, I was conscious of a great relief, but also an equally great misery. The Hall was no longer the Hall with Susie away. The report of my possible marriage had got whispered about, and many attributed her seclusion to the fact that she loved me, and her indisposition and retirement were occasioned by the thought of my union with another.

As to that union, I no longer desired it. It tortured me; I seemed to recoil from Florence's brilliant talk and careless laughter. The selfishness of her disposition, which could not sympathize with mine, I began at last to comprehend; and instead, I craved, like a starving man, for Susie's sweet, consoling presence.

But I had gone too far to draw back. I was Squire Orton now; and Florence, as her father, urged on the wedding; so, after a quiet marriage and brief honeymoon, I brought home my bride to the Hall.

Susie, to avoid remarks, occasionally consented to join us in the drawing-room; but the exceeding pallor of her complexion, her wasted features, and depressed manner, were fitting causes for her seclusion. I felt I had murdered her also.

Never once had we two met alone. One day I had encountered her in the corridor, but, with a low, affrighted cry, she had fled from me.

Her aversion, coupled with the ever constant presence of my dead victim, could not fail soon to break down my constitution, and affect my disposition. I grow gloomy—morose.

I had first tried what constant change of society and excitement would do, thereby delighting Florence; but it would not answer—it only made the nights worse, and I adopted seclusion. My wife complained, persuaded, was angry. Each was equally futile. That haunting figure, the remembrance of Susie, and the eager longing for her presence, had made my wife's influence naught. "The longing for her presence?" Yes, too late, I found I loved Susie, with that deep, calm love which never dies.

Florence did not guess *my* secret, but she knew my affection had gone from her; *hers* I had never possessed. She had wished to be mistress of Orton Hall, and she was finding the fruit so coveted, bitter—bitter at the core.

Suddenly a change took place in her—she no longer pleaded nor complained. The expression of her handsome face was stony impassibility. She regarded me curiously, sometimes timidly, and rather avoided my company. I readily fell into her humour, for it suited me.

One morning, on awakening, I found her absent from my side. I looked round, no one was there except my awful attendant.

Since my crime, when sleep, long courted, once quitted me, it never again returned till night; so, rising, I dressed quietly. My wife did not appear, and, gently, I opened the door of her dressing-room. She was there, attired in her customary morning toilette, and writing hurriedly. On becoming aware of my presence, hurriedly she slipped the paper beneath some others, and coldly asked what I wanted.

"Merely to see where you were," I rejoined, turning away.

Shortly after, I heard her bell ring for her maid. Then, in a few moments, the quick beat of a horse's hoofs on the gravel drive attracted me to the window. It was a groom riding from the hall at full speed.

The indifference between Florence and me had reached such a height, that one never interfered in the other's concerns; so I went back to my reading till the hour for breakfast, during which Florence was unusually silent, and I could not fail to perceive was nervously anxious about something; but, occupied with the morning papers, I paid little heed to her.

The meal had nearly concluded, when the footman brought in a card. At the same moment the footman ushered in a Mr. Midhurst—a county magistrate—and two men. Before we could exchange the ordinary salutations, Florence approaching between us, said, in a quick, hurried tone, "Mr. Midhurst, I wrote you this morning that it was in my power to surrender to justice a criminal now at large. I do so. I order—I command the arrest of that man, my husband, for the murder of Squire Orton, whose body you will find in Fellbrig Pit."

I had leaped to my feet, and now stood confounded—aghast.

"Madam!" I cried; "are you aware of what you state?"

"Perfectly, sir!" she answered, frigidly. "What, waking, you deny; sleeping, you have confessed. Night after night," she proceeded, in a kind of triumph, "I have listened, trembling, to the wild sentences uttered in slumber. I have watched the nightmares which have tortured you, till the whole occurrence has been confided to my ear. Yes, the meeting—the cruel blow—the concealment of the body—the ever-haunting presence—*everything*. Murderers, sir, should not marry! Mr. Midhurst, I swear to you, yonder is Squire Orton's assassin! You know whether to arrest him or not."

There must have been that in my quivering face which confirmed her words, for the magistrate, making a sign to the constables, they approached me. I retreated, casting my eyes round for a means of escape. None offered; the windows were locked. So, seizing a chair, I resolved they should not take me easily.

The men had recoiled a step before my threatening attitude, when, abruptly, the door was thrown open, and, as white as death—her lips hueless, her large eyes bright and glistening— Susie Mayfield glided in. Passing by them all, advancing, she threw her arms about me.

"Back!" she then exclaimed, authoritatively, addressing the men. "That woman lies! Sydney Orton is innocent of this deed, and you shall not harm him. If yonder faithless wife denounces him, *I* say he is guiltless. My word is equal to hers. You have no proofs—none. You shall not take him."

Florence laughed mockingly.

"Certainly it is right that *you* should be his shield and champion, Miss Mayfield," she said—"the assassin of your best friend. Mr. Midhurst, I have done *my* duty; do yours, as you please or not."

"Mr. Orton," remarked the magistrate, gravely, "I am deeply sorry for this; but after the accusation has been made in *such* a manner, I cannot pass it over. Men, arrest Mr. Sydney Orton."

As they drew near, Susie's arms tightened about me. Her sweet, scared face was raised to mine; her eyes beamed affection as alarm; while her trembling lips sought vainly to be firm, as she whispered, assuringly, "Do not fear, Sydney; they *dare* not hurt you. I alone know the truth, and they shall kill me before I confess it—they shall, they shall!"

But at the touch of the constables' hands, her courage gave way, and, shrieking, she resisted their efforts to remove her. I imagined they were handling her roughly, and my love took fire, to the forgetting of my own safety; and, like a tiger, I flew upon them. A scuffle ensued; but I was weak in their grasp. They flung me down. My chest heaved with painful gasps. A moment, I lost consciousness. Then the scene had changed. Feeble, languid, I was lying on a sofa, my coat off, a tight bandage about my arm, the lassitude of illness upon me; and, wearily, I raised my heavy lids.

I was yet at the Hall; and on the hearth-rug, by the fire, stood Susie, talking earnestly with my ghostly companion, whose shape was far more solid and defined, while his expression was irritable rather than angry.

"Dear guardian," Susie was saying—she always called him thus—"I beseech you yield to his desire. The trouble, the disappointment may kill him. Oh, consent to his marrying her! She is handsome——"

"Handsome, Susie!" interrupted the spirit, sharply. "Yes, so are you. But you are the good, the kindest, the best; while she is a heartless flirt, I tell you, whose brainless head is full of only her splendid self. She would but marry yonder foolish lad to be mistress of this old place; and I will not, by yielding, have *him* ruined and my money squandered. He is not the first this girl has wilfully driven to despair. She wouldn't look at him if he were penniless; and I took care to let old Bradlaw know to-day that he will never be otherwise, unless I approve his selection of a wife."

"But, guardian, if he love her?" pleaded Susie.

"He does *not* love her; he is only fascinated as a child might be with the brilliant hues of a snake."

"Oh, guardian! Yet, think; she may be all you say; yet the heart is powerful. Love may change her; she may be different to poor Sydney."

"Susie, you are a darling, brave, noble, generous girl, thus to plead this coquette's cause," said the spirit, taking his *protégée*'s face fondly between his hands, and gazing into the brown eyes. "Noble, indeed, when you are aware that you yourself have given your heart and warm affection to my worthless nephew!"

Susie uttered a little cry, and quickly covered her crimson face with her fingers; then, pleadingly looking up, she said, "Dear guardian, who have been to me as a father, why should I conceal the truth from you? But, oh! please, never—never tell him."

"My child, if he has not the eyes to discover the rich gem he might call his, do not think I would debase you by informing the idiot of his blunder. No, let him take his course; I shall take mine. There, do not fret; all danger is passed now; he'll soon be better, since Doctor Gruge has bled him. It was merely a fit."

As he ended, he left the apartment.

Left it, and *my side also*. What! was he not a spirit, after all? Doctor Gruge, and bleeding! Had I been ill? I directed my eyes to my arm; it was bandaged. Had all which had passed been a dream—the visions of delirium? It must be so; in which case, Squire Orton was alive, I was *not* a murderer, neither was I married to Florence Bradlaw.

The inexpressible delight I experienced at these facts was too much for me, and I fainted. When I came to, the lamp had been lowered. Through the withdrawn window curtains, I saw the moonbeams without glittered on vast tracks of snow, while the rich fire-light illumined the apartment within, its red mellow tint throwing out in clear relief Susie's graceful figure as she sat pondering over it. Her face was sad, and I was sure she was weeping. How beautiful, how good she looked! Uncle Orton had said correctly. If with my own eyes I could not discover the priceless gem which might be mine, I deserved none to point it out to my dull brain.

Yes, the delirium had passed, leaving me a wiser man. Of all that had occurred, two events alone were real. First, that Florence Bradlaw had refused me, *because* I was not master of the Hall. Secondly, that Susie Mayfield loved me with her entire heart.

"Dear Susie!" I murmured.

In an instant, a bright smile on her lip, thinking I needed aid, she was by my side. Somehow, I got her hand in mine, and would not let it go. Her bent, averted face showed my touch had at once told my meaning; nevertheless, my lips speedily removed all doubt.

Half an hour after, the entrance of Squire Orton startled Susie away from the sofa. The expression of his features was singular; they displayed satisfaction, blended with a dash of pity. Heightening the lamp, after congratulating me on my recovery, he said, not looking at me, "I have some startling news; I wonder if you can bear it, Syd?"

"Indeed! What is it, uncle?" I asked.

He glanced keenly at me, then added, "Miss Florence Bradlaw eloped this evening with Colonel Harrison."

"Really!" I rejoined, so quietly that it was he who started, not I. "May she be happy."

My wish was not realized, as a case two years later, in the Divorce Court, proved.

Squire Orton regarded me in amaze, which yet further increased, as I added, "Uncle, I am resolved to get married; I trust you will approve of the wife I have selected. Susie, my darling, come to me."

The Squire looked from my extended palm to Susie's blushing cheeks; then striding forward, and clasping my hand as he never yet had clasped it, he exclaimed, "Heaven bless the boy, he has come to his senses at last! Syd, that fit we found you in, lying before a perfectly roasting fire, has saved your life. This shall be a happy Christmas to all of us, my dear, dear lad!"

Need I say it was so? We three saw it in, seated about the glowing logs, my arm around Susie's waist, and listening to the merrily clashing bells, bearing tidings of joy to all hearts, as I told my listeners the story of Squire Orton's Ghost.

CPSIA information can be obtained
at www.ICGtesting.com
Printed in the USA
BVHW070531131122
651571BV00007B/726

THE VALANCOURT BOOK OF
VICTORIAN CHRISTMAS GHOST STORIES

VOLUME TWO

THE VALANCOURT BOOK OF

VICTORIAN CHRISTMAS GHOST STORIES

VOLUME TWO

Edited with an introduction by
ALLEN GROVE

VALANCOURT BOOKS
Richmond, Virginia
2017

The Valancourt Book of Victorian Christmas Ghost Stories, Volume II
First published December 2017

Introduction © 2017 by Allen Grove
This compilation copyright © 2017 by Valancourt Books, LLC

Published by Valancourt Books, Richmond, Virginia
http://www.valancourtbooks.com

ISBN 978-1-943910-88-5 (hardcover)
ISBN 978-1-943910-89-2 (trade paperback)
Also available as an electronic book.

All Valancourt Books publications are printed on acid free paper that meets all ANSI standards for archival quality paper.

Cover by Henry Petrides
Set in Dante MT

CONTENTS

INTRODUCTION

Christmas, Ghosts, and the Nineteenth Century

Henry James's *The Turn of the Screw* (1898) opens with a group of men and women sitting "round the fire, sufficiently breathless" as they share strange tales in an old house on Christmas Eve. In W. W. Jacobs's "Jerry Bundler" (1901), we find half a dozen travelers at an old inn in late December "talking by the light of the fire" as the conversation turns to supernatural tales. At the end of the final story in this collection, the narrator and his friends sit "about the glowing logs" on Christmas day to hear a ghost story. Again and again in the pages of Victorian literature, we find that ghost stories are just as much a part of the holiday as gifts and Father Christmas.

While stories of hauntings, murder, and fear might seem a strange way to celebrate the birth of Christ, the connection isn't as odd as it might at first appear. For one, storytelling was a sure way to find comradery and entertainment during the darkest time of the year. Also, some ghost stories perfectly fit the spirit of the Christmas season. The most famous of them, Charles Dickens's *A Christmas Carol*, reveals that a healthy dose of fear can actually transform one into a better person. Through his interactions with the novella's ghosts, Scrooge learns to value family and friends, and he even discovers the pleasure that comes from spending money on Christmas gifts. The story struck an enduring chord, for the perennial stage productions, audio performances, and movie adaptations make clear that Dickens's ghosts are as popular today as they were when the tale was first published in 1843. We find the influence of Dickens in this collection of tales as well, and in "A Terrible Retribution; or, Squire Orton's Ghost," the story's supernatural events bring about a transformation in the narrator that leads to a "happy Christmas to all."

The association between ghosts and Christmas, however, did

not begin in Victorian times. December 25th, after all, is most likely not the actual birthdate of Christ, but the date of pagan festivals such as the Roman Saturnalia that celebrate the winter solstice. The solstice marks the moment when darkness begins to give way to light, and the dying world begins to be reborn. It doesn't take much of a stretch to recognize it as a time when the living and the dead are most likely to encounter each other. Even within British fiction, the associations between ghosts and Christmas predate the Victorians. Horace Walpole published the first Gothic novel, *The Castle of Otranto*, using his private printing press at Strawberry Hill on Christmas Eve in 1764. The novel features several ghosts and supernatural beings, including one that walks out of its painting frame, a phenomenon we find repeated in "The Ghost of the Treasure-Chamber," one of the stories featured in this collection.

While the origins aren't Victorian, the popularity of ghost stories certainly peaked in the nineteenth and early twentieth centuries. The timing has much to do with shifts in the publishing industry. In the 1790s, Gothic novels were all the rage, and Ann Radcliffe's *The Mysteries of Udolpho* (1794) and *The Italian* (1797) were two of the most widely read works of the decade. Readers craved fiction with shadowy villains, mysterious screams, secret passageways, and castles and manor houses with haunting inhabitants. Matthew Lewis's *The Monk* (1796) went through four editions in two years as readers devoured his violent tale of ghosts, demons, and sexual transgressions. While these works featured hauntings, they were also three- and four-volume novels that little resembled the short stories that would find an adoring audience just a few decades later. Access was also an issue, and the typical eighteenth-century reader couldn't afford novels. So while haunting tales were popular, books were expensive, short stories were not yet a popular genre, and magazines had not yet reached their heyday.

This would all change in the Victorian period as cheaper and faster methods of both printing and paper manufacture were developed. By the mid nineteenth century, numerous weekly and monthly periodicals featured fiction, poetry, essays, local news and gossip, cartoons, and other forms of entertainment. Long

before television, radio, movies, and the internet, a family's evening amusement often involved the sharing of magazine content
by lamplight. In the pages of *Bentley's*, *All the Year Round*, *Punch*,
Temple Bar, *The Argosy* and numerous other periodicals, we find
stories and essays crafted to entertain and unite families in the
evening hours. Many of these magazines would take advantage
of the growing popularity of Christmas by devoting entire editions to Christmas content that included ghost fiction.

Indeed, the rise of magazines and the rise of Christmas went
hand-in-hand. In the early 19th century, Christmas was a little-
celebrated holiday, one that wasn't even recognized by many
employers. Queen Victoria would play a large role in changing
the holiday's status, in part because her husband Prince Albert
brought to England many Christmas practices from his native
Germany. Writers such as Washington Irving in the United States
and Charles Dickens in England also played an important role
in transforming the holiday through their representations of
Christmas celebrations similar to the ones we know today. It was
during the nineteenth century that Christmas trees, gift giving,
holiday decorations, and even the roast turkey became dominant
elements of the holiday.

While the connections between ghosts and Christmas might
make some sense, the actual popularity of haunting tales during
the Victorian era is rather odd. After all, the eighteenth-century
Enlightenment never really ended, and faith in science and reason
only continued to grow during the nineteenth century. Within
the pages of this anthology we find mention of electric lights,
rapid transportation by train, and the telegraph. The Victorian
era is also marked by the appearance of the first automobiles and
the publication of Charles Darwin's important theories of evolu-
tion. More and more of the world around us was being explained
by science, and even religious faith seemed to be under attack by
scientific progress.

The stories collected here often reflect this rational and
empirical world through their narrators. While we sometimes
encounter Poe-like madmen such as the narrator of Coulson
Kernahan's "Haunted," many are quite the opposite. The speaker
in "Number Two, Melrose Square" is a translator who values

"hard practical work" and describes herself as a "plain matter-of-fact woman of the nineteenth century." More often the rational, level-headed characters are men, for medical advancements of the nineteenth century were often unkind to women. Hysteria and other neurological disorders were largely considered female problems. Drawing on these stereotypes of female nervousness and sensitivity, ghost fiction is filled with women whose weak minds make them susceptible to ghosts. In "The Ghost of the Treasure-Chamber," the narrator is "naturally of a very nervous and excitable temperament." Many of these stories forecast the most famous ghost story centered on female nervousness, Charlotte Perkins Gilman's "The Yellow Wallpaper" (1892).

Ghostly Images

In "The Ghost Chamber," we encounter another type of popular haunting in Victorian literature: portraits. While there is obviously nothing supernatural about a painting, it captures a time that no longer exists. A portrait can function much like a ghost, a long-dead visage staring stony-eyed into a shadowy room in a castle or manor house. We find such hauntings in Eliza Lynn Linton's "Christmas Eve in Beach House," James Grant's "The Veiled Picture," and Emily Arnold's "The Ghost of the Treasure-Chamber."

A new nineteenth-century technology—the photograph—can play a similar role to a painted portrait as it captures a moment that ceases to exist in the living world the instant the camera's shutter closes. Moreover, the limitations of early photography with its long shutter times often transformed its subject into a ghostly image. When the shutter is open for seconds or even minutes, anything in motion will appear as nothing more than a ghostly shadow, if it appears at all. Louis Daguerre's 1839 photo of Boulevard du Temple transformed a busy Paris street into an eerie scene depopulated of everyone but a man standing still to get his shoes shined. Numerous street scenes of the 19th century reveal ghostly, transparent shadows of people who failed to stay still long enough to make a full impression on the photographic plate.

These ghostly images certainly made their Victorian viewers think of ghosts, and they also led to numerous efforts to pass off these ghostly images as actual ghosts. Spirit photography became popular in the 1860s as William Mumler in Boston gained a reputation as both a medium and photographer who could capture photos of his clients with the ghostly images of dead loved ones standing behind them. Mumler was just one of many spirit photographers in England and America in the second half of the 19th century, and the time was marked with a widespread interest in the invisible forces in our world that escape our senses. We see evidence of this in "The Ghost of the Treasure-Chamber," a story that features Mr. Delaware, a "clairvoyant and mesmerist" who puts the narrator into a trance in which she receives a vision central to the story's mystery. Belief was not universal. The narrator of "The Steel Mirror: A Christmas Dream" notes that he is not a believer in "spirit-rapping," a popular method of communicating with the dead by Victorian spiritualists.

In our contemporary world in which cameras are cheap and ubiquitous, we tend to think of a photo as something that captures a snapshot of reality. The limitations of Victorian photography, however, meant that photographs weren't necessarily thought to capture the world as it is, but to transform it or even capture alternate realities. James Grant's "The Veiled Portrait" begins with the narrator discussing the "Unseen World" and the idea that the "darkness is full of light." This was a widely held idea, and many Victorian ghost hunters believed that cameras would be able to capture invisible energies that elude human perceptions. In 1891, Michael Solovoy wrote in the *Journal for the Society for Psychical Research* that "it seems to be a generally accepted fact that rays of light which the human eye *cannot* see *can* be photographed, and that images invisible to the human eye can affect the sensitized plate." This belief remains with us in the twenty-first century, and cameras were frequently used in the popular television show *Ghost Hunters* to document paranormal activity.

Whether or not a camera has ever actually captured the image of a ghost is debatable, but there's no denying that film can, in fact, capture rays of light that are invisible to the human eye.

The hypothesis of Victorian ghost hunters was proven true in 1895 when Wilhelm Conrad Röntgen placed his hand between a Crooke's tube and a fluorescent screen to see the world's first X-ray. An X-ray is clearly not a ghost, but to the Victorian imagination it might as well have been. Periodicals were quick to publish haunting images of skeletal hands stripped of their flesh with metal rings and bracelets floating hauntingly around the bones. The language surrounding these images in the sensationalized periodicals of the 1890s was not of medicine and science, but of ghosts and the graveyard. Much like the winter solstice is a time when the living and dead can mingle, the X-ray image revealed the deathlike skeleton lurking beneath the surface of its living subject.

Grant Allen's "Wolverden Tower" (1896) was quick to incorporate this new scientific advancement. While "The Veiled Portrait" of 1874 references the "Unseen World," Allen's story, published shortly after the discovery of X-rays, presents imagery that Röntgen's rays clearly inspired. When Maisie enters the vault of the dead, she finds that "her face and hand and dress became momentarily self-luminous; but through them, as they glowed, she could descry within every bone and joint of her living skeleton." Later in the story, she observes others whose bodies became "self-luminous" so that for each "the dim outline of a skeleton loomed briefly visible." In descriptions such as these, we find a possible explanation for the continued popularity of supernatural tales at a time when superstitions were rapidly yielding to scientific reason and progress. The reality was that the scientific and technological advancements of the age created as much fear and wonder as they dispelled, and science ironically worked to confirm the existence of ghosts rather than debunk it.

Ghost stories are meant to surprise and scare us, but at the same time their conventions bring a certain level of pleasure in their familiarity. The stories here don't disappoint on this front. We find vacant old houses whose rents are surprisingly cheap (warning: there's a reason!) We discover secret rooms and hidden staircases. We find sinners whose crimes come back to haunt them. We find haunted rooms, haunted objects, and haunted minds. Many of the stories here are by little known or anonymous authors, but in their pages we find echoes of Edgar Allan Poe, Charlotte Brontë, Henry James, Charles Dickens, M.R. James, Mary Shelley, and many other popular and influential writers of dark and disturbing tales.

The stories in this collection vary widely. We find ghosts that are malicious and ghosts that are benevolent. Some stories unquestioningly feature supernatural beings, while the hauntings in others are traced to natural causes or the chimera of a disturbed mind. Whatever the nature of the ghosts, the stories in this anthology give us a glimpse into a Victorian world that we often look back on with nostalgia. That world, however, hasn't entirely left us. As the days grow cold and short, shut off the television, phone, and computer. Turn off the lights, but light a few candles to help dispel the darkness (except in the shadowy corners of the room). Stoke the fire, and gather family and friends around. Embrace the living, enjoy the holiday season, but recognize that the dead aren't that far away. Now, it's time to read ...

Allen Grove
Alfred University
September 2017

Allen Grove (Ph.D., University of Pennsylvania) is Chair and Professor of English at Alfred University where he teaches courses such as Tales of Terror, Gothic Fiction, Literature and Science, and the Romantic Movement. His research and teaching often explore the interplay between sexuality, science, and genre in gothic fiction. He has previously introduced several editions for Valancourt Books, and he has also written introductions for Barnes & Noble Books and Race Point Publishing for works including *The Strange Case of Dr. Jekyll and Mr. Hyde*, *Dracula*, *Frankenstein*, and *The Lost World*.

NOTE ON THE TEXTS

The stories in this volume are reprinted verbatim from their original periodical appearances, with the exception of a very small number of obvious typographical errors that have been silently corrected. The use of single quotation marks in "White Satin" has been changed to double to match the other stories.

The sources for the stories are as follows:

"A Real Country Ghost Story" first appeared in *Bentley's Miscellany* in January 1846.

"The Ghost of the Treasure-Chamber" first appeared in *Time* in December 1886.

"Number Two, Melrose Square" first appeared in *All the Year Round*, edited by Charles Dickens, on December 6 and 13, 1879.

"The Weird Violin" first appeared in *The Argosy* in December 1893.

"Walsham Grange: A Real Ghost Story" first appeared in the *Illustrated London News* Christmas Number in 1885.

"Haunted!" first appeared in *Time* in November 1885.

"The Steel Mirror: A Christmas Dream" first appeared in *Routledge's Christmas Annual* for 1867.

"White Satin" first appeared in the *London Society* Christmas Number in 1875.

"Nicodemus" first appeared in the *Belgravia* Annual in 1867.

"Wolverden Tower" first appeared in the *Illustrated London News* Christmas Number in 1896.

"Christmas Eve in Beach House" first appeared in *Routledge's Christmas Annual* in 1870.

"The Necromancer, or, Ghost *versus* Gramarye" first appeared in *Bentley's Miscellany* in January 1842.

"The Veiled Portrait" first appeared in the *London Society* Christmas Number in 1874.

"The Ghost Chamber" first appeared in *Ainsworth's Magazine* in January 1853.

"A Terrible Retribution; or, Squire Orton's Ghost" first appeared in the *Bow Bells* Supplement on December 6, 1871.

Albert Smith

A REAL COUNTRY GHOST STORY

ALBERT SMITH (1816-1860) *was one of the most popular writers of his day and well known as a humorist for his contributions to the magazine* Punch. *His wit and humor are on display in the opening pages of this story, which begins in a light-hearted vein before turning its focus to the uncanny happenings of one particularly tragic Christmas. Smith's story first appeared in* Bentley's Miscellany *in January 1846.*

> " 'Graut Liebchen auch? Der mond scheint hell!
> Hurrah! die Todten reiten schnell!
> Graut Liebchen auch vor Todten?'
> 'Ach nein! Doch las die Todten.' "—BÜRGER's *Lenore*.

IF THE FOLLOWING NARRATIVE WERE NOTHING MORE THAN A mere invention, it would have very little in it to recommend it to the notice of the reader; but detailing, as closely as possible may be, some circumstances which actually occurred, and which were never accounted for,—no case of spectres found to be finger-posts or pollards in the morning, nor dim flickering lights seen in churchyards at midnight, afterwards proved to have been carried by resurrection-men or worm-catchers,—it may form a fitting addition to the *repertoire* of unaccountable romances, which, taken from the pages of Glanville and Aubrey, are narrated at this fire-side period always in time to induce a dread of going to rest, and a yearning for double-bedded rooms and modern apartments.

For our own part, we believe in ghosts. We do not mean the vulgar ghosts of every-day life, nor those of the Richardson drama, who rise amidst the fumes of Bengal light burned in a fire-shovel, nor the spring-heeled apparitions who every now and then amuse themselves by terrifying the natives of suburban localities out of their wits. To be satisfactory, a ghost must be the semblance of some departed human form, but indistinct and vague, like the image of a magic lanthorn before you have got the right focus. It must emit a phosphorescent light,—a gleaming atmosphere like that surrounding fish whose earthly sojourn has been unpleasantly prolonged; and it should be as transparent and slippery, throwing out as much cold about it, too, as a block of sherry-cobler ice. We would go a great way upon the chance of meeting a ghost like this, and should hold such a one in great reverence, especially if it came in the dreary grey of morning twilight, instead of the darkness which its class is conventionally said to admire. We would, indeed, allow it to come in the moonlight, for this would make its advent more impressive. The effect of a long cold ray streaming into a bedroom is always terrible, even when no ghosts are present to ride upon it. Call to mind, for instance, the ghastly shadow of the solitary poplar falling across the brow of Mariana in the 'moated grange,' as Alfred Tennyson has so graphically described it.

Once we slept—or rather went to bed, for we lay awake and quivering all night long—in an old house on the confines of Windsor Forest. Our bedroom faced the churchyard, the yew-trees of which swept the uncurtained casement with their boughs, and danced in shadows upon the mouldering tapestry opposite, which mingled with those of the fabric until the whole party of the "long unwashed" thereon worked, appeared in motion. The bed itself was a dreadful thing. It was large and tall, and smelt like a volume of the Gentleman's Magazine for 1746, which had reposed in a damp closet ever since. There were feathers, too, on the tops of the tall posts, black with ancestral dirt and flue of the middle ages; and heavy curtains, with equally black fringe, which you could not draw. The whole thing had the air of the skeleton of a hearse that had got into the catacombs and been starved to death. The moonlight crept along the wainscoat, panel after panel, and we could see it gradually approaching our face. We felt, when it did so, that it would be no use making the ghosts, whom we knew were swarming about the chamber, believe that we were asleep any more. So we silently brought all the clothes over our head, and thus trembled till morning, preferring death from suffocation to that from terror; and thinking, with ostrich-like self-delusion, that as long as our head was covered we were safe. Beyond doubt many visitors flitted about and over us that night. We were told, in fact, afterwards, that we had been charitably put in the "haunted room"—the only spare one—in which all kinds of ancestors had been done for. Probably this was the reason why none of them let us into their confidence; there were so many that no secret could possibly be kept. Had we been aware of this interesting fact, we should unquestionably have added ourselves to the number of its traditional occupants long before morning, from pure fright. As it was, we left the house the next day,—albeit we were upon a week's visit,—with a firm determination never to sleep anywhere for the future but in some hotel about Covent Garden, where we should be sure of cease-less noise, and evidences of human proximity all night long; or close to the steampress office of a daily paper. But this by the way; now to our story.

On the left bank of the Thames, stretching almost from the little village of Shepperton to Chertsey Bridge, there is a large, flat, blowy tract of land, known as Shepperton Range. In summer it is a pleasant spot enough, although the wind is usually pretty strong there, even when scarcely a breath is stirring anywhere else: it is the St. Paul's Churchyard, in fact, of the neighbourhood. But then the large expanse of short springy turf is powdered with daisies; and such few bushes of hawthorn and attempts at hedges as are to be found upon its broad sweep, are mere standards for indolent ephemeral dog-roses, dissipated reckless hops, and other wild and badly brought-up classes of the vegetable king-dom. There are uplands rising from the river, and crowned with fine trees, half surrounding the landscape from Egham Hill to Oatlands; one or two humble towers of village churches; rippling corn-fields, and small farms, whose homesteads are so neat and well-arranged, that they remind one of scenes in domestic melo-dramas, and you expect every minute to hear the libertine squire rebuked by the farmer's daughter, who though poor is virtuous, and prefers the crust of rectitude to all the *entremets* of splendid impropriety. The river here is deep and blue,—in its full country purity before it falls into bad company in the metropolis, flowing

gently on, and knowing neither extraordinary high tides of pleni-
tude, nor the low water of poverty. It is much loved of anglers—
quiet, harmless folks who punt down from the "Cricketers," at
Chertsey Bridge, the landlord of which hostelry formerly bore
the name of *Try*—a persuasive cognominution for a fishing-inn,
especially with regard to the mighty barbel drawn on the walls
of the passage, which had been caught by customers. Never did
a *piscator* leave the house in the morning without expecting to go
and do likewise.

But in winter, Shepperton Range is very bleak and dreary.
The wind rushes down from the hills, howling and driving hard
enough to cut you in two; and the greater part of the plain, for
a long period, is under water. The coach passengers used to
wrap themselves up more closely as they approached its boundary. This was in what haters of innovation called the good old
coaching times, when "four spanking tits" whirled you along
the road, and you had the "pleasant talk" of the coachman, and
excitement of the "changing," the welcome of "mine host" of
the posting-inn, and other things which appear to have thrown
these anti-alterationists into frantic states of delight. Rubbish!
Give us the railway, with its speed, and, after all, its punctuality;
its abolition of gratuities to drivers, guards, ostlers, and every
idle fellow who chose to seize upon your carpetbag and thrust it
into the bottom of the boot, whence it could only be extracted by
somebody diving down until his inferior extremities alone were
visible, like a bee in a bell-flower. When Cowper sent to invite his
friend Bishop Spratt to Chertsey, he told him he could come from
London conveniently in two days "by sleeping at Hampton;"
now you may knock off eighteen out of the twenty miles, from
Nine Elms to Weybridge, in fifty minutes.

In winter (to return to the Range) the pedestrian seeks in vain
for the shelter of any hedge or bank. If the wind is in his teeth,
it is no very easy matter for him to get on at all. Once let it take
his hat, too, and he must give it up as utterly lost—all chance of
recovery is gone: and if the snow is on the ground and the moon
is shining, he may see it skimming away to leeward for a wonderful distance, until it finally leaps into the river. And this reminds
us that it was winter when the events of our story took place; and

that the moon was up, and the ground white and sparkling.

It had been a sad Christmas with the inmates of a large family-house near the village end of the Range. For Christmas is not always that festive time which conventionality and advertisements insist upon its being; and the merriment of the season cannot always be ensured by the celebrated "sample hampers," or the indigestion arising from overfeeding. In many houses it is a sad tear-bringing anniversary; and such it promised to be, in future, at the time of our story, now upwards of fifty years ago, for the domestic circle of the Woodwards,—by which name we wish to designate the family in question. It is not, however, the right one. The eldest daughter, Florence, a beautiful girl of twenty, was in the last stage of confirmed consumption. Her family had been justly proud of her: a miniature by Cosway, which is still in existence, evidences her rare loveliness when in health, and as the reckless disease gained upon her, all its fatal attributes served only to increase her beauty. The brilliant sparkling eye with the fringe of long silky lashes; the exquisitely delicate flush and white *teint* of her skin; the bright arterial lips and pearly teeth: all combined to endow her with fascinations scarcely mortal.

"The beauty," beyond all comparison, of every circle of society into which she entered, Florence Woodward had not remained unconscious of her charms. Her disposition in early girlhood was naturally reserved, and to those casually introduced to her, cold and haughty; and this reserve increased with her years, fanned by the breath of constant flattery. She had rejected several most eligible matches, meeting the offers of one or two elder sons of the best families in the neighbourhood with the coldest disdain, even after having led each of her suitors to believe, from the witchery of her manner, fascinating through all her pride, that he was the favoured one; and although at last they felt sure that their offers would be rejected, if not with a sneer, at least with a stare of surprise at such presumption, yet the number of her admirers did not diminish; in many instances it became a point of vanity as well as love. The hope of being, at last, the favoured one urged them on, but always with the same result. She looked upon their hearts as toys,—things to be amused with, then to be broken, and cared for no more.

A year or two before the period of story she met Frank Sherborne one evening at the Richmond ball. The Sherbornes had formerly lived at Halliford, within a mile of the Woodwards, and the two families were exceedingly intimate at that time. They had now left the neighbourhood some years, and Florence was astonished to find that the mere boy, who used to call her by her Christian name, had grown to be a fine young man in the interim. Whether it was to pique some other admirer in the room, or whether she really was taken, for the few hours of the ball, with the lively intelligence and unaffected conversation of her old companion, we know not, but Sherborne was made supremely happy that evening by finding himself dancing each time with the *belle* of the room; and when he was not dancing sitting by her side, lost in conversation. He was fascinated that night with the spells she wove around him, and he returned home with his brain almost turned, and his pulses throbbing, whilst the thoughts which recalled the beautiful face and low soft voice of Florence Woodward excluded all other subjects. His feelings were not those attendant upon a mere flirtation with an attractive woman, in which gratified self-conceit has perhaps so large a share. He was madly, deeply in love.

To be brief, his intimacy with the Woodwards was renewed, and Florence led him on, making him believe that he was the chosen above all others, until he ventured to propose. In an instant her manner changed, and he was coldly rejected, with as much *hauteur* as if he had only been the acquaintance of a single dance. Stunned at first by her heartlessness, he left the house and returned home without uttering a word of what had occurred to his family. Then came a reaction, and brain-fever supervened; and when he recovered he threw up all his prospects, which were of no ordinary brilliancy, and left home, as it subsequently proved, for ever: taking advantage of his mother's being a relation of Sir John Jervis to enter the navy on board the admiral's ship, and do anything in any capacity that might distract him from his one overwhelming misery.

No sooner was he gone than Florence found, despite her endeavours to persuade herself to the contrary, that she also was in love. Self-reproach and remorse of the most bitter kind seized upon her. Her spirits drooped, and she gave up going into society, and albeit her pride still prevented her from disclosing her secret to a soul, its effect was the more terrible from her struggles to conceal it. Day by day she sank, as her frame became more attenuated from constant yet concealed fretting. Winter came, and one cold followed another, until consumption proclaimed its terrible hold upon the beautiful victim. Everything that the deepest family affection and unlimited means could accomplish was done to stop the ravages of the disease; but although her friends were buoyed up with hope to the last, the medical men knew that her fate was sealed, from the very symptoms, so cruelly delusive, that comforted the others. She was attended by a physician, who came daily from London, and an apothecary from a neighbouring town. From the latter we received this story some time back. He was a young man, and had not long commenced practice when it took place.

He had been up several nights in succession, and was retiring to rest about half-past eleven, when a violent peal of the surgery bell caused him to throw up the window and inquire what was wanted. He directly recognized the coachman of the Woodwards upon horseback, who told him that Miss Florence was much worse, and begged he would come over to Shepperton immediately. Sending the man at once away, with the assurance that he would be close upon his heels, he re-dressed hurriedly, and going to the stable, put his horse to the gig himself,—for the boy who looked after it did not sleep in the house,—and then hastily putting up a few things from the surgery which he thought might be wanted on emergency, he started off.

It was bright moonlight, and the snow lay lightly upon the ground. The streets of the town were deserted; nor indeed was there any appearance of life, except that in some of the upper windows of the houses lights were gleaming, and it was cold— bitter cold. The apothecary gathered his heavy night-coat well about him, and then drove on, and crossed Chertsey Bridge, under which the cold river was flowing with a swollen heavy tide, chafing through the arches, as the blocks of ice floating on it at times impeded its free course. The wind blew keenly on the summit of the bridge; but as Mr. —— descended, it appeared

more still; and when he got to the "gully-hole," with its melancholy ring of pollards—(wherein a coach and four, with all the
passengers, is reported by the natives once to have gone down,
and never been seen again)—it had almost ceased.

We have said the moon was very bright—more so than
common, and when Mr. —— got to the commencement of
Shepperton Range, he could see quite across the flat, even to the
square white tower of the church; and then, just as the bell at
Littleton tolled twelve he perceived something coming into the
other end of the range, and moving at a quick pace. It was unusual
to meet anything thereabouts so late at night, except the London
market-carts and the carriers' waggons, and he could form no
idea of what it could be. It came on with increased speed, but
without the slightest noise; and this was remarkable, inasmuch
as the snow was not deep enough to muffle the sound of the
wheels and horse's feet, but had blown and drifted from the road
upon the plain at the side. Nearer and nearer it came; and now
the apothecary perceived that it was something like a hearse, but
still vague and indistinct in shape, and it was progressing on the
wrong side of the road. His horse appeared alarmed, and was
snorting hurriedly as his breath steamed out in the moonlight,
and Mr. —— felt himself singularly and instantaneously chilled.
The mysterious vehicle was now distant from him only a few
yards, and he called out to whoever was conducting it to keep the
right side, but no attention was paid, and as he endeavoured to
pull his own horse over, the object came upon him. The animal
reared on his hind legs and then plunged forwards, overturning
the gig against one of the flood-posts; but even as the accident
occurred he saw that the strange carriage was a dark-covered
vehicle, with black feathers at its corners; and that within were
two figures, upon whom a strange and ghastly light appeared to
be thrown. One of these resembled Florence Woodward; and the
other, whose face was close to hers, bore the features of young
Sherborne. The next instant he was thrown upon the ground.

He was not hurt, but scrambled up again upon his legs immediately; when to his intense surprise nothing of the appalling equi-
page was to be seen. The Range was entirely deserted; and there
was not a hedge or thicket of any kind behind which the strange

apparition could have been concealed. But there was the gig upset, sure enough, and the cushions and wrappers lying on the snow. Unable to raise the gig, Mr. ——, almost bewildered, took out the horse, and rode hurriedly on over the remaining part of the flat, towards the Woodwards' house. He was directly admitted, being expected; and, without exchanging a word with the servant, flew upstairs to the bed-room of the invalid. He entered, and found all the family assembled. One or two of them were kneeling round the bed, and weeping bitterly; and upon it lay the corpse of Florence Woodward. In a fit of coughing she had ruptured a large vessel in the lungs, and died almost instantaneously.

Mr. —— ascertained in an instant that he had arrived too late. Unwilling to disturb the members of the family, who in their misery had scarcely noticed his arrival, he drew the nurse from the room, and asked how long she had been dead.

"It is not a quarter of an hour, sir," replied the old woman looking on an old-fashioned clock, that was going solemnly with a dead muffled beat upon the landing, and now pointed out the time—about ten minutes after twelve: "she went off close upon midnight, and started up just before she died, holding out her arms as though she saw something; and then she fell back upon the pillow, and it was all over."

The apothecary stayed in the house that night,—for his assistance was often needed by the mother of the dead girl,—and left in the morning. The adventure of the night before haunted him to a painful degree for a long period. Nor was his perfect inability to account for it at all relieved when he heard, some weeks afterwards, that young Sherborne had died of a wound received in the battle off Cape St. Vincent, on the very day, and at the very hour, when the apparition had appeared to him on Shepperton Range!

We have often heard the story told, and as often heard it explained by the listeners. They have said that it was a curious coincidence enough, but that Mr. —— was worn out with watching, and had gone to sleep in his gig, pulling it off the road, and thus overturning it. We offer no comments either upon the adventure or the attempt to attribute it to natural causes: the circumstances have been related simply as they were said to have occurred, and we leave the reader to form his own conclusions.

Emily Arnold

THE GHOST OF THE TREASURE-CHAMBER

This rare story first appeared in Time *in December 1886 and seems never to have been reprinted. No information about its author appears to be available. She signed her story "Emily Arnold" and is credited in the magazine's table of contents as "Mrs Henry Arnold," making her most likely the same person who published the three-volume novel* Monks-Hollow *under that name in 1883.*

I

YES, I HATED LEAVING INDIA WHERE I HAD BEEN SO HAPPY for six years with my dear father, who was the colonel of a crack cavalry regiment at Allahabad. And now I was ordered home, for my health had begun to fail under the scorching sun and enervating climate.

Home, did I say? Alas! England was no home to me. All that were nearest and dearest to me were in India, and I felt that my heart would break at leaving my dear old dad, to whom I had been all in all since my mother's death, which had occurred when I was only fourteen. But it was no use grieving over the inevitable. I had to go; and, as I had no wish to make our parting the harder by useless tears, I tried my best to conceal my sorrow, and I fancy my father did the same. Never can I forget the day when he saw me on board the steamer with my chaperone, Mrs. Somers; there was a long, lingering embrace, a few broken words, and then the gulf of waters widened between us, and his dear grey head and upright form faded from my sight, as the vessel ploughed her way through the smooth, green waves.

Upon landing, I was to go to some relatives, my mother's own sister, the Trevalyons, who lived in Cornwall at Tregarthlyn Castle.

"By Tre, and Pol, and Pen,
You may know the Cornish men."

The Trevalyons were a very old Cornish family, who had held Tregarthlyn ever since the reign of Elizabeth; but, of late years, bad times had come upon them; they had grown poorer and poorer; a succession of spendthrift heirs had wasted the substance; and my aunt, with her son and daughter, had much ado to make both ends meet. At all events, I was to stay with them for a time, the doctors being certain that the fresh Cornish air and bracing salt breezes would prove most beneficial to me.

I was naturally of a very nervous and excitable temperament, and was a good deal interested at finding that among the passengers was the celebrated Mr. Delaware, the clairvoyant and mesmerist, then on his way to England.

To tell the truth, I was just a little frightened of him, he was so tall and thin and solemn-looking, with large pale eyes, which seemed to read one's inmost soul. I felt his piercing orbs fixed on me more than once during the first week on board, and I took care to keep out of his way. But one evening the captain announced that Mr. Delaware had kindly offered to entertain us with some of his spiritual manifestations and mesmerism.

Of course we were all very eager to witness the performance, which proved to be decidedly wonderful. It consisted of thought-reading, writing upon a slate by invisible agency, and in mesmerising most of the crew, who were invited upon the platform for the purpose.

As I was leaving the saloon at the end of the evening, the captain asked me to go with him on deck, and, having received permission from Mrs. Somers, I followed him. It was an exquisite night, bright and balmy; the sky, one vast sheet of purple, brilliant with stars; the moon, a huge globe of silver, illumining the wide expanse of gleaming waters.

Like most sensitive persons, I was peculiarly alive to beauty in every shape and form, and, breathless with delight, I leant against the side, and watched the phosphorescent light from the great green rollers, as they glided away to leeward. But my reverie was interrupted by a voice close by me.

"A lovely night, Miss Jocelyn."

I started, and looked round. There, at my elbow, his tall, thin figure erect, his glassy eyes fixed on mine, was Mr. Delaware!

I assented coldly, for I was somewhat annoyed at the intrusion, but nothing daunted, he continued,—

"You have the true artistic temperament, I can see; you are emotional, and keenly susceptible to beauty. Is it not so?"

"How can you tell?" I replied, interested, in spite of myself.

He laughed. "I am used to studying faces, yours is a very characteristic one. You would make an excellent trance medium and clairvoyante."

"Should I?" I exclaimed, much astonished. "Could you mesmerise me?"

"Easily," he returned, smiling; "let me try."

I hesitated. "Will you promise not to make me do anything foolish?"

"Yes, on my honour as a gentleman; you shall only tell me what you see, and the captain shall stand by you all the time."

I felt horribly nervous, but eventually curiosity got the better of my fears.

I endeavoured to make my mind as blank as I was directed, and fixed my eyes upon those of Mr. Delaware. The sensations I experienced were curious; first, a hazy mist seemed to obscure all surrounding objects, through which Mr. Delaware's eyes alone penetrated; then I lost consciousness, and, as in a dream, there arose before my mental vision a fair but wintry landscape, bounded by frowning hills, whose peaks seemed to touch the grey sky-line. Overlooking the valley stood an old picturesque building with castellated battlements, clothed with a tangle of creepers.

As I gazed at it, the light faded, a dim obscurity succeeded the shafts of sunshine, a cold blast seemed to turn my blood to ice, as from the gathering gloom, there approached a tall figure, enveloped in a martial cloak which hid its features. I heard a deep voice mutter:—"To you a task is given; see that you perform it.

"She, who through love the treasure seeks,
    Puts nerve and courage to the test;
    But woe betide her if she fail
    The Phantom Knight's lost bones to rest."

As I stood in breathless horror, unable to stir a limb, the figure raised its arm, a skeleton hand emerged from the heavy folds of the cloak, and touched my elbow. A scorching pain shot through me, I uttered a shriek,—— and awoke to find Mr. Delaware bending over me anxiously.

"Well?" he said interrogatively.

"How strange!" I murmured, passing my hand over my eyes. "But why did you hit me? You must have done so, for my arm hurts me dreadfully," and I pulled up the loose sleeve of my dress, and looked at it; but there was nothing to be seen.

"I have not touched you," replied Mr. Delaware. "Was your vision pleasing?"

"No—not very," I returned, thoroughly puzzled. "I saw a castle and a figure."

"Probably foreshadowing what is to happen, Miss Jocelyn," said the mesmerist.

"Heaven forbid!" I exclaimed; and then I wished him and the captain good-night, and went to my cabin, not a little upset and nervous.

I wrote down the doggerel verse I had heard, lest I should forget it, and retired to rest with my head full of the vision I had seen.

But my sleep was dreamless, and I awoke next morning ready to laugh at myself for my fears, and to think what a fool I had been to allow Mr. Delaware to practise his uncanny arts upon me.

When I met him, I briefly asked him to say nothing about it, as I did not wish Mrs. Somers to know how foolish I had been.

"I cannot understand," I said, "how you managed to make me unconscious. I quite lost myself for a time."

"You were unconscious for ten minutes," he replied, regarding me gravely. "It is simply the extraordinary power that a strong and trained will has over a weaker one. And you, pray forgive me for saying so, are of a highly-strung organisation, and so peculiarly susceptible to magnetic and spiritual influence."

"Do you believe in spirits?" I asked, much interested.

"Certainly I do; and I have every reason to think that the vision you saw last night came direct from the spirit world. You will know one day; when you do, will you tell me if I am right in my belief?"

I promised, feeling vaguely uncomfortable; the subject then dropped, nor did we again allude to it.

II

Mrs. Somers and I were landed at Plymouth one chilly day in the beginning of November. She was going on to London next morning, after she had handed me over to the tender mercies of my relations, whom I had expected to meet me.

We drove to Chubbs' well-known and comfortable hotel, and were duly ushered into a cosy oak-panelled apartment, a blazing fire burning on the hearth, the table laid appetisingly for dinner. I pulled off my hat and cloak, and knelt down on the hearth-rug to warm my chilled hands, whilst Mrs. Somers bustled about with her numerous parcels and bags, worried her maid, interviewed the waiter, and finally departed to arrange her belongings for the night. I was feeling terribly forlorn and homesick, and an inexpressible longing came over me to have my dear old dad's loving arms round me once more; with trembling fingers I drew from my neck a thin gold chain to which was attached a locket; I opened it, and with brimming eyes looked at his dear, kindly face; alas! it would be many weary months before I saw it again. I was just making up my mind for the luxury of a good cry, when the waiter announced a visitor. It was my cousin, Derrick Trevalyon, whom I had not met since I was a tiny child.

I sprang to my feet, as he came forward and took my hand, with such frank, honest sympathy in his dark grey eyes, that my heart warmed to him at once. And then he was so handsome! After all, beauty is a gift of the gods, and its sway is omnipotent. It is all very well for wise people to depreciate it, saying that it is but skin-deep, and that charms of mind are better than those of person. But, in my humble opinion, beauty wins, hands down. Would Helen of Troy, or Ninon de l'Enclos, or Cleopatra, have received a quarter of the meed of love and adoration they exacted, had they been plain women, were they as sagacious as Minerva herself?

Derrick Trevalyon was exceptionally handsome.

He was tall and finely built, with straight, clear-cut features, resolute grey eyes, and fair hair, which would have curled all over his well-shaped head had it not been too closely cropped.

"And you are Ruby?" he said, in low penetrating tones, still holding my hand in his firm clasp. "You are not much altered from the little girl I used to play with. My mother is longing to receive you. She sent you her best love, and regretted that she could not come with me to meet you, but this is one of her bad days."

"I am so sorry," I replied, withdrawing my hand, and motioning him to a seat by the fire. "Is Aunt Eleanor a great sufferer?"

"Yes, at times she has dreadful attacks of neuralgia;" and then he added, half to himself, "Poor mother, she is but ill-fitted to bear trouble."

Our *tête-à-tête* was interrupted by Mrs. Somers, who welcomed my cousin very cordially, and we sat down presently to a cosy little dinner, admirably served, after which Derrick insisted upon carrying us off to the theatre, where he had secured a box.

The next morning I parted from Mrs. Somers with many expressions of regret, and the sincere hope that we might meet again ere long, and then Derrick and I started for Tregarthlyn Castle, which was some miles north of Penzance.

It was growing dark when we arrived at the lodge-gates and drove up a long avenue of fine old elms, whose leaves were now whirling down in showers in the wintry blast.

At the end of the avenue, the castle came into full view, but it was too dark to discern it, though there seemed to be a singular air of familiarity about it, which troubled me considerably. In another minute Derrick had sprung out, and was assisting me to alight.

"Welcome to Tregarthlyn, my fair cousin," he said, heartily. I ran up the stone steps, and entered the hall, where I was folded in my aunt's warm embrace.

"My dear little Ruby," she said, kissing me affectionately, "how

glad I am to see you; you must be tired to death with your long
journey, and cold too. I hope Derrick has taken care of you," and
she led the way to the drawing-room,—such a pretty, quaint, old-
fashioned apartment, sweet with the breath of flowers,—where
I was placed in an arm-chair, and my aunt removed my hat and
furs, and chafed my cold hands in her soft warm ones. The tea
stood ready on a little Chippendale table in front of the hearth,
and whilst she poured me out a cup, I had time to look at her.
She reminded me of my dear, dead mother, and had altered but
little in the last twelve years; her features were delicate, she had
Derrick's eyes, and her pretty, wavy, fair hair was now plentifully
besprinkled with grey. She looked almost too young to be the
mother of such a stalwart son.

As I sat there enjoying the warmth, Derrick plying me with
hot scones and cake, the door opened and a girl entered.

She was not in the least like Derrick or my aunt, being short
and dark, with black hair and laughing brown eyes; such a pretty
girl! She greeted me as warmly as her mother had done, saying,
"I am so glad you have come to spend this winter with us. I have
sometimes been rather dull without a companion, so I shall thoroughly appreciate your society. We must teach you to skate, and
there are lovely walks and rides about here. I hope you will soon
be at home with us and will not feel strange."

I replied that I felt at home already, which I think pleased my
aunt, for she patted my cheek approvingly. When she presently
suggested that I might like to go to my room, my cousin Beatrice
accompanied me.

"I thought you would prefer to be near me," she remarked,
as, after ascending the broad oak staircase, we traversed a long
corridor, with doors on one side, and finally entered a room at
the end, which was simply yet comfortably furnished, and contained a bookcase in which I saw several of my favourite authors
and poets, a couple of arm-chairs, and a writing-table; and, better
than all, it opened into Bee's bedroom, which gave me much
inward satisfaction. I found her a bright, clever, and amusing
companion, and she chatted away to me whilst she helped me to
arrange my knick-knacks, and get ready for dinner.

The next morning I awoke early, and springing out of bed, ran to the window, and looked out over the gardens, which extended far into the valley beneath, through which ran a streamlet spanned by a couple of rustic bridges, and foaming over huge boulders covered with lichen. In the misty distance was a chain of hills, whose rugged tops were hidden by clouds.

Those hills seemed strangely familiar to me. Where had I seen them?

Like a lightning flash came the recollection of Mr. Delaware, and his interview with me.

As I stood spellbound, unable to believe the evidence of my own senses, the fog gradually rolled away, and there before me lay the landscape of my vision!

A sensation of utter bewilderment, not unmixed with fear, seized me; I dreaded I knew not what. But I longed to go out and get a view of the castle, which was impossible from my present position, so I dressed quickly, and, going downstairs, let myself noiselessly out of the hall-door, and ran down the grassy slope of the lawn, until I reached a thicket of arbutus and laurel, which I had noticed from my window.

Then I turned and faced the castle. Yes, there it stood, the very embodiment of my dream! the sun sparkling on the old diamond-paned windows, and tinting the few leaves left upon the trailing creepers a vivid crimson.

I felt as if turned to stone; and a great reverence for Mr. Delaware, and his spiritual arts, rose in my impressionable mind. As to the rest of my vision, I dared not let myself think of it, it was all too uncanny, too horrible. But my unpleasant reflections were abruptly ended by my cousin Derrick, who emerged from a side path in knickerbockers and gaiters, a gun over his shoulder, and who seemed unfeignedly pleased and astonished at seeing me.

"Good morning," he said, taking off his cap, and the sun shone on his bright face and clustering brown hair; he looked so brave, and frank, and handsome, that my fears left me as if by magic.

"You are early; I'm afraid you did not sleep well."

"Yes I did, capitally; but I was possessed of a demon of curiosity, and was obliged to come out. Now, you shall show me over the grounds."

He gladly assented, and we made the tour of the gardens,

which were extensive and very lovely, though Dame Nature had it a little too much her own way. Where there had been an army of gardeners were now only two; the acre or so of glass was unused, and falling into decay. The stables were the same; the fine stud reduced to a couple of old hunters, and a rough pony. My heart ached to see the ruin, the desolation, that had fallen upon what was evidently once a splendid estate.

I suppose my tell-tale countenance must have betrayed my feelings, for Derrick turned to me half-laughing, yet with an undercurrent of bitterness which he could not conceal; "It is the old story, Ruby; we must cry Ichabod, the glory has departed. The sins of the fathers are visited on the children. Do you know that in four months we must turn out of here?"

"Is it possible?" I cried aghast.

"Yes, we can no longer keep the wolf from the door. We have struggled on for years; the castle was heavily mortgaged during my father's lifetime; now they mean to foreclose—we can do nothing. My mother has enough to keep her from starving. As to myself I mean to get a tutorship; thank Heaven, my college education will ensure me that! It is hard to give up the old place that has been ours for so many generations, but beggars mustn't be choosers."

There was a break in his voice, he turned away and busied himself with his gun.

I felt very grieved, but could think of nothing to say to comfort him.

Presently he continued, "The worst of it is that there is a rumour that an immense quantity of treasure lies concealed somewhere in the castle."

My heart stood still.

"Treasure?" I repeated eagerly.

"Ah, then you have never heard the legend of the Trevalyons, nor of the ghost which is supposed to haunt Tregarthlyn. But how pale you are, Ruby; perhaps I had better postpone my story."

"Oh no; tell me now," I urged, and drawing my sealskin closely round me, for I shivered intensely, I seated myself upon one of the seats on the terrace which flanked the south side of the building.

"Well, there was once upon a time, during the reign of Charles I., a certain Sir Guy Trevalyon. Of course he was a staunch Royalist, and something of a freebooter too, I'm afraid, judging by all accounts. This worthy knight was in close attendance upon the King, and was among the escort sent to convey the Queen Henrietta Maria to England. Later on he was despatched on a secret mission to Spain, and whilst there a quantity of Spanish treasure in the shape of money, drinking cups, flagons and chalices, all in pure gold, fell into his hands, and was brought here for concealment. Six months later, during the civil war, Tregarthlyn Castle was stormed by the Roundheads, who were successfully repulsed by Sir Guy; but after the siege was over the knight was found to be missing, and was never again heard of. What became of him, or the treasure, Heaven only knows. Every successive heir to the estate has searched the place, but to no purpose."

"Have you?" I asked breathlessly.

"Yes indeed; you may think me a fool, but I have had surveyors and architects here for a month at a time. We found one secret chamber opening with a sliding panel from the picture gallery, but nothing more. There is an old doggerel rhyme about it; it runs something like this—

"'She, who through love the——,'"

he broke off suddenly as I started forward, crying, "No, no, there must be some mistake—it can't be."

"Why, Ruby, what is the matter? you don't mean to say you are frightened?"

I tried to smile, but I felt horrified; what did it all mean? Only too well I knew the remainder of the rhyme, for it haunted me. I had it written down in my desk at this very moment.

"I don't see much chance of any lovely young maiden braving the ghost of Sir Guy for my sake," he went on; but his tones seemed muffled and far away. I have a vague impression that he turned to me with keen solicitude in his glance; then he, the castle, everything, faded into a dark mist; a ghastly terror seemed to shake my very soul, and I fell forward, unconscious.

When I recovered myself I was in the warm breakfast-room, my aunt bending anxiously over me with a bottle of smelling salts.

"My dear child," she said, "how you frightened me. I have been scolding Derrick for taking you out without any breakfast. You must remember, dear, that you are somewhat of an invalid, and quite unused to our cold climate."

I sat up, and tried to smile. "Please don't scold Derrick; it was all my fault."

"Then you must promise me not to attempt to get up another morning until you are called. Now you must have some breakfast."

At the mention of that somewhat overrated meal I began to think I was very hungry; and so, much to Derrick's satisfaction (he seemed terribly put out by my sudden collapse, poor fellow), I allowed myself to be ensconced in a warm nook by the fire, and did ample justice to aunt's hospitality. In the afternoon Bee offered to show me over the castle, and I gladly assented.

It was a rambling, old place, big enough to put up a regiment of soldiers. Two wings were entirely closed, and only saw daylight when it was necessary to remove the dust that gathered upon the time-worn furniture and brocaded hangings, relics of past generations.

Everywhere I saw the same evidences of decay, of poverty, that I had noticed out of doors; it was indeed sadly apparent that the glory of the Trevalyons had departed. When we entered the picture-gallery, which ran the length of the north wing, and was shut off by heavy folding doors, the sun was setting, and darkness was coming on apace. We passed down it, our footsteps making no sound upon the tapestried floor, the eyes of the dead and gone Trevalyons following us as eyes will do in an oil-painting, Bee pointing out to me the most noteworthy of them. I'm afraid they were mostly a lawless race, given to cards, dice, and wine, and more apt to love their neighbours' wives than their own lawful spouses.

"This is the celebrated Sir Guy," said Bee stopping short at a full-length picture of a knight in armour, his plumed casque in his hand; "he is supposed to haunt the castle. Isn't he an old fright?"

I looked up at the dark and saturnine countenance above me with something of awe; certainly I felt no inclination to speak so irreverently of the Phantom Knight. His bold, black eyes gazed straight out from the canvas in a defiant stare, and—could it be fancy?—they seemed to me illumined as with an inward flame.

I glanced hastily round. Was it a shaft of sunlight that had caused that unearthly radiance? No, the gallery was already shrouded in darkness.

With a sudden feeling of terror I turned to Bee, who had gone on, and said in a half-whisper, "I don't like this place, it is eerie; let us go downstairs," and seizing her arm, I hurried her towards the door, and we ran down the corridor as if all the ghosts imaginable had been at our heels.

Bee threw herself, breathless and laughing, into a chair when we reached the drawing-room.

"I declare you have given me quite a scare," she said as soon as she could speak. "What on earth did you see or hear? I expect Derrick frightened you this morning with his silly stories."

"I wish you would not laugh about it," I returned rather pettishly; "I detest ghosts and all that sort of thing."

Bee jumped up and kissed me in her usual impulsive fashion.

"Poor little coz! she looks like a ghost herself with her pale face, and her wondering blue eyes."

"Am I really so hideous?" I asked plaintively, with an anxious glance at the adjacent mirror.

"Oh, alarmingly so," laughed my mischievous cousin. "That is, if one can be hideous with lovely, rippling, auburn hair, eyes like violets, and a little face like a wild rose."

"You are too poetical to be truthful, I am afraid," I returned severely; "but, tell me now, have you ever seen the ghost?"

"I? No, never, thank heaven! Sir Guy has not troubled me. He evidently thinks I am far too material a person to be honoured with his spiritual attentions. But with an ethereal being, like yourself, it may be different. I should not be at all surprised if he paid you a visit, if only out of deference to your personal charms. I have always heard that he was a great admirer of beauty; quite a gay Lothario in fact."

This was too much; I was feeling horribly nervous and

unstrung, and here, to Bee's utter dismay, I burst into a fit of hysterical weeping.

In an instant she was on her knees beside me, her arms clasping my waist, her pretty, soft, rosy face pressed to mine, whilst she whispered contritely, "My little darling cousin, do forgive me. I am a brute to tease you. I did not mean a word of it, but I am not accustomed to the society of such a delicate little flower as you, so you must forgive me. Sir Guy is a myth, no one that I know of has ever seen him, or any other ghost. Of course, all old places boast of one; it is the proper thing to have, like old silver, old port, and ancestral portraits." So she petted and cheered me, until gradually I recovered myself, though it was some time before I could quite shake off the nervous, uncomfortable feelings that had risen in my breast since my arrival.

III

THE days slipped away very quickly, and I soon felt quite at home and happy with my relations, though there was scarcely any hour in the twenty-four that I did not think, with a swelling heart, of my dearest old dad, so many, many miles away. I grew rapidly stronger and better; the pure Cornish air, laden with the briny breath of the broad Atlantic, blew a faint colour into my cheeks; and perhaps a hidden happiness, which I scarcely yet realised, lent a brighter colour to my eyes. Yes, I was happy; for I felt that Derrick Trevalyon loved me! I was not a child, and I had had a certain amount of experience in the ways of mankind in India, so I was not likely to deceive myself. I read his secret in the ardent gaze of his honest grey eyes, in the fervent clasp of his hand, in the tender inflection of his voice when he addressed me; and gradually the conviction dawned upon me that I reciprocated his affection. And with that knowledge came the belief that it was in me to do something—what, I could not determine—to help him at this crisis.

As the time passed his resolute young face grew graver and graver; on more than one occasion I found my aunt in tears, which she vainly endeavoured to conceal; and even my irrepressible cousin Bee seemed sad and anxious. Only too well I knew the cause. In three months they would be homeless! I had never learned the value of money; my father was scarcely a rich man, but we had always had enough for comfort, if not luxury; but now I longed for wealth as ardently as the most inveterate miser could have done.

I had now quite got over my old fear of Sir Guy Trevalyon, and in fact passed an hour or so every day in the gallery, which commanded a magnificent view of the surrounding country, whose exquisite hills and dales I was constantly sketching.

We spent a very pleasant Christmas Eve. The rector of the adjacent parish, and his noisy family, together with some distant neighbours, were our guests, and after dinner we had charades, finishing up with a dance. The next day there was a Christmas Tree for the village children, at which Bee and I had worked hard for some weeks, and an entertainment at the schools for the old men and women.

On New Year's Eve we were bidden to a dance at Viscount Ruthlyn's, about ten miles away, to which festivity both Bee and I were looking forward with feverish eagerness. We had seen a good deal of the Honourable Gerald Trevor, his lordship's eldest son, during the last few weeks. Scarcely a day passed without bringing him over upon some excuse or another, and he seldom went away without a glimpse of Bee's pretty face, and some of her saucy speeches ringing in his ears. In truth, she snubbed him unmercifully; but he seemed to like it, possibly because it offered such a complete contrast to the reception he usually met with at the hands of the fair sex, being the heir to large possessions. We started off in high spirits for the ball, Derrick having expressed his satisfaction at our appearance, which we secretly agreed left nothing to be desired,—we were dressed alike in white tulle— and arrived safely, in spite of the slippery state of the roads and the snow that had been falling during the day. Dancing had commenced, and all the notabilities of the county were footing it merrily. The old oak-panelled rooms were gay with flowers and holly, whose shining crimson berries gleamed like fire amongst the myriads of wax-lights.

During the evening, Derrick and I found ourselves in the cool depths of the conservatory, where rare exotics bloomed in a wealth of ferns and creepers. Almost hidden behind some giant palms was a cushioned lounge; I sank down upon it with a sigh of content, and commenced fanning myself.

"Hark," said Derrick, listening intently, "it is twelve o'clock; there go the bells. Can you hear them?" and as he spoke, the wild musical ring of many iron tongues announced the death of the old year, the birth of the new.

> "Ring out wild bells to the wild sky,
>   The flying clouds, the frosty light;
>   The year is dying in the night;
>   Ring out, wild bells, and let him die."

So I quoted softly as Derrick leant towards me and took my hand in his.

"God bless my dear little cousin, and give her a very happy year," he said tenderly, looking into my eyes.

"I should like to wish you the same," I commenced shyly, for his earnest gaze somewhat disturbed me.

He dropped my hand, and, turning away, picked a spray of Cape Jessamine.

"Do you know I am going to London to-morrow?" he asked abruptly.

"No, are you really?"

"I am going to interview a gentleman, who requires a tutor for his son. You may wish me luck if you like."

My eyes filled with tears, his tone was so bitter, so unlike himself.

"Derrick," I said earnestly, "I wish I could help you. I would give all I possess to be able to do something for you all. I wonder what that rhyme means."

I stopped suddenly, half frightened at the light that flashed over his face.

"'She who through love the treasure seeks,'" he said gently. "Ruby, don't tempt me to tell you what I have been longing to say for days past. I am a poor penniless beggar, who has no right to think of love, or any such luxury."

"Don't say that, Derrick; what has money to do with love?"

"A great deal, my sweet romantic little coz; the world cannot get on without it."

I looked up at him, our eyes met, and then somehow, Derrick's arm slipped round my waist, and my cheek found a comfortable resting-place on his shoulder, whilst he whispered that he adored me, had done so in fact ever since he saw me at Chubbs' Hotel,— a forlorn, tearful little figure, kneeling by the fire.

I went home in a dream of happiness, and, as I bade Derrick good-night, promised to be down the next morning to give him his breakfast before starting for London.

On reaching my room, I told Bee I was tired to death, and shut the door leading into her apartment. There was a bright fire in the grate, and, after undressing, I slipped on a warm dressing-gown, and sat down to consider the state of affairs. The fixed idea in my head was still how I could help my darling. What on earth was the meaning of that doggerel rhyme? Why had I been troubled with that extraordinary vision on board the *Victoria*, if nothing was to come of it?

I sat there thinking and thinking until the fire went out, and I awoke to the fact that I was intensely sleepy and very cold. I got into bed, but I could not sleep; over and over again I recalled my curious interview with Mr. Delaware. He had said that I was peculiarly susceptible to spiritual influence. Surely, the spirits would not harm me if what I desired to know was to benefit those I loved. With a sudden, but irresistible impulse, I rose, took my candle, and stole noiselessly out of the room, along the corridor, to the picture gallery.

I paused for an instant with my hand on the door.

What mad act was I about to do? I knew not—but I was in that stage of exultation when fear is unknown. I turned the handle slowly and entered.

The cold moonlight, pouring in at the uncovered windows, fell athwart the picture of Sir Guy Trevalyon, standing grim and forbidding in his suit of mail.

I went up to it, scarcely conscious of what I was about, but feeling vaguely that I was acting under the guidance of a superior will; I fell upon my knees, and held out my arms imploringly to the portrait. "Great Shade," I murmured, "help me to find this treasure. If it be true that thou walkest through these walls seeking rest, I pledge myself to give thee Christian burial if thou wilt grant my prayer, for the sake of thy descendants, now in such trouble."

Was my petition impious, do you think? I know that it came from my heart; as I ended, my eyes fixed upon the scornful ones above me, a radiant flame, as of an expiring ember burned in them. I almost fancied that those dark harsh features softened as they looked down upon me. I rose from my knees, and was advancing towards the door, when a deep sigh, which was almost a groan, startled me.

In an access of terror I flew along the corridor, and regaining my room locked the door, and jumped into bed.

But I was too nervous, too excited, to sleep.

Great Heaven! what had I done? Invoked the spirit of the dreaded Sir Guy?

A crowd of horrible impossibilities overwhelmed me; I dared remain no longer by myself. I went into Bee's room, and asked her to let me share her bed, to which she willingly consented; and after a long time I fell asleep.

IV

How long I had slept I know not, but I suddenly awoke with a violent start. I glanced at my companion, she was slumbering sweetly, I sat up and looked fearfully round the room. The night-light was burning dimly; outside the window was nothing but darkness, the moon had disappeared. How silent everything seemed.

Hark! what was that sound? Surely in the distance I could hear the clank of armour; as it were the echo of a mailed footstep ascending the staircase.

I listened intently, but my heart beat with such suffocating throbs as almost to render me deaf to all else. Every nerve in my body seemed strained to its utmost tension. In breathless suspense I waited; yes, there it was again, that muffled but steady footfall, coming slowly along the corridor towards our room.

Nearer and nearer it approached; and, oh horror! *stopped at our door!*

That door was locked, for I had turned the key myself when I came in. The handle was softly turned, it opened, and there entered a tall figure enveloped in a long grey misty cloak. It advanced to the foot of the bed, and, raising its arm, beckoned to to me with a skeleton finger.

I sat fascinated, an icy terror numbing my limbs, paralysing my faculties, my eyes fixed on those of the figure, which glittered like a lambent flame from beneath the folds of the cloak.

As I gazed spellbound, I seemed to hear the words, "You have summoned me—*you must follow me.*"

But I could not have moved a limb. At last I realised the fearful consequences of my rash act, and with a wild cry to Heaven for mercy, I turned, and, flinging myself upon the pillow, hid my face. I seized my cousin, and in a whisper implored her to wake; I shook her, I even pinched her, but though usually so light a sleeper, she remained immovable. Then I wondered if my grisly visitor had departed, but I dared not look up. Unable to endure the agony of suspense any longer, with a desperate effort, I at length ventured to peep out. Oh God! there it stood; its flaming eyes still fixed on me, its fleshless hand still beckoning.

Then as I watched it there came over me something of the same curious sensation I had experienced when Mr. Delaware mesmerised me. It seemed as though I became partially unconscious, my material self remaining motionless and inert, whilst my spiritual faculties were singularly clear and acute. In a dream of horror,—such horror that even now the remembrance of it curdles the very blood in my veins,—yet impelled by an irresistible attraction, I slipped gradually out of bed, and advanced towards the apparition.

It turned, and led the way to the door, which opened, and we emerged into the corridor. How ghostly, how quiet the old house seemed! only the clank of the phantom's footsteps disturbing the slumbering echoes. Where was Derrick? I wondered. What would he do if he could see me now, a little white figure flitting along in the wake of the lost Sir Guy. Suppose I should never see him again! Ah! and my poor old dad, what would he ——? a frenzied shriek came to my lips but I stifled it; after all it was my own fault, and I must suffer for my impious rashness.

We came to the door of the picture-gallery; it opened of its own accord. The gallery was full of light, but, oh Heaven! not the light of the blessed day, nor of the moon; but the phosphorescent glare that comes from the putrescence of a charnel-house. The place seemed alive with misty forms; impalpable shapes, perhaps of the dead and gone Trevalyons, glided past me, and faint whispers and sighs sounded in my ears. Probably they were wondering what reckless mortal was this who dared to brave the spirits of the departed. I glanced at Sir Guy's portrait—*it had disappeared!*—only the frame remained.

The ghost paused at the sliding panel which Derrick had shown me, it flew back; he entered, then beckoned me to follow. I would have given worlds to refuse, to run away, to scream, to do anything that would alarm the household; but I could not. My lips were dumb, and the strong magnetic attraction, impossible to resist, that had dragged me from my bed, now forced me to go on. I stepped into the recess, the panel closed; I was a prisoner!

Sir Guy advanced to the end of the small room; I saw his hand raised to a portion of the wainscot, it fell back, and presented to my astonished gaze a steep stone staircase. Down we went. It must have been pitch-dark, but we needed no candle; that pale, phosphorescent gleam accompanied us. The stone steps were dank and slippery with slime, whilst noisome creatures that foster in the dark—horrible toads and bats, that filled me with loathing—slunk away at the strange light, and the clank of armour. If only I could have screamed aloud it would have been some relief to my agonized brain, but I was powerless to utter a sound. I counted the steps as we descended. There were three flights of a hundred each.

At length we came to a huge iron door, bolted and barred. It opened at our approach, and we passed into a kind of vaulted chamber built of great blocks of stone. The ghost laid his hand upon one—it was the centre of the fourth tier—an enormous piece of solid masonry swung back, discovering a smaller room. Here, Sir Guy came to a standstill; he beckoned me nearer, I obeyed him and, looking round, I saw by the light he emitted a pile of gold cups, goblets, drinking vessels of every kind and shape, chalices and crosses set with gleaming jewels. But what was that figure seated by the table on which the treasure was heaped? It was habited as a cavalier, while the remains of a plumed hat hung from the back of a chair.

As I gazed at it in horrified silence, it raised its bent head from the table, and looked at me. It was a skeleton, the fleshless, grinning skull glaring horribly in the faint obscurity. Then an icy breath seemed to freeze the marrow in my bones, and a voice said, "I have granted your request; see that you fulfil your promise to me, or you will be lost for ever."

The ghost turned to me, casting his fiery eyes upon mine, he raised his hand, and laid it upon my arm, just as he had done in the vision. A scorching pain shot through me, and served to loosen my tongue. I gave one awful shriek which rang through the vaulted dungeons; a shriek which did not seem to me like my own voice, and frightened me as much as it did the bats; then the ghostly figures, the golden treasure, all faded away in a thick crimson mist, and I remembered no more.

V

WHEN I regained consciousness I was lying at the foot of Sir Guy Trevalyon's picture; I raised myself on my elbow and looked around; the sickly rays of the cold wintry morning were stealing through the windows. My teeth were chattering—my head throbbed and burned, but I noticed that Sir Guy had returned to his frame, and stood grim and grisly as when I last saw him. Presently there was a sound of voices outside; hasty footsteps ran along the corridor, and my Aunt Beatrice and a couple of frightened maids appeared, looking thoroughly scared and anxious.

"What is the matter, my dear child?" said my aunt, helping me to rise; "your scream awoke us. Why are you in here? you must surely have been walking in your sleep. Even Derrick, in his distant room, heard you."

I looked from one to the other dazed and wondering. How could they have heard my shriek at the bottom of that awful stone staircase, beneath the ground? Then suddenly a fear, a doubt, and a great joy came upon me; I flung myself into my aunt's arms, and burst into alternate tears and laughter, "I have found the treasure-chamber," I cried. "Yes, I have found it; there are three flights with a hundred steps in each."

"Good Heaven!" exclaimed my aunt seriously alarmed; "the child is raving. We must get her to bed; she is evidently very ill. Sarah, ask Mr. Derrick to ride off at once for the doctor—at once, mind."

"I am not ill," I gasped, "I have found the treasure;" but I could say no more, a sudden feeling of utter horror and fear of what I had endured overcame me and choked my utterance. I remember but little of what followed; I was carried to my room and put to bed.

When the doctor came he said I must have had some very severe shock, and considered my condition serious, with grave symptoms of brain fever. I think I must have told them all my story in my delirium. For three days I was a raving lunatic, and terrified those about me with my piteous appeals to them to save me from Sir Guy Trevalyon. But, thank God! I pulled through; and when I was well enough to be moved into another room, Derrick himself carried me in his strong arms into aunt's cosy boudoir, and there I told them the story I have endeavoured to relate here, from my mesmeric trance on board the *Victoria* to the discovery of the hidden gold.

"I am afraid you don't believe me," I said as I ended, and I noticed that Aunt Eleanor looked at me anxiously, with an incredulous expression on her gentle face; she evidently thought I was still wandering. But Derrick knelt down beside me. "My little darling," he said, tenderly, seriously, "I believe everything you tell me; and I will go at once and prove the truth of your words."

"You can't go alone," I entreated. "Wait till to-morrow, and get Gerald Trevor to accompany you. I will send him a note at once, and Lord Ruthlyn shall come too."

He did so; and the next morning Gerald arrived with his father. When Derrick explained why he required their presence they were tremendously excited and curious.

We accompanied them to the picture gallery; they opened the sliding panel and entered the tiny recess. I pointed out the spot which Sir Guy's finger had pressed. There was a moment of breathless suspense—then incredulity turned to awe, for the partition flew out as I had told them, and disclosed the stone staircase.

I gave one glance at it; then, shivering with horror, I hid my face on my aunt's shoulder, and she and Bee led me away.

My story is told. They found everything exactly as I had related, but they could not unclose the iron door which Sir Guy had opened with a touch. Two locksmiths had to be summoned from the town, and it was accomplished at last; the solid masonry in the stone chamber swung back, as I described, and disclosed the long-lost treasure that Sir Guy had brought from Spain, and which probably caused his ruin. The figure seated at the table was doubtless that of the missing knight, who had been caught a prisoner in this secret chamber by the untoward closing of the aperture, which opened by a spring from the outside. It is needless to say that his remains were carefully collected, and interred with full honours in the Church of Tregarthlyn, and later on I had a brass inserted in the ancient pavement to the memory of the Phantom Knight. Besides, did I not owe him a debt of gratitude for his kindly conduct to myself?—and I was so horribly afraid of his visiting me again.

Amongst the treasure were found many Spanish doubloons, and broad gold pieces; enough, thank God! to free Tregarthlyn from the mortgages and debts encumbering it, and to enable my Derrick to hold up his head amongst the greatest in the land.

That summer he and I sailed for India for our honeymoon, my dear father coming over to England to give me to him.

Whether I ever did descend those awful stairs with the ghost of Sir Guy Trevalyon, or whether, under the influence of some powerful supernatural influence, I evolved what I have related from my inner consciousness, I know not; but it is a singular fact that I still bear upon my arm the print of those four skeleton fingers; and, what is more, my two little children have also the sign manual of the ghost of the TREASURE-CHAMBER.

Theo Gift

NUMBER TWO, MELROSE SQUARE

*First published anonymously in two weekly parts on December 6
and 13, 1880 in Charles Dickens's magazine* All the Year Round,
*the story's authorship was revealed in 1889 when it was reprinted in
Theo Gift's volume of weird tales* Not for the Night-time. *"Theo
Gift" was in fact the pseudonym of* DORA HAVERS (1847-1923),
*who is also remembered for having collaborated with E. Nesbit in
writing stories for children. One of the most accomplished and effective tales in this volume, it serves as a warning to be wary of under-
priced rental properties, particularly those with sinister servants.*

CHAPTER I

I AM ASKED TO STATE AS CLEARLY AS POSSIBLE why I gave up
the house in Melrose Square, Bloomsbury, as suddenly as I did,
and what happened there. The landlord says that I have given
it a bad name, and prevented him (owing to certain paragraphs
which have lately appeared in one of the daily papers) from letting it to another tenant. That is why I have been called upon to
make this statement, and I will do so accordingly as briefly and
exactly as possible. If the landlord be further hurt by it, I cannot
help it. Had I been allowed I would far rather have avoided ever
saying or thinking anything more on the subject. To me it is still
an inexpressibly painful one.

I first entered Number Two, Melrose Square, rather late in
the afternoon of November 15, 1878; that is, just about a year
ago. It was a furnished house taken for me by a friend who was
slightly acquainted with the landlord. She had also, on his recom-
mendation, engaged for me a temporary servant, and it was this
woman who opened the door for me as I alighted from the cab
at it.

She was not a pleasant looking person; and I remember my first impression of the house was that it looked dark and cheerless, and not so inviting by any means as my friend had described it to me. She, however, had seen it on a bright morning in October, when the sun was shining and the leaves were still ruddy on the trees, while I was entering it under the treble disadvantages of twilight, soaking rain, and a sky low and dense, and sooty enough to suggest its being compounded of nothing but exhalations from the river of black mud which lined the streets and made the pavements foul and slippery on every side. No house could look pleasant under such circumstances, and I had not come to London for pleasure, but for hard practical work. I had undertaken the translation of a book which necessitated my constant vicinity to the British Museum for at least six months, and the house in Melrose Square was at once so convenient for the purpose, and so exceedingly—I had almost said ridiculously—low rented that it seemed as though it had been left empty specially for my accommodation. It would have required something more than a little outward dreariness to damp my spirits on my first arrival.

Inside it was rather more cheerful. The entrance hall, it is true, was dark and narrow; but Mrs. Cathers, the servant, had lighted a bright fire in the dining-room, and the tea-things were already set out on the table. I began to think that the woman's face belied her character, and that I should not have to suffer from want of attention at any rate; altogether I sat down to tea in very good spirits, and afterwards wrote a letter to brother John, with whom I had been staying ever since I let the cottage after our mother's death. It had been a long visit—not too long for him, I hope; but Mrs. John was fussy in her kindness, would make a visitor of me, and fidget if I shut myself up for an hour with my writing. On the whole I had rather looked forward to being my own mistress again. This evening I did not mean to do anything, however. The journey from the north had been as long and tiring as such journeys always are, and I hardly felt equal to getting out any occupation; while in the room where I was sitting there was certainly nothing to interest me or amuse my thoughts.

It was a medium sized apartment, with a rather dingy red Turkey carpet, furniture in the orthodox brown leather and mahogany, and a wall-paper of dull orange striped with maroon. There were one or two very bad oil-paintings, and an engraving, not at all bad, representing Judas casting down the thirty pieces of silver in the Temple; a bookcase in one corner, but locked and with no key in it; and over the chimney-piece a mirror covered with yellow gauze. I have a particular objection to gilding covered up with yellow gauze anywhere or at any time; but in this case the glass was covered as well—a precaution as senseless as it was hideous; and I made up my mind to remove the eye-sore on the morrow. For that night I was too lazy, and about nine o'clock rang for Mrs. Cathers to bring me my candle that I might go to bed. She went upstairs with me. It was rather a winding staircase, and my bedroom was on the second floor. I had to pass the drawing-room landing, and a window a little way above just where the stairs took a curve. I remember looking through this window and trying to discover what view it had, and being disappointed because the gloomy blackness of the night without only gave me back a vision of myself reflected in the glass with Mrs. Cathers's decidedly unprepossessing features a little in my rear. For the moment, indeed, I fancied there were two Mrs. Cathers, or rather a second head a little below hers; but of course that was only a flaw in the glass, and I laughed at myself for the momentary idea that this second head had been more like an old man than my middle-aged servant woman. That is all I recollect of the first night; for after unpacking my trunks I made haste to bed, and slept so soundly that it required more than one knock at my door to arouse me in the morning.

I spent the whole of the next day at the Museum, only returning at dusk to a late dinner. It was still raining then, and the house looked as dreary as it had done on the previous evening. It did not face the square itself—which, indeed, hardly deserved the name, being only a narrow oblong enclosure where a score or so of melancholy trees shook down their last yellow leaves on a wilderness of tall grass and rank weeds, and round which all the house seemed to have acquired an air of damp and gloom. It opened into a little narrow street turning out of one end of the square, and cut off by iron posts and chains from being a thoroughfare to anywhere; and on that side it was divided from the next house by an archway leading down a long entry to some mews in the rear. The house on the other side, that looking into the square, was empty. So was the one immediately in front, and the big, gaunt letters, "To Let," stared me whitely in the face from the dingy window above and below. It was not a cheerful place; but, as my friend wrote me, when I asked her to find me nice apartments near the Museum, a furnished house in a square, and with a servant included, for positively less money than you would pay for three rooms in anything like a decent street, was a thing to be grasped at, not despised; especially as I could be so much more my own mistress than in the latter place, and could ask Tom and Hester up from their barrack quarters to spend Christmas with me. So I tried to shut my eyes to the exterior look of things and went inside. Here there was one improvement at least—the yellow gauze was gone. I had stripped it off the mirror the last thing before leaving the house in the morning, as also from the glass in the drawing-room, which, though the gilding of the frame was decidedly shabby, was to my great amusement as carefully guarded as the other.

I went up to the latter apartment after dinner. Mrs. Cathers had suggested that "Of course I would not do so, as the dinin'-parlour were so much more cosy;" but I did not agree with Mrs. Cathers. That orange paper with its maroon stripes, and the grim old engraving of Judas, with the horrible expression of the traitor and the sinister, leering faces of the high priests and elders, were depressing to my spirits. The very force and realism of the picture made me feel as if the room were one in which it would be possible to plot a crime. Besides, a house in which a drawing-room is unused, except for company, is never a cosy or homelike one to me; and I knew that Hester felt still more strongly on the subject. I was determined that she should find me and my work-basket and books established there as a matter of course when she came.

Neither books nor work were much called into requisition on the present evening, however. There was a pleasant fire burning in the grate, and two candles on the little round table by the sofa, where the last number of the Cornhill, with a new novel, lay awaiting my perusal; but a day's continuous writing and my dinner combined had made me sleepy; and after reading a few pages and finding that I was getting into a dreamy state, and mixing up the crackling of the fire with the roar of surf on a sunny beach, and my own position on the sofa with that of the Scottish heroine in a fast-flying cutter, I gave it up, blew out the candles, and composed myself for a nap till tea-time.

Do these details appear irrelevant to you? They are not so in reality. I mention them to show you that nothing of what I may afterwards relate can be accounted for (as has been falsely suggested) by my being in an excited, overwrought state, worked up by loneliness or the writing and reading of sensational romances. I was in perfect health. I had lived alone for weeks, and sometimes months, when my dear mother was visiting her married children. I had been simply following my regular profession, which this day lay in the translating a number of dry, scientific rigidly matter-of-fact letters, had walked home, eaten a plain dinner, and read myself comfortably to sleep with one of our healthiest and most-bracing English writer's descriptions of sea-coast scenery. Bear this in mind as I wish you to do, and then listen to what follows.

I woke from my nap with a start, caused by the falling of a coal into the fender. How long I had slept I could not tell; but I had that instinctive consciousness, which I daresay most people have experienced, that it was a long time, much longer than I had intended; and this opinion was confirmed by the sight of the tea-things standing on the table, where Mrs. Cathers had evidently placed them without rousing me, and also by the fact that when I touched the teapot I found it was almost stone-cold. Vexed with myself I rose quickly to my feet and began putting the fire together; for it had got so low and dead that the room was almost dark. Indeed, I feared at first that there was not sufficient vitality in it to light a candle, and so enable me to see what time it was, and whether it was worth while beginning any occupation; but a few skilful touches with the poker soon dispelled this idea and produced a bright, wavering flame; and I stood up again, meaning to get a spill from the mantel-piece and light it at it. As I did so my glance naturally fell on my own face in the mirror before me, and I said to myself aloud, and smiling as one sometimes will when alone: "Well, Miss Mary Liddell, you have made your head into a furze-bush! It's a mercy Mrs. John isn't here to see you, or——" My voice broke off suddenly at that word; for in the act of uttering it, and smiling to myself at my dishevelledness, as I have said, I saw that I was not alone in the room.

Standing at the farther end of it, almost opposite to the grate, and reflected in the mirror by the ruddy light, was a woman: a woman I had never seen before. That she had not been there five minutes back when I awoke I could almost have sworn; for I had looked all round the room; and dim as the light was, I could see well enough that there was no one else in it, and that the door was closed. It was closed now, and how she could have opened and shut it again without my hearing her, unless during the moment that I was poking the fire, I could not imagine. The curious thing was that she did not look at or speak to me even now; but stood perfectly still, her face turned towards the door as if in the attitude of listening, and with all the appearance of a person belonging to the house, seeing that she was not dressed for walking, but in a loose sort of morning gown of white cambric, with deep ruffles down the front and at the wrists, and wore her hair loosely plaited down her back. I noticed this at the first glance as adding to the strangeness of her presence there at all; but in the same moment the fire shot up in a brilliant flame throwing a bright light on her face, and almost nailing me to the ground as my eyes read the expression on it. In all the years I have lived, in all the years I may yet have before me, I never have seen, I trust I never may see, such an expression on any human being's face again! For it was a young face, that of a girl, almost a child; and would have been pretty but for the awful, corpse-like pallor which overshadowed the brow and cheeks, and the hopeless, unutterable depth of misery and fear, of utter despair, and ghastly, speechless, livid horror, all blended in one single effort, an intensity of listening, which seemed to absorb every nerve and power: listening to something outside the door, something which seemed from her starting eyeballs and the hopeless quiver in her lower jaw to be drawing nearer and nearer; for her slender, feeble body seemed to shrink with each breath, and draw itself farther and farther back, as though from some loathsome, terrible animal which she could see in act to spring, or as though—— It was all visible in the sudden leaping up of that flame. The next moment it died down again, and I turned round sharply!

The woman was gone!

How I felt I cannot tell you. It has taken many words to write all this, but it did not require the space of one minute to see it. It must have taken you many seconds to read, but it did not take a dozen heart-beats to feel it in all its ghastly, inexplicable mystery. I was still breathless with the surprise of seeing her there, there in my room, which only a moment before had been empty save of myself; and she was gone—disappeared! The door had not opened. There was no sound, no cry, not even the lightest footfall. The house seemed wrapped in the most impenetrable silence. Even the noises in the street were hushed; and I was there alone in the firelight with the unlit spill in my hand. I suppose I rang the bell violently; for I remember listening to the sound of it jingling far away in the basement regions, and then ringing again and again, and waiting, with my heart beating like an alarm-clock, and my hands quite cold and damp, for Mrs. Cathers to answer it.

She made her appearance at last. It may not have been as long as it seemed. One does not tell time accurately at such moments; but it was long enough to give me time to recover myself a little, and to feel annoyed with the woman for the marked sullenness and unwillingness in her whole manner as she entered with the conventional query: "Did you ring, ma'am?" She was carrying a large kerosene lamp, and the sudden glare of light, as well as the sound of her voice, surly as it was, restored me further.

"I should think you heard me ring several times," I answered. "Did you meet anyone on the stairs just now? I have been asleep longer than I intended, and I did not hear the door open; but——"

"Yes, ma'am, you 'ave been asleep," Mrs. Cathers interrupted me in a tone of greater injury than before. "And if I didn't answer of your bell the minnit it ringed, it was in cause of my bein' that tired of waitin' up I'd dropt into a doze myself a-sittin' in my cheer. P'r'aps, ma'am, you don't know as it's twelve o'clock?"

"Twelve o'clock!" I repeated. Had I really slept so long? "Why did you not wake me when you brought up the tea?" I added, looking at the woman in surprise.

"Why, m'm," she said peevishly, "I would have done so, in course, if you 'adn't said at dinner as you were tired; an' when I come up you were sleepin' so sound I didn't like. Dreamin', I should think you was too, by your 'air," the woman put in with a sudden furtive glance at me.

I had not been able to catch her eyes once before. She kept them rigidly fixed on the lamp she carried, never even looking about her; and, indeed, there was something now so unpleasant in her glance, that I felt almost unwilling to go on speaking to her. Still, if anyone had got into the house without my knowledge—anyone of feeble mind, or in great terror! Writing this as though I were in the witness-box, I can solemnly aver that so free was my mind from any morbid or romantic fancies that, even then, I could not think of my visitor as having any supernatural element.

"Have you let anyone into the house without my knowing?" I asked, rather sharply. "Or is the hall-door open? If you have been asleep yourself, you might not hear anyone come in at it; but I believe someone did just now—a woman. She was in this room a few minutes ago."

Mrs. Cathers looked at me again, this time with barely veiled contempt.

"You 'ave been dreamin', ma'am," she said coolly. "The 'all door! Why, it 'ave been shut an' locked ever since dusk, an' as to me lettin' anyone in, I'd not think of such a thing. There ain't no one in this 'ouse but you and me, nor there hasn't been, man or woman either. Lor, to think what queer dreams some folks 'ave! But I thought as you were give that way, when I 'eard you mumbling to yourself in your sleep."

I did not believe her, for I knew that I had not been dreaming; and there was something in the woman's whole manner which made me distrustful of her, and more especially of her almost impertinent determination to force a ready-made solution of my query on me. Why should she be so anxious to persuade me that I had been dreaming, when, as a matter of fact, she could have no idea of my grounds for speaking as I did? On second thoughts, I decided to say no more on the subject at present; but, simply observing that she ought to have woke me sooner, told her to light me up to bed, and make haste to her own. I could not have stayed longer just then in that drawing-room by myself, and I am perfectly willing to own that until I was safely in bed, with my room door locked, I avoided looking about me as carefully as Mrs. Cathers had done. I was honestly frightened and bewildered, and my mind was in a whirl. It was a comfort to me when three, striking from a church-clock hard-by, and followed by the crowing of an over-wakeful cock, showed me that the actual night was past, and gave me confidence enough to let me sleep.

The following day, the 17th of November, was bright and sunny; and I awoke, feeling more cheerful, and able to reason with myself quite calmly as to the last night's occurrence. Looking back upon it thus, through the medium of sunlight and a refreshing sleep, I could only conclude that, however unlikely and foreign to all my previous experience, I had simply been the victim of some strange optical delusion, though how produced, and whence arising, I could not tell. Against any other idea, that, for instance, which had already presented itself to me, of some mad or imbecile girl being concealed in the house with Mrs. Cathers's connivance, I guarded by looking into every room and cupboard immediately after breakfast, and, after locking up those which I did not require for present occupation, depositing the keys in my desk.

I spent the greater part of that day like the last at the British Museum, and afterwards called on some old friends in Russell Place, and stayed to dinner with them. I had been half in hopes of carrying off one of the girls to sleep and spend a few days with me, for the strange vividness and reality of the last night's vision, and the ghastly sense of horror and mystery encompassing it, had left a sufficiently strong impression on me still to make me wishful for some other company than my own. I was not exactly afraid to be alone, but my nerves had received an unpleasant shock, and I wished to assist myself to recover from it. I was disappointed, however, both the daughters being away on a visit in the country; but their father, one of the kindest and most genial men living, insisted on seeing me home at night, and even came in and sat for half an hour or so talking to me, greatly, as I judged from her face, to the discontent of Mrs. Cathers. Indeed, the sourness of her expression, when she saw me return accompa-

nied by a clergyman, even attracted the old gentleman's attention, and caused him to observe laughingly to me:

"Why, Mary, my dear, one would think you were a jealous
wife, with a husband partial to pretty servant girls, and had
chosen the most repellent you could find accordingly. Does your
Abigail always present such an unamiable appearance?"

She was to have her amiability further tried. My kind friend, to
whom I had half jestingly mentioned the previous night's fright,
insisted on looking over the house with me before he left, so as
to "set my mind at rest," he said; and Mrs. Cathers resented the
proceeding so much that she came up to me in the middle of it,
and, without taking any notice of Mr. L——'s presence, asked
me, in her strongest tone of ill usage, whether I objected to her
going to bed: "seeing as how it were past twelve before she got
to rest last night, and just on eleven now, and having been hard at
work since——"

I told her shortly that she might go to bed as soon as she
pleased. When you are used to nice old family servants with
gentle, respectful ways, this sort of coarse incivility grates on
you, and as I bid my kind old friend good night, a few minutes
later, I told him, smiling:

"Well, I think I shall take your advice in one respect before
Tom and Hester come, although she is rather a jealous wife. I
shall look out for a pleasanter maid."

I said this, with the hall-door in my hand—he will bear witness now, how cheerfully, and how little the thought that I should
never require another maid in that house, or sleep another night
there, had occurred to me. Indeed, I can safely say that such an
idea had never been further from my mind. I went back to the
dining-room quite cheerfully too. Originally, I had intended
going to bed very early, and had even, by an impulse which I was
ashamed to put into words, re-covered the mirror with its hideous
yellow veil; but the evening with my cheery-hearted friends had
so restored my natural spirits that I felt divided between laughter
and blushes at my own folly in so doing, and finding a little pile of
letters and proofs which had come for me by the last post lying on
the side-table, I sat down to look over them, and speedily got so
absorbed in the task as to forget altogether how time was passing.

I was aroused from it quite suddenly by a feeling which I cannot explain, but yet which was strong enough to make me lift my head with a start, and look sharply around: a feeling that someone was in the same room with me!

CHAPTER II

I said at the end of the first part of this statement that I was aroused from my occupation by the sudden sensation that someone was in the room with me. It was not so in fact. One glance round the formal gas-lit apartment, with its rather skimpy curtains looped flatly against the wall, and its utter absence of anything like dark corners or ghostly recesses, was enough to assure me of my error; but the feeling remained with me all the same, and grew stronger instead of passing away. It almost seemed as though someone were seated at the same table with me, breathing near me, occupying the very next chair; and then gradually there stole over me the same sensation I had had before with regard to this room, as if some crime, some deadly, sickening sin which appalled me even while I was utterly ignorant of its nature, were being plotted and worked out in it—something too hideous to be rendered into words, but to which I, by the very fact of my presence there, was being made a party. It was then, at that moment, that the thought of what I had seen in the mirror last night came into my mind. I was exactly under the drawing-room floor where it had stood—the vision-woman with that awful, unspoken mystery of horror and despair in her livid cheeks and dim, dilated eyes. Was this unknown, unguessed-at wickedness being woven and worked out against her? Was she up there now, waiting?

I had been sitting down, holding my letters in my hand, trying honestly and hard to think of them and nothing else. I could not do so any longer. I stood up abruptly. There was a trembling in my limbs and hands, and my forehead felt cold and moist. All the while I was putting up my papers my eyes would keep wandering by a sort of fascination to the mirror. I could see nothing in it. The gauze prevented me; yet it seemed to me more than once as if the reflection of something—some moving figure, not mine, had passed across it; as if, but for the veil—— I could not bear it, and went out quickly from the room, shutting and locking the door behind me. There was no light in the hall or upon the stairs, except the candle I carried. After putting that ready for me, Mrs. Cathers had turned out the gas. I went upstairs with swift steps; swiftest in passing the drawing-room door.

I have said the staircase took a bend here and crossed a long window, which in daylight lighted it from top to bottom. This window gave on the dead wall of a neighbouring house about eight feet distant. There was no blind to it. As on the first night, it frowned on me in black, unsheltered nakedness when I turned the corner. As on the first night, I saw myself reflected at full length in it, the candle in my hand, the buttons and fringes of my dress, the—— My God! but who, who or what was that behind me, that crouching figure which froze me to the spot, actually paralysed with dread—a dread which was all the more over-mastering because I had heard no faintest rustle or sound to give me warning of it.

Believe me or not; but just below me, creeping slowly with soft, gliding, noiseless steps, was the figure of a man!

At the moment he was not on the same angle of the stairs with me. The banisters separated us, and at first the light only fell on his head: the head of an old man, bald, with tufts of greyish-white hair hanging in coarse, shaggy locks over the large, red, wrinkly ears, and a short, stubbly beard, white too—an old man with stooping shoulders and heavily corrugated brow. The face beneath was inexpressibly evil and repulsive: evil and repulsive in the loose, hanging, sensual lips; evil and repulsive in the cruel, vindictive eyes almost hidden under their overhanging brows; so evil and repulsive in every line and curve of the hoary head and brutal, wolfish jaws, that even if met by daylight in a crowded street one would instinctively have shuddered and shrunk away from contact with him. How much more so now when illumined by an expression of such deadly, sinister determination that the very sight of it seemed to chill one's heart and limbs, and deprive one even of the power of a cry for help.

In that moment of mortal, agonised terror, longer in seeming than all the years of my past life, I felt as though in the presence of some ferocious animal; some creature without pity, without conscience, without soul, whose very glance must foul and destroy if it once fell on one.

For that was the strangest part of it, adding in one way to the mystery and horror of his presence. This creature, man or devil, never looked at me; seemed, if it were possible to believe such a thing, unconscious even of my presence. Like the vision-woman of last night, its eyes were fixed straight before it. Like the vision-woman of last night, they never blinked or wandered once, but seemed concentrated in one fixed, deadly stare; a stare which had for its object the drawing-room door! Could it be—was it possible, or was this some horrible, fevered dream?—that she was there now, cowering behind that door; a woman, young, almost a child, alone in the night, utterly friendless, utterly helpless, waiting and listening in an anguish of fear beyond words, beyond hope, beyond even prayer, for the approach of this very man who, step by step, was gradually drawing nearer to her—the man whose unseen presence had made the room below horrible with meditated crime, whom I had thought to leave behind me there!

I could see the whole of him now. Inch by inch with a stealthy, crawling movement, as though he were raising himself by the wrinkled, sinewy hand, which grasped the rail of the banisters so close to me that it almost touched my dress, rather than by the use of his feet. He had gained the landing outside the drawing-room door; and I saw that he was clad only in trousers and shirt—the latter open at the throat so as to show the wrinkled, hairy skin; also that he carried in his left hand an ordinary table-knife with a black horn handle, the blade of which, worn to a point like a dagger, had evidently been recently sharpened. I saw, too, for the first time, that he was not alone. Close to his side, and alternately rubbing herself against his legs and the knuckles of his left hand, was a big, yellow, gaunt-bodied cat, with an unusually large head, and one eye bleeding and sore from some recent wound. There was something peculiarly horrible about this cat, horrible even in the almost obtrusive way in which she lavished her caresses on her sinister companion, and then, leaping forward, crouched down at the door, smelling at it and turning her sound eye on her master as if aware of his object and inviting him to hurry with it. Still without a word, and seeming indeed to hold his breath between his clenched teeth, he struck at her with the knife to drive her off; and then, gliding closer to the door, gave one furtive glance around him, and tightening his hold of the weapon, laid his hand upon the lock.

That broke the spell which held me, and had held me till then numb and speechless; and as the handle slowly turned under those cruel, sinewy fingers I shrieked aloud, shrieked again and again, till the whole house rang with my cries of fear and horror; shrieked, and springing wildly forward, saw——nothing! a blank, empty space, where a moment before had been man and animal, and let the candle fall out of my nerveless fingers down between the banister and far below, clattering into the darkness.

What happened next, or how I got there, I shall never know; but it was early dawn when I recovered consciousness, and I was lying face downwards on the floor in my own room. Someone— Mrs. Cathers it was—was trying to lift me up; but at first I did not recognise her, and the touch of a hand only wrung a faint cry from me, and made me go off again into a second fainting-fit. I suppose she must have got some water then and dashed it in my face; for, when I next revived, both it and my hair were dripping with wet, and I opened my eyes and saw her bending over me. But I was still only half-conscious. I did not know where I was or what had happened to me, and my first effort of returning life was to cling to this woman, so repugnant to me usually, and moan out faint contradictory entreaties that she would stay with me, that she would not leave me; and then, at the same time, that she would run to that poor girl and save her. "Oh, do go to her; do, do, or he will kill her. He will have killed her by now."

"Killed her! Why, ma'am, whatever are you talking on? There's no one in the 'ouse but you an' me. There ain't, indeed. On my conscience there ain't." This, or something like this, Mrs. Cathers kept repeating; but I hardly heard or understood. The frenzy of terror, only half subdued by exhaustion, was still on me; and when I found she would not move I tried to rise, and failing, burst into a fit of hysterical weeping, which lasted so long that Mrs. Cathers got quite frightened. She ran for some brandy and poured it down my throat, and this partially revived me; but by this time I was as weak as a child, and the woman had to half lift, half drag me on to the bed, and then stoop her head low to hear my whispered request, urged with tremulous eagerness, that even if she were sure that there was no one in the house, she would send at once to the friends I had been with last evening, and beg Mrs. L—— to come to me. To my surprise and sorrow, however, this Mrs. Cathers would not do. She had a hundred reasons to the contrary. There was no one to send, and I was not well enough to be left, and if I liked to write to Mrs. L—— later she would put the note in the pillar; all of which did not satisfy me; for with all my suspicions of the woman revived by her reluctance to carry out such a simple and natural wish, I could not feel sure that any letter I might write would reach its destination. Besides, a better idea had come into my head, and finding her obstinate on that score, I begged her to help me to dress, and call a cab, declaring that I would go to the L——'s myself. That would save all delay, and they would take care of me. I could not and would not sleep another night in that house.

Mrs. Cathers lost patience.

"Tush, ma'am! What's the matter with the 'ouse?" she said rudely, and pressing me back on the pillows with a hand strong enough to be unpleasantly suggestive in my weakened state. "There's not a soul stirred in it but yourself after the gentleman went last night, and nothing ain't happened excep' that you've nearly druv yourself into a fever an' got a fit of the hystericks with the bad air in that beastly Museum, and writin' mornin', noon, an' evenin', too, as is enough to drive anyone mad. I expect you was reg'lar wore out, and most like fell asleep aside of your bed a-sayin' your prayers, and got awful nightmares in consequence, as was only natural. Why, you was cryin' out and struggling in one still when I came upstairs. And now just you lie down, ma'am, an' take a sleep to quiet you. Why, bless you! you'll be all right when you wake, and thankful to me I didn't let you go rampagin' about when you wasn't sensible what you was sayin' or doin'."

I looked up in the woman's face and saw that it was useless to try either argument or command on her; for there was a darkly obstinate expression about her mouth which told me she meant to have her way. Perhaps if I pretended to give in to her, and lay still for a while, I might be able to get up later and leave the house without any further appeal to her. That any such appeal would be futile I felt sure. Indeed, her resoluteness in keeping me in the house and preventing me from speaking to other people, with her peculiarly persistent avoidance of asking me any question, either now or on the previous night, as to what had happened, preferring to put forward a made-up story of her own as though she were going through a programme learnt by rote beforehand, made me certain that she either knew more of the secrets of this gloomy house than anyone suspected, or was in the landlord's pay to keep them from being brought to the light of day at any cost, even of life or reason, to a tenant. Put before yourself what would be the natural curiosity, wonder, and sympathy of most women of the lower orders on such an occasion, and I think you will come to a similar conclusion.

Acting on this idea I made believe to yield to her way of thinking, and also to her making me a cup of tea, which she declared would do me all the good in the world. In truth I was both thirsty and anxious above all things to regain strength enough to carry out my purpose; and, therefore, when she brought me up a large breakfast-cup full, I raised myself and drank it off greedily, although it struck me in so doing that it was not good tea, and had a strange bitter flavour. The next moment I felt myself sinking heavily back and my eyes closing. I opened them with an effort, and looked at Mrs. Cathers. There was a smile on her face; but it seemed to be getting fainter, as though I saw it through a thickening mist; and when I tried to say, "You have given me a narcotic," my voice sounded thick, and the words seemed to lose themselves between my teeth. Before they were fairly uttered, sound and sight, too, had faded away, and I was fast asleep.

How long I slept I do not know, but I should judge it was about four hours. Narcotics, especially in strong doses, have rather a curious effect on me. They both operate and lose their power far more rapidly and thoroughly than with most people. It wanted a few minutes to eleven when I awoke, and, with the exception of a slight headache, I felt at once that both my perceptions and my memory were quite clear. My bodily powers, too, had come back in a great degree; for though I felt much weaker than usual I was quite able to rise, and lost no time in dressing myself for walking, and putting up my money and a few valuables in a small hand-bag as softly and swiftly as possible. My intention was to leave the house, if possible without seeing Mrs. Cathers again; and at first I seemed likely to succeed. There was no sign of her on the stairs as I passed that awful window, now blank and bare, and filled with raw, white daylight; or in the drawing-room, the door of which stood wide open; and as I hastened down a shudder ran through my limbs, and a feeling of sickness came over me, when I noticed, what I had not seen before, a large brownish stain, which had been partially obliterated by scraping and washing, on the stencilled wall just outside the room.

There was no sign of Mrs. Cathers in the hall either, and the whole house was as still and silent as if she too had dosed herself off to sleep. It was, therefore, an unpleasant shock to me when I lifted the latch of the front door, expecting next moment to be in the street, to find that it was locked and the key gone. The dining-room too was in darkness, the shutters being still up and barred; and a feeling of nervous dread prevented me from giving more than a hasty glance into it. I preferred to boldly invade the kitchen regions, and, if I saw Mrs. Cathers, desire her to let me out by the area door. She could hardly refuse; and if she did, there were enough passers-by at this time for me to easily attract someone's attention. I went downstairs accordingly. They were narrow stairs, and, though clean enough at present, had evidently not been kept so by previous tenants, for they were stained with blackish spots and patches nearly all the way to the bottom, as though something had been spilt down them, and soaking into the wood remained there. I noticed too that the wall on one side had been whitewashed for about three feet up at a much later period than the rest.

To my surprise Mrs. Cathers was not in the kitchen below; nor in her own room, which adjoined it, and the door of which standing open showed me that her bonnet and shawl were gone from the peg where, on my previous visits to the basement, I had always seen them hanging. It flashed upon me then that she had gone out on some errand of her own, trusting to my being sound asleep, and probably meaning to return before the influence of the narcotic had worn off; and when, to my intense relief and thankfulness, I discovered that she had omitted or forgotten to fasten the area door behind her, I felt as though a heavy weight had been rolled off my heart, and a sudden resolution came to me to profit by her absence by endeavouring to discover some clue, if any existed, to those horrors nightly enacted upstairs. It did not seem likely that I should; but at least I had courage to try.

The kitchen and lower offices generally I had examined before, and found them all alike, dreary in the dreariness of dark November days, rather bare and very clean. Mrs. Cathers's room remained; but that came under the same category. There was not even anything lying about in it. She kept all her possessions in a small trunk, which was locked. There was no looking-glass in the room; and the key was inside the door. Did she fasten herself in at night, and remain so, unmoved by any shrieks or cries for help from upstairs? There was nothing to be learnt here.

I had only one more place to visit, a small yard at the back of the house. Originally, perhaps, it had been a garden; for there were a couple of lilac-bushes and a holly at one end of it; but these had evidently not borne a leaf for years, and being coated with a thick garment of soot stood up against the dank, mildewed walls like black spectres. They were high walls, so high that even if there had been any sun it could hardly have forced an entrance; and the ground beneath was black, too, and sodden with moisture. At one side there was a huge tub for rain-water, and a pile of old bottles; at the bottom a worm-eaten, tumbling-to-pieces summerhouse. That was all. I do not know what took my steps to the last-named place. Standing there under the low leaden sky, and half hidden by the spectral lilac-bushes, it presented an appearance even more gloomy, sinister, and desolate than the rest; yet something within me, something which I could not resist, seemed to force me to the door and compel me to look inside. There was nothing to be seen there at first—nothing, at least, but a pile of wood heaped up on one side, and a rusty old chopper lying across some of the billets with which Mrs. Cathers had evidently been chopping them up for her fire; but as I stood gazing, something living seemed to move at one end of the wood-stack; and to my unutterable horror—a horror which must have been felt to be understood—there came out a large yellow cat, very gaunt and rough-skinned, with an unusually big head and only one eye.

For the moment I thought I should have fainted again. This animal, hideous in itself, and the very facsimile of that whose horrible gambols I had witnessed the previous night, seemed like a part of that ghastly scene risen up again in proof of its reality; and for a minute or so the walls of the building seemed to swim round with me, and I was forced to lean on the wood-stack to save myself from falling. Then I saw that the ground where the animal had been crouching was hollowed into a hole, partly by her own claws, partly, perhaps, by chopping billets on it; and at the present moment she had returned there, and was licking and growling over a bone, which, from its whiteness and the earth on one end of it, appeared to have been disinterred in the process. It was a very small bone, not bigger than that in a rabbit's fore-leg or a human finger; and close by I saw a gleam of something else, also white, showing through the loosened mould. Conquering my repugnance I stooped down, and with a shrinking beyond all words, and which gives me a sick feeling now to think of it, drew out this white thing, discovering it to be a second bone resembling the first. A few blackish fibres like threads were hanging from it, and to it a fragment of stuff—muslin, apparently—was adhering.

The cat lay still, watching me all the while with her one vicious eye, and growling furtively. With an involuntary gesture of disgust I dropped the bone almost as soon as I had touched it, but the bit of muslin had got caught on my finger, and obliged me to look at it more closely. It was a scrap of cambric about nine inches long and two broad, hemmed at one side and gathered at the other, like a frill or ruffle; but it had evidently been torn roughly from the article of dress to which it belonged, and one end was stained with some dark brown liquid, which had dried and caked it into a hard, crumpled mass.

Like a frill or ruffle! Like—like—good God! was it only a fancy?—the ruffles at her wrist; and stained with——

How I left that horrible house I hardly know; but five minutes later I was outside it in the open street, and I have never entered it again. For several weeks I lay very ill in Russell Place; so ill that Hester was sent for from Aldershot to help the L——'s in nursing me; and as soon as I was well enough to be moved she took me back there with her, and afterwards returned with me to the North, where I have remained quietly almost ever since. On the second day of my illness Mrs. L—— and my brother-in-law went to the house in Melrose Square. Mrs. Cathers was there, and opened the door to them, professing great alarm at my absence and entire innocence as to the possibility of anything in the house being the occasion of it; but when she found that one of their first objects was to summarily send her about her business her manner altered, and she sturdily refused to go, declaring that she had been put into the house by the other lady and the landlord, and that no one had any right to send her off at a moment's warning because a poor, weak-minded lady had got a fever. She had done all she could for her, and tried to keep her quietly in bed; though as to drugging her that was all an invention, and she would swear she had not. Let them take her to a magistrate and try; and if the poor, silly woman would get up and go out what could be expected but she would get worse? Why, she had seen at the very beginning what a nervous, hysterical state she was in; and had told the landlord she did not much like being alone with such a person; and the least she expected was a month's board and wages in compensation. Tom had written to the landlord already, and an angry interview and correspondence ensued; the latter gentleman persisting in treating all suspicion of there being anything wrong in the house as equally childish and insulting, had the ground of the summer-house dug up, and triumphantly pointed out that there was nothing buried there (this was a week after my visit to the spot, and who could tell what had been done in the interim?) and spoke of me uniformly as a poor, nervous bibliomaniac, worked up into a brain-fever by a disordered digestion and an overwrought brain. Indeed, he even threatened to claim a quarter's rent, declaring that the house had been taken for six months; but my brother-in-law fought this valiantly, and he had to be content with the month's rent he had received in advance.

As to Mrs. Cathers, she disappeared during the quarrel between her superiors, and was heard of no more. My firm belief is, and always will be, that she was aware of the evil character of the house, and was heavily paid by the landlord to act as servant to his tenants in it, and cast a slur on anything they might declare they had seen there. He, of course, spoke of her as a person of the highest character, and pointed to the fact that none of my property had been disturbed in my absence as proof thereof.

But what was the explanation of the mystery? What was the dark secret of this house, so strangely shadowed forth to me, a plain matter-of-fact woman of the nineteenth century? After minute enquiries among the neighbours and shopkeepers in the vicinity, I can only say I do not know! The mystery is still unexplained: the secret still hidden in those dreary walls, never probably to be unveiled on earth.

All that the lawyer and Mrs. L——, acting for me, could find out in their research was this: The house had been untenanted for a year and a half before I took it; the last people who lived there being a blind old lady with her husband and two servants. The aged couple used to go to bed very early, and the servants slept downstairs, and never spoke of having heard or seen anything out of the common; but one night the husband, having to come downstairs for his wife's medicine, must have missed his footing, for he was heard falling to the bottom, and was picked up speechless and dying. The blind widow went away after that, and the household broke up.

Who had the house before them? Oh, a young couple; but they only stayed a week or so, and left suddenly. Reported in the neighbourhood that the landlord turned them out; said they were not respectable people.

And before that? Before that it had been empty a good while, ever since the old gentleman lived there who owned it and was uncle to the present landlord. Married? No; nor likely to have been; a very ill-favoured old gent, and not pleasant in his manners either. Had a ward living with him, however—a young lady; but she was said to be a sad invalid, never went out, and no one ever saw her, except now and then at an upper window. They went away all in a hurry to France—indeed, no one knew till they were gone; for they were not sociable people, only kept one servant, latterly a charwoman who did not sleep in the house, and had no acquaintances in the neighbourhood. Folks said the young lady died abroad, and perhaps her guardian found the house lonesome without her; for though he came back after a time he did not stay. Anyhow, he was dead, too, now; for that was how the house came to the present owner, who had never lived there himself, but let it just as it stood, furnished.

Dead! And there was an end of the clue, if any had existed. It could be traced no farther. Probably it never will be now, since, as I have said, the man and his ward are both dead; though how she died, or where, no one will ever know save God, who looks down on every ghastly secret of this earth and suffers them to lie hidden in His hand until the Day of Judgment. Anyhow, the house is there now, empty. You may pass it any day and read the big "To Let" in sprawling letters on a card in the dining-room window. No one has ever opened the shutters in that dreary room. A rumour has got about that Number Two is haunted, and that evil sights are seen there; and the landlord cannot let it in consequence. That is why he is now threatening me with an action for libel; and if he chooses he may, of course, carry it out. In my defence I can only make a plain statement, the same that I have written here. Let anyone else make what further examination he pleases, and draw his own conclusions.

Anonymous

THE WEIRD VIOLIN

Stories of haunted antiques or other cursed objects were popular in the Victorian era, and violins in particular often figured in weird and ghostly tales, the most famous of which is J. Meade Falkner's novel The Lost Stradivarius *(1895). "The Weird Violin" originally appeared anonymously in the long-running monthly magazine* Argosy *in December 1893, just in time for eerie Christmas reading.*

THE GREAT POLISH VIOLINIST, S——, WAS STROLLING aimlessly about the town, on a sunny, but cold afternoon, in November of a certain year. He was to play, at night, at one of the great concerts which made the town so musically famous, and, according to his usual custom, he was observing passers-by, looking in shop windows, and thinking of anything rather than the approaching ordeal. Not that he was nervous, for none could be less so, but he came to his work all the fresher for an hour or two of idle forgetfulness, and astonished his audiences the more.

Turning out of the busiest street, he ambled into a comparatively quiet thoroughfare, and, throwing away an inch of cigar-end, produced a new havannah, lighting up with every sign of enjoyment. Now, it was part of his rule, when out on these refreshing excursions, to avoid music shops, and he had already passed half-a-dozen without doing more than barely recognise them. It is therefore very remarkable that, walking by a large music warehouse in this quiet thoroughfare, he should suddenly stop, and, after remaining in doubt for a few moments, go straight to the window, and look in.

He had not seen anything when he first passed, and, indeed, he had merely ascertained, out of the corner of his eye, that one of the forbidden shops was near. Why, then, did he feel impelled to return?

The window was stocked, as all such windows are, with instruments, music, and such appurtenances as resin, bows, chin-rests, mutes, strings, bridges and pegs. An old Guanerius, valued at several hundred guineas, lay alongside a shilling set of bones, and a flageolet, an ocarina, and several mouth-organs were gracefully grouped upon a gilt-edged copy of "Elijah."

Amongst the carefully-arranged violins was a curious old instrument the like of which the virtuoso had never seen before, and at this he now stared with all his eyes. It was an ugly, squat violin, of heavy pattern, and ancient appearance. The maker, whoever he had been, had displayed considerable eccentricity throughout its manufacture, but more especially in the scroll, which, owing to some freak, he had carved into the semblance of a hideous, grinning face. There was something horribly repulsive about this strange work of art, and yet it also possessed a subtle fascination. The violinist, keeping his eyes upon the face, which seemed to follow his movements with fiendish persistency, slowly edged to the door, and entered the shop.

The attendant came forward, and recognising the well-known performer, bowed low.

"That is a curious-looking fiddle in the window," began the artist, at once, with a wave of his hand in the direction of the fiend.

"Which one, sir?" inquired the attendant. "Oh, the one with the remarkable scroll, you mean. I'll get it for you." Drawing aside a little curtain, he dived into the window-bay, and produced the instrument, whose face seemed to be grinning more maliciously than ever.

"A fair tone, sir," added the man, "but nothing to suit you, I'm sure."

As soon as Herr S—— touched the neck of the violin he gripped it convulsively, and raised the instrument to his chin. Then, for a few moments, he stood, firm as a rock, his eyes fixed upon the awe-stricken attendant, evidently without seeing him.

"A bow," said the musician, at length, in a low voice. He stretched out his disengaged hand and took it, without moving his eyes. Then he stopped four strings with his long fingers, and drew the horse-hair smartly over them with one rapid sweep, producing a rich chord in a minor key.

A slight shiver passed over his frame as the notes were struck, and the look of concentration upon his face, changed to one of horror; but he did not cease. Slowly drooping his gaze, the performer met the gibing glance of the scroll-face, and though his own countenance blanched, and his lips tightened, as if to suppress a cry, the bow was raised again, and the violin spoke.

Did the demon whisper to those moving, nervous fingers? It almost seemed to be doing so; and surely such a melody as came from the instrument was born of no human mind. It was slow and measured, but no solemnity was suggested; it thrilled the frame, but with terror, not delight; it was a chain of sounds, which like a sick man's passing fancy, slipped out of the memory as soon as it was evolved, and was incapable of being recalled.

Slowly, when the last strains were lost, the great violinist dropped both arms to his side, and stood for a few moments, grasping violin and bow, without speaking. There were drops of perspiration on his forehead, and he was pale and weary-looking; when he spoke, it was in a faint voice, and he seemed to address himself to something invisible.

"I cannot endure it now," he said. "I will play again to-night."

"Do you wish to play on the instrument at this evening's concert, sir?" inquired the dealer, not without some astonishment at the choice, much as the performance had affected him.

"Yes—yes, of course!" was the reply, given with some irritability, the speaker having apparently roused himself from his semi-stupor.

As the dealer took back the fiddle, he chanced to turn it back uppermost. It was a curiously marked piece of wood, a black patch spreading over a large portion, and throwing an ugly blur upon the otherwise exquisite purfling.

"See!" gasped the artist, pointing a shaking finger at this blotch, and clutching at the shopkeeper's shoulder. "Blood!"

"Good gracious!" ejaculated the other, shrinking back in alarm. "Are you ill, sir?"

"Blood, blood!" repeated the half-demented musician, and he staggered out of the shop.

It was night, and the concert-room was crowded to excess.

The performers upon the platform, accustomed as they were to such sights, could not but gaze with interest at the restless sea of eager, expectant faces which stretched before them.

That indescribable noise, a multitude of subdued murmurs, accompanied by the discordant scraping of strings, and blowing of reeds, was at its height; now and then a loud trombone would momentarily assert itself, or an oboe's plaintive notes would rise above the tumult; and, in short, the moment of intense excitement which immediately precedes the entrance of the conductor was at hand.

Suddenly, the long-continued confusion ceased, and, for an incalculably short space of time, silence reigned. Then a storm of deafening applause burst forth; necks were craned, and eyes strained in vain attempts to catch an early glimpse of the great violinist who was to open the concert by playing a difficult Concerto of Spohr.

It was noticed, that as the virtuoso followed the grey-haired conductor to the centre of the platform, he was unusually pale; and those who were seated at no great distance from the orchestra, observed also that he carried a curious violin, instead of the Stradivarius upon which he was wont to perform.

A tap on the conductor's desk, a short, breathless silence, and the sweet strains of the opening bars issued from the instruments of a hundred able musicians.

The soloist, with a sinking at the heart which he could scarcely account for, raised the violin to his shoulder, and saw, for the first time, that it had been re-strung. As he invariably left stringing and tuning to others, this would appear to have been a matter of no moment, and yet it had a strange effect upon him. Again that shudder passed through his body, and again he unwillingly met the glance of those diabolical eyes upon the scroll. Horror of horrors! was the face alive, or was he going mad?

The band, which had swelled out to a loud forte, now dropped to a pianissimo. The moment had arrived. Herr S—— raised his bow, and commenced the lovely adagio.

What had come to him? Where were the concert room, the orchestra, the anxious crowd of people? What sounds were these? This was not Spohr, this sweet melody so like, and yet so unlike the weird music which he had played in the dealer's shop. What subtle magic had so acted upon those strains that their horror, their cruel mockery had entirely vanished, and sweet, pure harmony alone remained?

It seemed to the player that he stood within a small, but comfortably furnished room. Two figures were in the room, those of a beautiful young girl, and of a dark, handsome, foreign-looking man.

There was something in the face of the latter which vividly recalled the face upon the scroll, and, strange to say, a counterpart of the violin itself rested under the man's chin.

The girl was seated at a harpsichord, and, as she played, her companion accompanied her upon his strange instrument. From the costume of both, the dreamer concluded that they were phantoms of a hundred years ago.

"Ernestine," the man was saying, in a low voice, as he passed his bow over the strings, "tell me to-night that you have not dismissed me for ever. I can wait for your love."

"It is useless," replied the girl—"oh, it is quite useless! Why importune me further? I could never love you, even if I were not already promised to another."

A savage light gleamed in the man's eye, and more than ever he looked like the face on the violin; but he did not immediately reply, and the music went on.

"You tell me it is useless," he said, at length, "and I tell *you* that it is useless. Useless for you to think of him. Do you hear?" he continued, lowering his violin, and leaning towards her. "You shall never marry him; I swear it by my soul."

The girl shrank from him, and the music ceased. Though he did not know it, the dreaming violinist had reached the conclusion of the adagio movement. He did not hear the deafening plaudits which greeted the fall of his bow; he knew nothing of the enthusiasm of the orchestra, or the praise of the conductor; he heard no more music.

Look! what is this? The girl has seated herself upon a couch, and her lover, his violin still in his left hand, is kneeling at her feet, passionately imploring her to listen. She expostulates for awhile, then repulses him and rises. A malignant fire darts from the furious foreigner's eyes; something bright gleams in his hand; he rushes forward, raises his arm to strike——

The presto movement had commenced, and an extraordinary circumstance soon made itself apparent to the audience. The violinist was running away with the band. Greatly to the horror of the conductor, the tempo had to be increased until a prestissimo was reached. Still the performer was not satisfied, there seemed no limit to his powers to-night; his fingers literally flew up and down the fingerboard; his bow shot to-and-fro with incredible swiftness; and yet the music grew quicker, quicker, until the unhappy conductor, who with difficulty pulled along the toiling band, felt that a fiasco was inevitable.

On, on rushed the fingers and the bow, faster, and faster still; a few of the bandsmen fell off from sheer exhaustion, and stared, horror-stricken, at the mad violinist. Some of the listeners rose in alarm, and many were only detained, by extreme anxiety, from bursting into loud and frantic applause.

Suddenly, with the loud snap of a string, the spell was broken. The orchestra, unable now to proceed, stopped in utter confusion, and a loud sigh of released suspense went up from thousands of throats. Then the whole mass rose in sudden horror, as the violinist dropped his instrument with a crash upon the platform, stared wildly around, clasped a hand to his side, and, with a strange cry, fell to the ground insensible.

For weeks the great violinist lay between life and death; then nature reasserted herself, and he recovered. But it was long, very long, ere he could again appear in public; whilst the weird and mysterious violin never again sent forth its strange and mysterious influence. It had been hopelessly shattered in that last night of its performance, which had well-nigh proved fatal to the world-famed player.

E. Morant Cox

WALSHAM GRANGE

A REAL GHOST STORY

One of the lighter tales in this collection, "Walsham Grange" first appeared in the Illustrated London News *Christmas Number in 1885. As readers of the first volume of our* Victorian Christmas Ghost Stories *series will know, such tales are about evenly divided between those featuring supernatural hauntings and those whose "ghosts" are revealed to have a rational explanation. The subtitle of this piece, "a real ghost story," is playfully ambiguous, hinting that it contains a "real ghost," though in fact the nature of the haunting turns more on the "real" or rational than on the ghostly. Little known today, E. Morant Cox was an illustrator of books for young readers in the late nineteenth century; this seems to be one of his few forays into fiction.*

WALSHAM GRANGE—I HAVE BEEN REQUESTED TO ALTER all the names—stood about six miles from the sea. A lonely, desolate old manor-house, with a bad name among the people round. Some horrible murder had been committed there in days gone by, and the house was haunted. Mudleigh was the nearest village, some three miles off, and queer tales were told by belated travellers of fearful shrieks, and strange lights flitting from room to room. It was, in fact, a regular haunted house of the old school.

Well, my great-uncle married, and wanted to settle down somewhere in the country.

"Look here, Ferriers," said his friend Brufton, "here's the very thing for you. Take Walsham Grange off my hands. My wife hates a country life, or I would live there myself. It seems a pity to let the old place go to wreck and ruin for want of a tenant. But no one will stay because of the nonsense about the ghosts. But you are a sensible man; and you shall have the place, grounds and all, for a mere song. And I tell you what, my boy, give a regular good Christmas party, fill the house with friends, invite us down, and we'll find out all about the ghosts, and you can see how the place suits you."

Ferriers was delighted at the notion; and they determined to go down together first, to see if they could discover anything before their wives and the guests arrived. They agreed to say nothing about the ghosts to anyone, especially the servants, who were to follow them as soon as possible. So off they started by the Exeter coach, having sent word to the caretakers to prepare for them.

Evening was just setting in when they reached Walsham Grange. They were delighted to find a capital repast ready for them, and were a good deal amused at the conduct of the old caretaker and his wife, who lived in a cottage hard by, and evidently dreaded staying so late in the great house, and were thankful when the time came to say "Good-night." After the constant rumble of the coaches, the old house seemed painfully quiet. However, they chat away merrily, when "Bang!" goes a door close by. They seize candles, and rush out, pistol in hand. Yes; the drawing-room door is shut. There is no draught. What on earth can have closed it? Oh! what's that? The door at the other end of the room is suddenly flung open. Ferriers runs up, sees something dark, and fires.

"I say, old fellow," says Brufton, trying to laugh, "don't do too much of that. It's bad for the furniture. That was your shadow."

Nothing more happened; so they persuaded themselves that it must have been the wind. And so, after a smoke and a glass of grog, they went to bed.

Next morning they thoroughly explored the whole place, but found nothing. In due course their families and guests arrived. Not a word was said about the ghosts; but after dinner, when they were all in the drawing-room, doors were suddenly heard slamming violently. Our friends eye each other askance. And, hark! What's that? A low wail, commencing far away at first, but gradually coming nearer and nearer, and culminating in one awful shriek! What is it? The ladies begin to scream and faint, and all the servants come rushing in, scared out of their wits. This helps to restore the scattered courage of the gentlemen; and, the last unearthly yell having died away, Ferriers proposes that the men should at once institute a search for "the miscreant, Sir, who is trying to frighten us." All the servants are there; and their unmistakable alarm shows plainly enough that they know nothing of the mystery. "We must go at once," says Terriers, "and discover the rascal. Ghosts? Pooh! Nonsense!" But, for all that the ladies would not be left alone. So it ended in the whole party going over the east wing, where the screams seemed to originate. The gentlemen were continually seizing each other in the gloom; and quite a struggle took place between two old gentlemen before either found out their mistake. However, this served to raise the company's spirits; and, as nothing could be seen or heard, they readily accepted the suggestion of a footman, "Perhaps it's cats, Sir." And so, feeling infinitely relieved, they all went merrily to bed.

An hour or so passed away in silence; when suddenly a yell of agony rang through the house. Shriek follows shriek in close succession. The ladies in their rooms are screaming, and adding to the general uproar: then one last frightful yell, and all is still once more!

The rest of the night passes quietly enough; and at dawn the household gets a little sleep. The servants, however, give warning first thing. Everyone looks scared and shaky at breakfast; and one guest, Mrs. Ross, is quite hysterical, sends at once for a chaise, and declares she shall die if she sleeps another night in the house. And so goes away, taking the only three unmarried ladies with her. She said she was just dozing off to sleep, when a strange creaking noise aroused her. At first she thought it must be the wood fire, which was still smouldering on the hearth, when, to her awful horror, she saw a panel of the high wainscot slowly sliding down, and behind it the most frightful couple she had ever seen—a masked man and an old woman. The former softly stepped into the room. Then she saw what she had not before observed. Bending lovingly over a cradle just before the fire was a beautiful girl. She was singing a quaint little lullaby as she gently rocked the baby to sleep. Suddenly she looked round and shrieked with terror as she saw the hideous form behind her, with one hand extended towards the cradle. A moment more and they were struggling together—anything to protect her child from the man. Then he drew his dagger; but the poor girl, in her endeavour to keep him from reaching the cradle, had pushed it nearer to the open wainscot. In an instant the old hag threw herself forward, and clutched the still sleeping child, uttering as she did so a loud yell of triumph. Shriek after shriek rang from the wretched girl. Then the man struck her down with his dagger and leaped through the panel, which was closed directly after him!

Mrs. Ross rushed to the door in an agony of terror; but, stumbling over a chair, fell senseless to the ground. When she recovered, daylight was streaming into the room; but there was no trace of girl or cradle, nor any sign that a struggle had taken place.

After Mrs. Ross had gone, a complete search was made in her room; but no sliding panel could be found. However, that night the gentlemen sat up, determined to discover the mystery. Well, just about a quarter to twelve up gets Mr. Woodbury, and says, "Look here, Ferriers; you're a sensible man; and you know you don't believe in ghosts; and I think it's not right for us to lend ourselves to such absurd folly; and, in fact, as a father of a family, I shall not consent—to—watch for a ghost. So good-night!" And off he goes to bed. After this, first one and then another gets up, glances at the clock, and says, each in more or less the same words, "Yes, you know it's only cats, Ferriers; and Mrs. Ross had nightmare. I agree with Woodbury; so good-night!"

At last Ferriers finds himself left alone. It wants just two minutes to twelve. He hesitates. Presently a dog begins to howl. This is too much—and Ferriers bolts. Well, the shrieks that night were worse than ever; and next day all the guests went away. Ferriers and his wife, of course, couldn't spend Christmas there alone, so they went too; and the old house was once more left dark and deserted.

So Walsham Grange was simply uninhabitable, much to the disgust of Brufton and my great-uncle Ferriers. Lights were seen burning more brightly than ever in the windows of the old place; and many a shepherd passing after dark was half scared out of his wits by the awful shrieks that echoed through the deserted house. Of course, the story about the ghosts, and the sudden departure of the guests from the Grange, made a great sensation in all the villages round, and kept everybody's tongue wagging for months. In town, too, all the guests were questioned over and over again by their friends, who constantly got up special dinner parties on purpose to hear all about the ghosts from the lips of one who had really been in a haunted house. But, while nearly all the visitors to Walsham declared they never had passed such a terrible time before in their lives, and would not enter the old house again for worlds, there were a great many friends who lamented bitterly that they and their husbands had not been invited.

Well, Christmas-tide was fast coming round again; and one day who should turn up but Ferriers' brother Jack, a young Lieutenant, on leave for Christmas, from his Majesty's ship Tackler, lately off the south coast endeavouring to put down the smuggling that went on there to an enormous extent. So Master Jack was full of anecdotes of hair-breadth escapes and adventures with smugglers both by land and sea.

"Ah, Jack," said Mrs. Ferriers, "that south coast is indeed a dreadful place!" And then she told him all about the ghosts at Walsham Grange.

But instead of laughing, as Ferriers half expected, the young fellow took very great interest in the story, got them to tell it again, and then quite frightened them by jumping up, banging the table, and shouting, "By George! I've got it! Hurrah! Look here, old fellow! You take the place at once from Brufton, and we'll go down together; and I'll warrant I'll clear the old house of its ghosts in a week!"

Now, Ferriers couldn't find a country house that suited him anything like as well as the Grange, and really hankered after it so much that he had been on the point of proposing to make a fresh attempt to oust the ghosts. So, seeing how much in earnest his brother was, he sprang at the idea.

Brufton was delighted. He, too, had long been contemplating another visit to the Grange, but did not like to ask Ferriers to help him again. Well, the end of it was, they all three settled to go down together. The ladies, however, much to Jack's amusement, would not hear of their going alone. If their husbands went, they must go too.

"Well," said Jack, "all the better; and better still if you will give another party, just as you did last year. But there's one thing you must leave to me. You must let me provide you with servants. Perhaps they won't wait very well at table; but you mustn't mind that. And they'll be rather fond of rum! However, directly the ghosts are laid I'll send them away, and you can get your own domestics down. Of course, the ladies can bring a maid or two; but don't take too many; and, above all things, don't let it be known that I sent the servants."

Jack started off at once to engage the attendants, and send them down to the Grange. And a most extraordinary lot they seemed, exciting general attention on their way to the coach.

Well, when the guests arrived at the Grange a few days later, they found half-a-dozen strapping damsels and as many men-servants ready to obey them. Their method of waiting at table was decidedly peculiar, and created a great deal of merriment. The first two or three nights passed away without any ghostly visitation, and everybody felt almost disappointed; but one evening a door was heard to bang in the disused wing, then another, then another. Everyone rushed out of the drawing-room, and saw to their astonishment all the servants, instead of being transfixed with terror, rushing wildly one after the other—maids and men—into the haunted wing. Then Jack, who was the first to disappear, came running back.

"It's all right," says he, "we've got him."

"Got whom?" scream the guests.

"Why, the ghosts," laughs Jack, "or one of them, at any rate. Here he is; look at him!" and just then up comes a party of the servants, bringing with them the ghost, certainly an awful-looking ruffian, white with rage and mortification at his discovery. He refused positively to say who he was, and how he came there; loudly regretting that his pistol had missed fire. Then a happy thought struck Jack.

"Tie him up tight to the balusters. Then come along to Mrs. Ross's room!" and there, sure enough, the panel by the fire-place stood open just as she had described it. "Follow me, my lads," cries Jack, snatching a lantern from one of the men, and jumping through the panel. Ferriers and Brufton were after him like lightning, followed by the servants. They found themselves in a narrow passage running inside the walls of several rooms, and leading to a winding staircase. After descending cautiously for some way, they see a light at the foot of the stairs. "Hullo! Jim," cries a voice, "have you woke 'em up a bit?"

"Ay! ay!" says Jack, bounding down the stairs, "that I have; and you, too, Brackenbury!" and before the man has time to recover himself Jack has thrown him to the ground and snatched his pistols from his belt. Some eight or ten men, sitting round a fire, are as quickly pinioned by Jack's followers. There was but very little resistance made, for they all seemed quite dazed at Jack's sudden onslaught. On examination, they find they are in an old cellar well stocked with casks of spirits, wines, silks, satins, and all kinds of excisable goods. Then Brufton and Ferriers understood why Jack was so anxious to know about the ghosts, for they prove to be a gang of the most notorious smugglers on the south coast!

Several women appeared on the scene, bewailing the capture of their husbands; and Brufton called Ferriers' attention to an old-fashioned cradle, that no doubt played part in the mock tragedy that Mrs. Ross had beheld. Indeed, ultimately Brackenbury confessed they had shammed ghosts to keep the house empty; and some ancient dresses they found in a chest enabled them to act part of an old legend connected with the house, while a subterraneous passage leading from the cellar to a wood at the back of the Grange, the entrance being completely hidden by thick ivy, afforded them a means of coming and going unobserved. Jack got his promotion for capturing the smugglers; and the servants, who, it is perhaps needless to say, were some of the Tackler's crew, got well rewarded.

But, after all, Brackenbury and his gang got off scot-free at the Assizes, for it could not be proved that they had smuggled these particular goods, nor even that the goods were smuggled. And neither Brufton nor Ferriers made any charge against them, feeling a kind of sympathy with their wild life; but the secret door was bricked up, and good care was taken that never again should they play the Ghost at Walsham Grange.

Coulson Kernahan

HAUNTED!

*This short tale, which can be read as either a story of the supernatu-
ral or of madness, first appeared in the British periodical* Time *in
November 1885. Like several other authors in this volume,* COULSON
KERNAHAN *(1858-1943) was a rather popular and prolific writer
in his lifetime, though he has been mostly forgotten today. This is
probably because his works, heavily tinged with religion and ardently
advocating military expansion and compulsory army service, have
not aged well, though given the impact of "Haunted!" one might be
tempted to wish Kernahan had written more fiction in this vein.*

A BITTER, STINGING TAUNT; A BURNING SENSE OF WRONG AND
hatred; a moment of wild, mad passion—and two human
lives for ever hopelessly wrecked and blasted! How strange and
unreal it all seems to me! Although I know that I must die to-
morrow, although I can hear the sound of hammer and saw as
they ply their ghastly task—yet, even now, I cannot bring myself
to realize that it is not some hideous dream from which I may
at any moment awake. But I know only too well that the vision
which I see ever before me, by day and by night, is no dream—
is no phantom. Would God that it were! I see myself and him
standing together again on that wild, craggy hillside. We are
talking of *her*, and there is an evil smile about his cruel lips as
he tells me carelessly that I need not trouble to send her any
more letters,—that she has commissioned him to inform me
that our engagement is at an end, and that she has promised to
marry him on his return to England. I hear the sneering tone
in his voice as he taunts me, when high words arise, with being
a pauper and a beggar; and then, as a burning sense of all my
wrongs seizes me, and a fierce thirst for revenge rushes through
my blood, I see myself raise the pocket-knife with which I have

been idly pruning an oak-sapling—I see myself raise it suddenly aloft, and in a fit of insane fury plunge it to the very hilt in his false heart!

It was but the work of a moment—a moment when I was goaded and maddened to such a pitch by the sense of all my wrongs, that I cannot believe God will hold me altogether answerable for what I did. The words had hardly died upon those lying lips before he lay dead at my feet, the warm blood gushing and gurgling from the spot where the knife was still buried. And yet I felt no horror for what I had done, no feeling of remorse came over me. Only a hideous consciousness that the corpse lay *there*, and must be got rid of in some way; because if it were so found, everything would point to me as the murderer. A sudden terror, a wild panic, possessed me. Although I knew there was none near, yet I felt that I could not breathe, could not think until I had hid it anywhere—anywhere out of sight, and out of mind. I seized it in my arms and staggered blindly on, hardly knowing what I sought, or whither I went. But fate favoured me, for my eye fell upon a long, narrow crevice in the limestone rock over which I was hastening. Panting and trembling with fear, I bent down and stuffed my burden through this opening, but it lay ghastly and bare before me, as though the very earth refused to receive the witness of my crime. With hands that shook with agitation, I seized a wedge of rock and forced it through the crevice as a covering, and saw, to my inexpressible relief, that the body had disappeared; so I hastily filled every chink with the stones and shingle that lay about, in order that no trace of my crime might remain. And then I stood up and thought of what I had done. God knows how little I ever dreamt that I should be a murderer. Only that morning I had read of the execution of some unhappy wretch, and had thought of him with horror and loathing, as of a foul thing between whom and myself there could be no kinship save that of our common humanity. And now I, too, was such an one as he! Yet I felt no remorse, no detestation of my crime. Only a dull, dead, dreamy feeling of some hideous illusion which possessed me, and which I strove to arouse myself from in vain. I knew there was little or no fear of discovery; that none, excepting myself, was aware of his being in Germany; and that, from his strange habits and uncertain movements, it might be months before he was missed. I thought it best, however, to leave the immediate neighbourhood, so that night I paid my bill at the hotel, and took the train to Rocheburg, a town some ten miles distant.

It was in vain that I tried to shake off the lethargy which oppressed me. All my thoughts were merged into one dull consciousness. As I looked at the faces of those around, they seemed to recede and withdraw to a distance, and even their voices had a weird, far-off sound. So strange and unreal did it all seem that I would repeat to myself in a mechanical way: "This is I, I, Richard Spalding," and try to shake off the spell that bound me, but it was in vain. I saw the faces of the people around, and answered when I was addressed, but they were the faces of dream-phantoms, not of living men and women.

One morning the manager of the hotel asked me if I would make one in a party which was going to drive to the famous caverns of Terrane. I said that I should be pleased to do so, or rather the automatic creature which moved and spoke in my name said so, for the real self was still wrapt in the dreamlike torpor. I have very little recollection of the drive, but I remember our arrival at the mouth of the caverns,—which I had heard were miles in extent, and the most wonderful in Europe. Our guide marshalled us in Indian file, I being last, and having placed a lighted torch in the hand of every third person, he led us into the grotto. Even in my dazed and wildered condition I was filled with wonder at what we saw. We passed through dark, icy caverns where gigantic stalactites and stalagmites writhed and twisted like huge reptiles around us. We crept, bent double, through slimy cavities and winding passages, where the chill water dripped monotonously about us; and then we emerged into an enormous cavern, so vast and lofty that the lurid light of our torches utterly failed to penetrate the unsearchable darkness that brooded around. The air, chill as in the halls of death, seemed heavy with a mysterious blackness, and above us there swept a fierce wind that howled and rumbled, like far-off thunder in the hollow womb of night. Then, as we stood there full of shuddering awe, as the wind lulled, we heard sweeping and rushing below the roar of mighty waters, and as the guide flung a torch into the gloom that encircled us, we found that we stood on the edge of a vast abyss, at the bottom of which we could see the inky gleam of black waters rolling sullenly below. And around crept and writhed foul, slimy, crawling things, that stole noiselessly away into the darkness, and above wheeled and circled clouds of strange bat-like creatures, uttering unearthly cries of blind, impotent anger.

What I have now to relate I cannot hope will be believed. It will be regarded, I doubt not, as the delirious dream of a madman— the creation of an over-wrought brain. But I know only too well that what I saw that fearful morning I *did* veritably and indeed see—that it was no illusion, no hallucination. Would to God that it had been! I have said that I felt no remorse for the crime I had committed, no feeling of detestation or horror, nor had I in any way brooded or dwelt upon the memory of my guilt. Had it been so, I could then have well believed that what I saw had no real existence, but was the creation of a diseased brain. But no thought of my victim was in my mind at the time. I can hardly realize now that I could so readily dismiss the memory of what I had done; but such was the case, and hence it was that what I then beheld came upon me with so fearful a shock.

I was the last of the party, the others having moved on some little way ahead; when suddenly a strange fascination seized and held me spell-bound, so that I could neither move nor stir, but stood rooted to the spot like one in a dream. I tried to call for help as I saw that I was being left behind, but all power of utterance seemed gone. And then a dreadful horror came over me, an awful consciousness of some evil presence. Slowly and mechanically I turned round, impelled by a strange fascination. I tried to resist, but all will-power and self-control had left me. At first I was aware only of a bluish, misty, phosphorescent light, and then a ghastly terror, that froze the very blood in my veins, seized me, for suddenly I saw rise up out of the inky darkness of a cavern behind me the form of a man—the eyes wide distended, and of a hideous red, fixed on mine with a look of hate, the mouth half-closed, but with the teeth showing like the teeth of a wild beast before it makes its spring; and the left hand pointing to a wound in the breast, where I could see gleaming out, even in the darkness, the blade of a knife!

It was but a moment, for even as I looked the awful apparition died away into the gloom, but in that moment (to me it seemed years) I recognised the face of the man I had foully murdered. A wild, exultant cry of devilish triumph seemed to ring in my ears, whence coming I knew not, and then a darkness blacker and more hideous than the impenetrable night of that awful cavern seized me, and I knew no more.

To-morrow I die, and God knows with what terror I shrink from the thought of that hour. And yet I doubt if the death which I so fear can be more awful than was the return to life and consciousness after that ghastly vision. At first I could recollect nothing, knew nothing, only that a death-cold numbness lay on heart, and brain, and limbs. Slowly I opened my heavy eyelids, to see if it were yet daytime, but everywhere round was an unearthly blackness, that folded me about like an inky cloak. I strove to pierce the gloom, till my strained eyeballs seemed as though they must crack and burst, but there was nothing save endless, impenetrable night. And then it came back to me, bit by bit. I was at Dover, at Calais, at Berlin, at Hartsburg, *he* was there; he who had been my curse and ruin, my evil spirit all through life. We stood together again, together on that wild, craggy hillside. He spoke of *her*, showed me the letters that told of her treachery, told me lightly that it was he who had robbed me of her, as he had robbed me of everything else. And then I saw it all again—the quarrel, that mad deed, the cavern, and, O God! that ghastly, hideous vision! And I was alone—alone in that fearful abode of death, alone with my own evil conscience, and the recollection of that awful apparition. My one terror was that it might reappear. The very thought of it made me shrink and shudder like a palsied man. I lay there on the slimy ground, with foul crawling things creeping over face and limbs, not daring to move lest I should see the red light of those ghastly eyes glaring, glaring, glaring down on me from the darkness. How long I remained thus I know not. It may have been hours, it may have been days; to me it was but one long, unchanging, eternal night. I knew that I could not live long so; that even if my brain did not give way under the torture I must soon die of terror. At last I forced myself, by a desperate effort of will, to rise and stand, but I turned sick and giddy at the thought of the awful abyss upon which I might be standing, and into which one single step might at any moment plunge me. I knelt down again, and crawled along on my hands and knees, feeling every inch of the ground as I went, until I came to the edge of the pit, and heard the black torrent of the river roaring and hissing sullenly below. Once the wish to throw myself over, and so end my misery, crossed my mind, but the thought of the unknown horrors which might be waiting for me in that hideous gulf made me shrink back again. And then I recollected that I had a small box of wax matches in my pocket I pulled it out, and with eager, trembling fingers opened it. There was only one left, but I felt that to see a light even for some few seconds would be an inexpressible relief. It would at least assure me that I still retained my sight, for I was haunted by an ever-recurring dread that I had lost it for ever. I struck the match and glanced tremblingly around. Horrible as was the midnight blackness that enshrouded me, the momentary gleam was still more horrible. In the darkness all was hidden, and there were no dim outlines and shadowy figures to terrify the imagination. As I looked around in the dim light of the taper, the limestone rocks and stalactites that hung about me took form and shape hideous beyond all description. Sheeted corpses and fleshless skeletons stretched white bony arms as if to seize me in their ghastly embraces. Strange beasts and reptiles seemed to glare from every side, and I beheld, or thought I beheld, red eyes of flame, which so burnt into my very soul, that I flung the tiny taper away, and buried my hands in my face to shut out the awful vision. And then the wind arose and howled and shrieked in the vast abysses, and below me I heard the hollow rush and roar of the angry waters, leaping against the slimy banks, as though impatient at being balked of their prey, so that I was seized with a sudden terror lest I might slip and fall into that watery hell, and I crawled back again with clammy limbs and parched lips. And ever in my mind there was the dread lest that awful vision should reappear; and ever I was rent and torn by the most terrible remorse that ever racked a human soul. At last I fell into a dream-haunted slumber, but, O God, what an awakening! What aroused me I knew not, but when I opened my eyes I saw a lurid light around, and there, right in front of me, was that hideous vision again—the ghastly red eyes fixed, and glaring down on me; the white teeth glittering like the teeth of a wild beast, and the hand still pointing to the wound in the breast, where the knife—my knife—was buried. And as I shrank back in horror and dread, I saw that it was no dream, no apparition or brain-phantom, which was before me.

It was the corpse of the man I had murdered, wet with the waters that had bourne it from the crevice where I thrust it to the cave-prison where I lay.

Yes, it was the corpse of the man I had murdered, come to bear witness against me. And then I heard a cry, "Good God! this is a murder!" And behind me I saw standing, with white, horrified faces, the party of guests from the hotel, whom the guide was taking over the caverns.

I was too remorse-stricken and broken to deny my crime, nor would it have availed me much had I done so. To-morrow I die, and must face the great Judge of all, to answer before Him for my sins. But no hell torments can be more awful than the agony of those black hours, and shall they not be taken into account?

W. W. Fenn

THE STEEL MIRROR

A CHRISTMAS DREAM

One of the more "Christmassy" entries in this volume, "The Steel Mirror" takes place on Christmas and features classic elements of the Victorian ghost story, including spectral images in a mirror and an ancient family legend of the supernatural. The author, WILLIAM WILTHEW FENN (1827-1906), *began his career as a painter but went completely blind at age twenty-five and turned to writing. "The Steel Mirror" first appeared in* Routledge's Christmas Annual *in 1867.*

WE HAVE MOST OF US, AT ONE TIME OR OTHER, HAD SOME experience in curious coincidences, mere matters of accident, which have fallen out so strangely as to wear the appearance of a forelaid scheme—coincidences which have given rise in men's minds to the idea of destiny, fate, or whatever we may please to call it; coincidences which, be they what they may, have, without doubt, been the basis of all superstition from time immemorial.

Presentiments, in a measure, are common to everybody, and even the most matter-of-fact individual may occasionally be swayed by them in spite of himself. Now, I flattered myself that I was one of these same individuals; I laid claim to no superfluous imaginations and fancies, I was no believer in ghosts or spirit-rapping, yet I leave it for others to judge whether what I am about to tell is, or is not, to be accounted for by purely natural laws, worked out by a chance combination of time, place, and circumstance.

Ever since I can remember, it had been our habit to spend Christmas with our old friends the Sequins, generally at their seat called "The Bower," not far from the principal town of a celebrated hunting county, about a hundred miles from London. It was a picturesque and thorough specimen of a time-honoured manor house, with scarcely a room, corridor, or passage, that had not a legend of some kind attached to it. The family, too, was one of the most ancient in England, and many were the tales connected with the daring deeds performed, and the knightly prowess displayed by its ancestors.

My father and old Sir George Sequin were contemporaries, and had religiously kept up the custom, which, I believe, had been even handed down to them by their fathers, of always dining together on Christmas-day. From them, Godfrey Sequin and I had again inherited the idea that things would go extremely wrong if the festive season was not spent in each other's company. He particularly had strong opinions on the point, and his anxiety that nothing should interfere with the custom sometimes bordered upon the superstitious.

Heirs to the jovial and kindly feelings of our fathers, we had carefully maintained this principle; but, as long ago my circumstances had so far changed as to render it impossible for me to entertain Godfrey and his wife in anything like their own style of living, the hospitality had been all on his side, and it had become a settled plan that we should go down to the Bower for a fortnight every Christmas.

I had been married some few years, when, just before one of these much-looked-forward-to expeditions, my wife was taken suddenly, but not dangerously ill, and there seemed every probability of our good old custom being broken through for the first time. The doctors pronounced it madness for her to think of taking a journey in the state of health she then was.

Letters passed to and fro between the Bower and Bloomsbury Square; devices and suggestions for surmounting the difficulty arose on both sides. I was to go with one of my girls, the other to remain with her mother; Sir Godfrey and Lady Sequin were to come to us; some plan must be adopted, if possible, to prevent our being separated at Christmas.

I did not myself feel the absolute necessity of this, but the Sequins held strong opinions about it. It would be terribly unlucky, we ought not to break through the rule whilst there was the slightest chance of maintaining it. Godfrey was even more urgent than his wife, and his letters had in them almost an imploring tone, bespeaking, as I fancied, an over anxiety and fear that something dire might happen if I failed to occupy my usual seat at his Christmas table.

Affairs remained in this uncertain state until within a few days of the 25th December, when my wife, having somewhat recovered, settled the difficulty by deciding, with that combined spirit of self-sacrifice and determination which some women display in emergencies, that, considering Godfrey's earnest wish, I ought to go down alone for a day or two at least. Her kind heart at once led her to set aside all her own feelings on the matter. She could not bear to think that my friend's happiness should be interfered with by any dislike she might feel at being left alone at such a time. She said that she should become quite superstitious herself, if she were to cause the breach of this old-established custom.

"After all," she continued, "what is it but a few days' absence; I should think nothing of it at any other season, and it is only imagination which leads one to attribute more importance to it just now; and I, you know, have very little imagination, whilst your friend Godfrey and his wife are made up of it."

Reluctantly, then, I settled to go. I say reluctantly, for the moment I had consented, a strange and unusual feeling of depression came upon me. I could not but admit the common sense of my wife's words, but nevertheless a, to me, ridiculous foreboding of evil, or, at the least, a sense of discomfort rooted itself in my mind. Apart from the joviality of Christmas meetings, I was the last person in the world to attribute any serious importance to their not being kept up, still I failed to get over the disquiet which the present arrangement had created.

However, I bade my wife and girls good-bye on the twenty-third, determining, that as Christmas-day fell on the Wednesday, to return, at the end of the week, instead of remaining as usual for the customary programme of hunting, shooting, etc. On my way down, everything seemed to combine to lower my spirits, the only other occupants of the railway carriage being a young widow lady, and her two little children. Her grief was very fresh, and it was with the greatest difficulty once or twice that she restrained herself from hysterical paroxysms of tears. The weather, too, was muggy and gloomy; thick mists had settled determinedly over all parts of the flat country through which my journey lay. Do what I would, I could not help contrasting the present state of the atmosphere with the crisp, frosty brightness and invigorating air which I remembered had set my usually elastic disposition bounding like a child's, when I travelled over the same ground a year ago.

The hearty welcome at the Bower only temporarily dismissed this demon of disquiet from my elbow, and I so continually relapsed into silence during dinner, that two or three of my old friends assembled at the house, and Godfrey especially, noticed my dejection, but dealt lightly with it, as of course my wife's absence, being universally regretted, at the same time also accounted for my own unwonted demeanour. The mirth generally, for some reason, was not as great, it struck me, as on previous occasions.

The following day, which was Christmas-eve, we were still very dull, and my own feelings considerably worse. I had grown horribly anxious, for the morning's post had brought no letter from my wife, although she had promised to write a line in the afternoon of the day I started. There was really nothing in this circumstance, yet somehow or other I was so unhinged that it had an effect upon me quite inconsistent with its importance. There were no means by which my mind could be speedily set at rest, for these were the early days of electric telegraphy, and the system of communication was very incomplete. Dankborough, the county town, was as yet without wires, and we were forty miles from the nearest telegraph station.

The arguments of Lady Sequin and her husband all failed to rouse and cheer me up, and in the most unnatural way my dejection rather communicated itself to them, for they began to feel, that perhaps it had been a little selfish on their part to insist on my presence, under the circumstances. It was the most dismal Christmas-eve we could remember; we voted it so by acclamation, vainly endeavouring to extract a joke from our universal opinion. On retiring for the night, my condition of mind, far from improving, became so deplorable that I thought I was losing my senses, or going to have a serious illness.

The picturesque, old-fashioned room allotted to me, called "The Mirror Chamber," was, I knew, noted in the annals of the house for several legends attached to it. None of these, however, lived individually in my mind, but highly wrought as it then was, this recollection communicated an uncanny ghostly appearance to the place, which it would not have borne, indeed, which it never had borne to me, on ordinary occasions.

In my present morbidly unhealthy state, it required a great effort to put out my candle, and turn into bed. After this was accomplished, the flickering light of the fire at times became so distressing that I could not persuade myself that I was alone in the room. I got out of bed, undrew the curtains, drew them back again, shifted the furniture, and generally worked myself into such a state of fever, that I quite lost all self-command, although at the same time feeling perfectly ashamed of the weak, unmanly part I was playing. Back again in bed, I tossed and tumbled from side to side, and when at last, worn out, I did begin to doze, the moaning of the wind at the casement, or the soft lapping sound of the dying embers falling upon the hearth, disturbed me with a start and a shock, which vibrated through my frame, as if there had been an earthquake.

I don't know how long I had been asleep, if asleep I really was (and this is the point which will ever remain a mystery in my mind), when a dream of such terrible reality came upon me, that to forget it, or, indeed, to believe that it *was* a dream, is next to impossible. At any rate, I was conscious of my exact position—conscious of the unnatural state of my mind—conscious of how and where I was, lying flat on my back, staring straight through the aperture, between the curtains, at the foot of my bed—conscious that I saw the bed dimly reflected in that relic of antiquity, a steel mirror, hanging opposite.

If I *was* in a dream, I was dreaming that I was awake, and awake in precisely the same place, and under the same circumstances, in which I knew myself to be; the same thoughts, the same feelings, the same surroundings were as vividly reproduced as any events in the most startling dreams ever are. The only difference being, that instead of dreaming of remote affairs and conditions, I was dreaming of the present—the positive, tangible present.

Here, then, I was lying, asleep or awake, as you please, when I became aware of a dim mist gradually overspreading the mirror, such as might be produced by human breath, increasing now, and then decreasing, just as if the action of the lungs in respiration made it fluctuate. This effect had continued for a minute or more, when I observed the reflected palm of a stealthy hand passed, as it were, straight across the steel, as though to wipe away the obscuring vapour, and then I saw upon the now unclouded metal—a face!—not the face itself, but palpably the reflex of one, as we may see our own in any glass! It appeared to be gazing at its eyes, yet there was no intervening form, no figure visible of which, I felt certain, this vision was but a reproduction.

Starting upright in bed, convulsively clutching the clothes, whilst cold drops of perspiration broke out upon my forehead, and my tongue clove to the roof of my mouth, I remained horror-stricken, for the face hitherto unrecognizable, now clearly showed itself to be that of a woman! the head and cheeks partially enveloped in something white. Rapidly increasing in distinctness, the white head-covering grew into the similitude of widows' weeds, as worn a few centuries ago, and the features! great powers! I shudder as I recall my sensations, plainly and unmistakably assumed the form of those of my wife!

The terrible truth of the likeness was made more manifest for a while, as the shape seemed to draw nearer; a spirt of flame, at the same time, springing brightly from the grate, showed the apparition with startling vividness. It was the last spark of light in the fire, which, burning brightly for one moment, instantly afterwards disappeared, leaving the room in total darkness.

I fell back in a swoon, from which I only slowly recovered as the dreary morning light was creeping through the shutters. Paralyzed though I was, by a multitude of bewildering sensations, I at last managed to dress myself, and hasten downstairs, firmly resolving, that if the post brought no reassuring news from home, I would go back to town immediately. It would be mere mockery attempting to enter into Christmas festivities under this roof.

I knew, from her active habits, that I should find Lady Sequin astir before any one else, and I went straight to her morning room, to communicate my intentions. She was unlocking the letter-bag as I entered, and her surprise at my early visit gave way, the moment she looked in my face, to a suppressed ejaculation of fear.

"What *is* the matter?" she exclaimed; "you are as pale as a ghost! Are you ill?"

"Yes, I think I am, dear Lady Sequin," I replied; "but pray tell me, is there a letter from Maria?"

We ran over the contents of the bag together; no, there was nothing for me. Then taking her hand, I continued, "I must have the dog-cart round at once, to catch the next train for London."

"Going back, and to-day! What for? Why, Godfrey will never forgive you!"

"I can't help it, I dare say it is very foolish, but you know the uncomfortable circumstances under which I came; you must have seen how distressed I have been for the last four-and-twenty hours; there is still no letter for me, and I cannot, after what I went through last night, endure this uncertainty any longer. Something *has* happened, or *will* happen, if I don't return at once."

"Gone through! And what have you gone through?"

"Why, such a night as I trust I may never pass again!"

Then, as the best means of explaining my reasons for leaving, I detailed my sensations, and the revelation of the mirror, adding my conviction that, dream or reality, it was a warning which I could not neglect.

As she listened, a shade gradually fell over her sunny countenance, and she gazed at me as earnestly as if she would catch the sense of my words before they fell from my lips. When I spoke of the widows' weeds, she sank half-fainting on a chair. A moment afterwards, raising herself with an effort, and looking up, with eyes full of a dreary abstraction, she said—

"Have no fear, my friend, have no fear. Do not leave us!—it is not, it is—not to you—but—no!—no! You never saw this, you dreamed it! Your heart was filled with thoughts of your wife—you fancied—you knew not what! You are not well. I have read that this" . . . . Then checking herself, she continued, "But why should you go? Pray do not leave us now."

I was moved beyond expression by the piteous sadness of her face, but still with the horror of the night fresh in my mind, I felt that depart I must.

It was with a choked utterance that I repeated my decision, adding, "I know the trains run to-day as on Sundays, and I shall have time to catch the parliamentary. Say anything for me you will, make any excuse you like, tell Godfrey that I have lost my senses, tell him what I have seen."

"Tell Godfrey!" she almost screamed, springing to her feet, and seizing my arm. "Tell *him!* no, not for worlds!" And her face flushed with excitement, and her eyes gleamed. "Breathe not a word of this either to him, should you see him before you start, or to any living soul. Give any reason for your departure rather than this; if friendship is not a mere word, promise me not to speak of it. Oh! promise me, promise me!"

The extraordinary vehemence and agony of her manner caused a strange revulsion of feeling in me. Why did she so earnestly implore silence? Promise! of course I would, but still I was determined to return home.

"God bless you, dear Lady Sequin," I said; "I would do all and everything for you and Godfrey, but, my wife, I must satisfy myself that no harm has come to her. Good-bye at once, good-bye, or I shall be too late." Leaving her with her face buried in her hands, I hastened out of the room.

An hour afterwards, without having seen Godfrey, or any of the guests, I was steaming towards London, my heart and mind busy with bewildering conjectures. How strange that my narration should so have affected my old friend's wife! Why should it have moved her so strongly? And what an agonized look she gave as she saw me drive away! The features reflected in the mirror were plainly those of Maria; to me, and mine alone, could there have been any meaning in what I had seen. How was it all to be accounted for? I knew not what to think, and it was only when I afterwards became acquainted with the legend attached to the steel mirror that the mystery was solved.

Occupied by conflicting thoughts, and giddy with suspense, I at last reached town after the terrible delays attending upon a slow parliamentary train, and it was late ere I rattled through the quiet streets of Bloomsbury, in the dusky twilight of the winter afternoon.

The relief which followed the surprised but reassuring words uttered by the servant, as she let me into my house, was perhaps the most pleasurable sensation I have ever experienced in my life.

"Nothing the matter?" No, of course not. Everything remained as I had left it; if there was a change, my wife was a little better, but startled beyond expression at seeing me. A few words explained all. Certainly Maria *had* written, not on the day I left, but the day after, that is yesterday, and I ought to have received her letter this morning, the morning of this identical Christmas-day. The servant had posted it in good time, had she not? No, that was just what she had not done, for, upon inquiry, she admitted that it might have been a little past six before she got to the post-office.

Mightily rallied was I by madame and her daughters for a dear superstitious old idiot; for remembering my promise to Lady Sequin, I did not tell them the cause which had mainly induced my return. I could simply attribute it to the want of news, and general apprehension of evil which possessed me. I spent a most unlooked-for, but not exactly merry Christmas evening, for great as was my relief, I found it impossible quite to recover myself, or banish from my mind the remembrance of the extraordinary effect my narration, and consequent departure, had had upon Lady Sequin. Poor Godfrey, too, how disappointed he would be—disappointed in the very thing upon which he had set his heart and pinned his faith. Unaccustomed, likewise, to ghostly influences, I felt it would take a day or two to shake *them* off. Ay, indeed, I might well think so, for even now I doubt whether they can ever disappear.

On Saturday, the third morning after my return, whilst looking for an answer to a note which I had despatched to Godfrey immediately on my reaching home, stating how groundless I found my fears to have been, and proposing to retrieve my lost character by again going down to the Bower, a letter in the handwriting which I knew to be that of one of our great friends, a never-failing Christmas guest of the Sequins, was put into my hands. Its place is here:—

"THE BOWER, DANKBOROUGH, *Dec.* 27.

"I have undertaken to break to you, as gently as may be, the details of affairs here since you so suddenly and unexpectedly left us on Christmas-day. Our good host could not recover your absence, and inveighed strongly against what he called your extraordinary and inexplicable behaviour. Throughout the day he harped upon it, and not having been quite himself lately, as I think we may all have observed, he did not take it so easily as he otherwise would. At dinner, too, he was more strong on the point than ever. There were a lot of our usual friends here, and whilst talking of you, he suddenly began to count their number, exclaiming, 'Why, bless my heart, if his absence does not make us thirteen at table!' And from that moment all semblance of good spirits deserted him.

"Lady Sequin likewise seemed affected by some mysterious influence, and was far from well. The result was the most dismal Christmas-day I have ever known in this house. Prepare yourself, my dear fellow, to bear up against what I know will be a terrible shock to you. The following day poor Godfrey, with some half dozen of us, rode over to Dankborough. Coming home, it was proposed that we should make a short cut across country; and off we went, rather glad of something to stir us up, and make a brisk finish of it.

"The speed and our spirits gradually increased, one or two raspers were taken with great success by Sequin, on a hunter he was trying for the first time. The brute had gone well so far, but in coming to a double post and rail, a rather narrow in-and-out, in taking his second rise, either missing his distance, or landing awkwardly, no one knows exactly how, he fell, rolling over we all suppose, upon Godfrey, for when we went back to the place, the horse was standing shivering with fear, and Godfrey lay stretched motionless on the ground—never, alas! to move again! We carried him home, and then—his poor wife! But I know that your eyes will be as dim, when you come to this part of my letter, as mine are now whilst I write."

Lady Sequin never recovered the shock. Her brain became partially affected. She had intervals, however, of perfect sanity. In one of these, and shortly before her death, she sent for me. Our interview was the most painful I have ever gone through. The result of it was a communication she made to me, and the purport of which ends my tale.

It appeared that only a few days before this fatal Christmas, she and her poor husband had come upon some hitherto undis-covered papers in the secret drawer of an old cabinet. Amongst several anecdotes and records of the Sequin family there was one which they read together, and which took great hold of the imagination of both.

The story ran, that such a vision as I had seen in the steel mirror, the ghostly reflection of a widowed woman, only appeared when a violent death threatened the head of the Sequin house. Its last coming was in 1746, when it had been immediately followed by the death of the first Sir Godfrey on the battle-field of Culloden. Many previous instances were also recorded of its appearance, always with the same result.

Anonymous

WHITE SATIN

This story, anonymously published in the London Society *Christmas Number in 1875, takes place around Christmas time against the backdrop of the Jacobite Rising (or Rebellion) of 1715, a failed attempt to restore the Catholic House of Stuart to the British throne. At the Battle of Preston in November 1715, the Jacobites were defeated, and many were taken prisoner and sentenced to death for treason. "White Satin" opens in December of that year, just after the Jacobite defeat, with Sir James Lisle, a Catholic linked to the Jacobite conspiracy, fleeing arrest. But the ultimate fate of Sir James and his family will turn on the intervention of a ghost.*

CHAPTER I

ROXLEY HALL

EVERY OLD HOUSE HAS A STORY OF ITS OWN, though it may remain untold, and perish with the crumbling walls that witnessed it. I know one that seems to me worth telling before it is forgotten, which it soon will be in a wonderful change of associations.

The Lisles of Roxley are not the first people who have been smoked out of their old home, but it was a shock to every one who knew the place to hear of its being let out in lodgings for miners.

To be sure there are black chimneys in the park and all round the place; and it would have cost a good deal to build cottages; and no doubt this arrangement is very saving and prudent. And there may be something absurd in the clinging to old associations, the reverence for fallen grandeur, which makes one feel that a visit to Roxley Hall now—squalid, crowded, noisy, dirty, with its stately rooms partitioned, whitewashed, hacked about, and its black, trampled garden—would be the saddest of pilgrimages. Still, I wish the house had been pulled down, and a red brick village built where it stands; for I mean no reproach to the miners when I say there is a place for everybody, as well as a time for everything.

It was on a spring day that I last saw Roxley; the house was empty then, but an old servant of the family lived at the gate and took care of it. The road runs, as it always did, through the middle of the place—a quiet road with wide grass margins, where the young Lisles used to canter their ponies. We drove up between the high, solid red walls of the house and yards, and an immense yew hedge, like a great green wall opposite, behind which were the kitchen gardens; walked under an arched gateway into a large square stable-yard, paved with round stones, and through another old ivy-covered gateway into the garden in front of the house. Part of this side was half timbered; the projecting windows in the gables looked down on a still, sad, pretty scene—a lawn with long grass growing, an empty fountain, a moss-grown sundial; then, beyond a sunk fence, the park sloping away in gentle undulations to the west, oaks and elms in all their varied tints of gold and green; the sun shining softly, reflected in the shallow water of an old fishpond down below, a lonely peacock sitting on the stone balustrade.

We entered the porch of black carved woodwork, and went through a small outer room into the hall. All the old furniture was still there—tapestry and carving and gilding of our great-great-grandfathers' days—and the Lisle portraits were hanging on the walls. Sir Henry had taken away all the modern append-ages of the place; he only came down now and then to see that it did not fall quite to ruin. I think at that time he had some idea of letting it, if he could have found a tenant; but we were told that the whole air was poisoned sometimes by the smoke which rose up from the valley, and people are not tempted to settle them-selves in such an atmosphere as that.

The library at Roxley was a long, dark room, divided into a number of recesses by screens full of books, as one sees them in a college library. One set of shelves in the bookcase opened with a spring, books and all, and showed a secret staircase in the wall behind it. The Lisles always used to make a mystery of that staircase, in a way which struck one as rather odd in these open-hearted modern days; but they have lost all interest in their old home now, and the secret has passed out of their hands. In the innermost recess of the library, opposite these movable shelves, there hung a full-length portrait of a lady in white satin, a Vandyck they say. I do not know what Sir Henry has done with it now, but I hope it hangs in a better light. Even in that twilight corner of the gloomy old library one could see how beautifully it was painted; the dark eyes looked down with a sweet solemnity, the pearls gleamed on hair and neck, there was a soft shadowy gloss on the stiffly-cut satin gown. And nobody knows who she was, this lady of Stuart days; but she must have been one of the family, for the old servant told us in a smothered voice, as we stood looking at her, that whenever any great misfortune came upon the Lisles—and they had often been very near ruin from various causes—this lady was to be seen walking about the house, carrying a large roll of papers in her hands; and as soon as she was seen, the misfortune was averted and the family regained its prosperity. Now nobody believes ghost stories, and I am not going to tell one; but this legend of the amiable Roxley lady—I wish we all had such an ancestress—was built upon a foundation of fact, on an event in the Lisle family; and as well authenticated, I assure you, as some stories you may have read when you were young in the History of England.

CHAPTER II

SIR JAMES

One snowy night in the month of December, 1715, Lady Lisle was sitting by the fire in the winter parlour—a long, low room in the south gable—working at her frame. Two candles were lighted on the high mantelpiece, but all the room was full of firelight; and there she sat in the glow in her handsome brocaded gown, with her powdered hair drawn back from a bright young face, full of thought and spirit, often pausing between the stitches, and sitting upright and very still, as if she were listening for an arrival. Presently it came: there was a little distant bustle in the house, and somebody in riding-boots came clanking hastily along the passage. Lady Lisle pushed her frame away, and ran out to meet him.

"Oh, my dear James, you are covered with snow!" cried she, as, after the first affectionate greetings, they came in hand-in-hand and stood before the fire.

"No matter, Kate; it will soon melt in this hot room of yours," said Sir James; and he looked down at her rather sadly, and pressed her hand tight between his own. He was a tall, rather heavy-looking man, sixteen years older than his wife, with a grave, deliberate, unexcited manner; she seldom saw him so much moved as he was that night, and as she gazed up into his face her own began to grow pale and anxious.

"Ah!" she said, "you have brought some bad news! Pray tell me at once. Richard is dead?"

"No; but he is in prison, and will be tried shortly with the rest. If he escapes it will be by a miracle," said Sir James, and he sighed. "These headstrong fellows pull their friends after them into the ditch. I suppose the name is enough. I have ridden pretty hard, for I left London at three o'clock this morning. There is a warrant out against me."

"Oh!" said Lady Lisle; and for a moment she drew closer to her husband, and laid her head against his wet shoulder. "But how dare they!—what does it matter? You have done nothing."

"I am on the wrong side—and a Catholic. And even if I were not myself at Preston, my brother was there."

"But against your wishes. I can tell them that. Oh! forgive me for taking his part! What are you going to do?"

"I must get away to-night, and as quickly as possible put the sea between me and them. Woolner will have a warrant to occupy the house, and to search for evidence of treason."

"To-morrow?"

"Scarcely to-morrow. In two or three days' time."

"I hate Mr. Woolner! And little Harry and I—shall we come away with you to-night?"

"The child would die on the journey. No; but you will be taken care of."

"By the Saints?" said Lady Lisle.

"No," he answered, rather absently. "Yes, the Saints, if you please—and old Baldwin. I can trust him. He will hide you for the present, and carry you, as soon as it is safe, to your aunt in Derbyshire."

"But, James! I cannot be left here. I must come with you."

"No," said Sir James, in his quiet, matter-of-fact way, stooping forward to warm his hands at the blaze. "You will do your duty, Kate; and that is to stay where I bid you. Dear, you have always been brave and wise; you will not change your nature now!"

He was not at all aware of the flood of self-reproach which, more than anything else just then, brought the tears to his wife's eyes, making the bright fire swim and dazzle before them. How often had she joined with his wild young brother in laughing at his goodness and gentleness! Well, she could make no amends now: he must ride off to exile across the snowy, desolate country, and she must submit to stay behind; there was nothing for it but obedience.

"You are mistaken," she said; "I am a foolish coward. But of course I must do as you bid me. Though, indeed, I thought it was a wife's business to follow her husband and share in his dangers."

"You will have no lack of danger," said Sir James. "Baldwin will warn you when these fellows are coming. But there is something for you to do here first. There are papers in this house that may well cost us all our heads—Dick's letters, and those of his friends, which should have been destroyed as soon as read. The careless rascal has left them all over the house, he tells me; there are three special letters from my Lord Derwentwater which must at all hazards be found and destroyed. Dick's letters to me are in the secret drawer of my table in the library; they also must be destroyed. And remember, Kate, you must not leave the house without those deeds which are in the chest in the hall, and those which are in the leather box in the fireplace cupboard in my room. If Woolner lays hands on them, I would not give much for young Harry's chance of succeeding his father here."

"You may depend on me," said Lady Lisle, nodding; "I'll carry them all away safely."

"I do depend on you," said Sir James. "Now I'll change these wet things, and be off as soon after supper as may be. Thorne goes with me. I told Farrer to pack me a change of linen. Baldwin is here now; I brought him with me from his house, being unwilling to leave you without some good protection."

Sir James went away upstairs without saying much more. Lady Lisle rustled off to consult with Mrs. Farrer over his outfit, and presently joined him in the nursery, where he was walking round and round the room with a rosy, sleepy boy of five years old in his arms. Many such partings there were in England then. Lady Lisle came up and kissed the little face that her husband held towards her.

"I know now something of what Hector felt," said Sir James, smiling.

"Ah! God grant that we three may meet again in safety."

"Amen! and that poor Dick may be with us; I fear more for him than for you."

"Poor Dick!" said Lady Lisle, sighing; and she stood by while Sir James kissed his son and put him back in his little bed, covering him up with large red hands that were as tender and careful as her own.

Then they went downstairs together to supper in the hall. Old Baldwin came in to take his master's last orders; a little man with keen eyes and a puckered yellow face. Even his voice trembled a little sometimes, and Lady Lisle was astonished at her own calmness. She felt no inclination to cry now—no, not even when Sir James had left her with a long embrace, mounted his horse, and ridden off with his man, Thorne, into the snowy night. She came back and stood by the hall-fire, while the servants watched her curiously as they went in and out. That evening was like a dream—but one of those dreams that leaves something definite behind it; something to be repeated over and over again, as if anything more was wanted to impress it on the mind:—Lord Derwentwater's letters to be searched for everywhere: Dick's letters in the secret drawer of the library table: the deeds in the chest in the hall: the deeds in the leather box in Sir James's.

CHAPTER III

TOO SOON

After standing for a few minutes deep in thought by the hall-fire, Lady Lisle took a little lamp from the table, and went silently out by a corner door, and along a short, crooked passage to the library. The room was cold and dark and desolate; every recess between the bookcases was a black little cavern into which her dim light seemed hardly to penetrate. She went on past them all to the end of the room, where Sir James's table and his great leather chair stood in front of the barred and shuttered window. Here she set down her lamp, sat down in the chair, pulled open a drawer, and put her hand to her head in some perplexity: she could not remember the trick of the secret drawer, which Sir James had shown her once: somehow it was inside this drawer, she thought—but where? and how was it to be opened? Sir James kept his private concerns very much to himself, and it was in a fit of unusual confidence that he had trusted his wife one day with this precious secret. And now the foolish thing had forgotten it!

"Well," she sighed to herself, "I'm more of a fool than I thought:" and then she rested both her elbows on the edge of the drawer, and with her chin in her hands gazed up at the dim, shadowy portrait on the opposite wall; dim at all times, but now a mere shimmer of satin and ghostly outline of face and form. "Oh, my dear madam, I've always loved you," said Lady Lisle— she was very childish still, poor thing. "Do, for pity's sake, tell me the trick of this drawer. I must find Dick's letters, you know."

But the lady, not being her patron saint, gave no answer to the appealing look and words, and Lady Lisle proceeded to poke and push in all directions. She had wasted about a quarter of an hour thus without any result at all, when hasty steps came tramping and blundering along the stone passage, and old Baldwin, groping his way and running up against the bookcases, at last arrived before his mistress, who closed the table-drawer with a sharp push.

"What do you want, Baldwin?" she said, rather sharply, for a new idea had just occurred to her, and it was provoking to be interrupted.

"My lady, my son's just come in with news. Mr. Woolner and the constables will be here in half an hour. They talk of catching Sir James, but they won't do that. They'll occupy and search the house, and you and Master Harry will be better out of it. If you'll please to hurry, my lady, there's a room in my house ready for you."

"Half an hour!" said Lady Lisle.

She had risen, but she sat down again, and stared with a wild, terrified look which frightened the old man. He was a little disappointed in her, too: his masters, the Lisles, were always brave and cool in time of danger, and here was Sir James's wife, who had parted with her husband so steadily, giving way like a child at the first shock. He stood and looked at her with a flash of something like contempt in his keen grey eyes.

"Half an hour," he repeated. "Ay, and plenty of time, too, for those who have their wits about them. Time to dress Master Harry and pack your jewels, my lady—though scarce time to sit and think about it," he muttered in a lower tone.

"Dress Master Harry! yes, surely. Dorcas will go with him of course. And listen to me a moment, Baldwin. Molly the cook-maid is about my size. Farrer can dress her in one of my gowns, muffled up well, and pretend in the morning that she has sent her off on some errand. She will be back to do her work, and the rest of the servants need not know—do you see—that I am not gone with Harry and Dorcas. What a famous plan!"

The old man was staring at his mistress now in complete bewilderment. She had certainly lost her senses—a dreadful blow indeed to fall upon the unhappy house.

"Madam—my lady, you are dreaming!" he said, almost angrily. "What harm can come to Molly the cookmaid?—Saints and angels! who'd have thought her wits were so lightly balanced!—My lady, will you be pleased to get yourself ready? Half an hour is none too much time, and we may as well be clear off before they come. That Woolner has the nose of a hound."

"Baldwin, I think you don't understand me," said Lady Lisle.

She was standing up now, quite grave and composed, though her cheeks were burning. "I can't leave the house. I promised Sir James not to leave it without collecting certain papers, which, if these people find them, may cost us all our heads. Therefore I shall stay here. No one will hurt me."

"Stay here! Madam, you are mad!" cried Baldwin impatiently. "Which does Sir James treasure most, think you—yourself or these papers? You will be arrested and packed off to prison. For heaven's sake think of your child!"

"But no one will know I am here. Not even the servants, except yourself and Farrer, and good Molly, who will be only too proud to represent me to-night in one of my gowns."

"Madness, madness! How would you hide yourself?"

Lady Lisle turned round and pointed to the bookcase behind her, but Baldwin only shook his head and groaned.

"I always loved to masquerade a little," she said, smiling. "You may assure yourself of one thing—those papers and I will leave this house together, or not at all. I mean to keep my word to Sir James.'

"But where are they? There's time yet—we might collect them now."

"And be caught in the act. No; they are scattered all about the house, and no one but myself knows where to look for them. I must be beforehand with Mr. Woolner. Be sure he is treated hospitably, Baldwin. And now we are wasting time here. Where's Farrer?"

She swept past the old man, who followed her with quick, trembling steps as she and her lamp hurried along through the shadows. Several of the servants were standing in the hall when their mistress came in suddenly upon them, her cheeks flushed and her eyes sparkling, but with an open, decided, commanding manner, which was a new thing in Lady Lisle. She stopped in the midst, still holding her lamp in her hand, and looked round on their agitated faces.

"Friends," she said, in a low, distinct voice, "I little thought we should part so soon. You will know that Master Harry and I are in good keeping. You will take your orders from Mr. Baldwin till Sir James or I return to you. I commend you to the keeping of

our Blessed Lady, who has a special care of faithful people. And—
yes, Baldwin, I'm coming—one word more. Have you ever had
reason to believe that this house was haunted?" She lowered her
voice almost to a whisper, and looked slowly and steadily from
one to another of the pale faces.

"No, madam," the murmured answer went round.

"I am not so sure about it myself," said Lady Lisle. "I have seen
something to-night; and it seems to me that I have heard some
old story of a lady who walks here in any time of misfortune.
But of this I am convinced, she means us nothing but good; and
this is my advice to you, should you meet her as you go about the
house, stand by and let her pass you quietly—do not speak to her,
or you may vex her; and we know not what power, for good or for
evil, may be given to such wandering spirits as these. Farewell!"

Lady Lisle walked out of the hall and upstairs, to her son's
room, where Mrs. Farrer and his nurse Dorcas were far advanced
in their preparations. Ten minutes later, two women muffled up,
one carrying the child, slipped out, under young Baldwin's care,
at a garden-door, and crept away across the pathless snow.

Not long after this, old Baldwin put his head in at the door of
the hall, and finding it empty, made a sign to some one behind
him. Slowly, noiselessly, and carefully shading the little lamp
she carried, a lady, with a white satin train thrown over her arm,
glided across the polished oak floor, and disappeared into the
library passage. The old man, following her on tiptoe, breathed
a blessing after her as she went. Then, in strange contrast to
that moment's mysterious stillness, the yard-gates outside were
shaken violently, rough voices shouted for admittance, and Baldwin, with a sudden angry stamp, hurried noisily to meet the servants who were crowding in.

"Hang the rascals! We must let 'em in, to be sure. No use holding out against a warrant, waste paper and false usurping rubbish
though it be."

"I've sent Molly and the girls to bed," said Mrs. Farrer. "Things
ain't so bad as they might be, after all. Mr. Woolner's a gentleman, or ought to be; and my lady and young master's safe at your
house by this time, Mr. Baldwin."

CHAPTER IV

A GHOST AND A MAGISTRATE

Mr. Woolner was a magistrate, and a country squire of good family, but much too sharp and lawyerlike for either of these characters, and generally disliked in consequence. It was a lucky time just now for an ardent Hanoverian; there were traitors to be caught, there was evidence to be hunted up; there were a hundred ways of deserving the gratitude of Government, and Mr. Woolner neglected none of them. He was a good deal disgusted, on arriving that night at Roxley Hall, to find the birds flown; but, after all, it did not matter much. Mr. Woolner comforted himself as he sat drinking Sir James's best port before the fire in the winter parlour, where, little more than two hours ago, Lady Lisle had been sitting at her frame. Old Baldwin had come in, and was standing respectfully before him. His quiet, submissive manner was rather pleasant to Mr. Woolner, who thought he could twist him round his little finger.

"So they're gone, are they?" said the magistrate. "Very wise of Lisle not to stay here to be trapped like a fox in his hole. I thought I should be too quick for him, though; but he's an old campaigner. As to the lady and the boy, we can lay our fingers on them at any time. I shall stay here quietly for the present, and look about me. I suspect there are papers in this house which will make the heads of certain gentlemen rather unsteady on their shoulders. Hey, what do you say?"

" 'Tis possible, sir," answered Baldwin. "But Sir James was never much of a writer."

"Ay, but that young fool, Dick, was scribbler enough for two. Why, when he was a mere lad he used to make verses by the score, more's the pity. Those verse-making fellows never come to good; if there's a right side and a wrong, you know where to look for them. His scribbling days are over, though, unless he takes to scratching rhymes on his prison-wall. Now you see, Baldwin," said Mr. Woolner, pouring himself out another glass, "what it is to belong to a nest of traitors. Sure to be blown up, sooner or later. Come, I always said you were a sensible fellow. Take my advice, and shake yourself free of 'em. You shan't lose your place; I'll keep you on if you deserve it."

"I beg your honour's pardon," said Baldwin gravely. "You will keep me on? I don't precisely take your meaning."

"Don't be an ass," said Mr. Woolner. "What do you suppose will become of this place? These masters of yours have looked their last on it, I can assure you. When their business is settled, who's more likely to step into it than the man who has deserved more of his Majesty's Government—more, sir, I tell you—than any other man from here to London? Come, you're not such a fool as you look. Not so clever as you think yourself, may be, but that's another thing. You have eyes enough to see your own interest."

"Well, sir, thank your honour, I hope I have," said Baldwin quietly.

"So, among other things, I want the deeds of this estate," proceeded Mr. Woolner. "I shall begin tomorrow morning to collect the papers, and look over them at my leisure. Seven o'clock—I am an early man; so all your lazy louts had better bestir themselves, if they don't want to be sent packing. Now, get along with you, and send my man Dodson. I shall do no more to-night."

Baldwin retired with a low bow, and Mr. Woolner presently tramped upstairs to the best bedroom, which Mrs. Farrer had grudgingly prepared for him.

But he was not destined to have a quiet night. At last in possession of Roxley Hall, for years the object of his ambition, he rolled from side to side of the great four-poster, listened to the wind howling in the chimneys, started at the creaking of the boards, and at last jumped out of bed, feeling quite sure that people were moving in the room underneath. He threw on some clothes, wrapped himself in a warm gown lined with fur—for the night was bitter, and cold winds seemed to find their way in at every joint and corner of the old house—took his sword and a lighted lamp, opened the door, and stole downstairs into the hall, feeling like a thief himself as he crept along. There were a few red embers still glowing on the hearth in the empty hall; they and his flickering lamp seemed to plunge the rest of the house in still deeper darkness. He stood still listening in the middle of the room. The wind howled frightfully outside, as if a thousand witches were careering on their broomsticks through the terrified air; the soft rush of frozen snow against the windows might have been the flick and rustle of their garments as they jostled each other, and went crowding past.

"Here's a night to be out in!" muttered Mr. Woolner to himself. "And of all the ghostly old holes I ever was in—I'll pull it down, and build a new house. I swear I will!"

Certainly the powers of the air were on the Jacobite side of the question that night; for this stout magistrate, in the prime of life, strong in possession and in loyalty, was almost unmanned by their wild clamour, and shivered as he walked across the hall and along the passage leading to the library. As his hand was on the door, a sudden puff of wind from some chink blew his lamp out.

"I'll open the door, however," said he. "This must be under my sleeping-room."

He opened it rather slowly, expecting to see nothing but darkness. The library was a long room, with an arched ceiling: this, and all the book-screens, with their separate shadows standing out, made it stretch away into the distance like the aisle of a church. In the background of the picture, in the innermost recess, a faint light was shining, and Mr. Woolner distinctly saw a figure bending over the open drawer of a table—a lady, in a long, strangely-cut satin gown, which gleamed white and grey and shadowy in the faint glimmer that seemed to fall from behind her.

She held some papers in her hands, which she was looking at earnestly. But the little noise at the door startled her: she stood suddenly upright, turned her head, her face being still in shadow, and gazed steadily for a moment down the room. Then she threw up both her arms in the air, still clasping the papers in her hands; the light vanished suddenly, and in the deep, black darkness Mr. Woolner heard nothing but a soft rustle, which seemed to recede into the distance. The howling wind had paused for a minute; he stood there till the cold and blackness and silence of the library became unbearable, and then turned round, locked the door behind him, and went back, with long, uncertain strides, down the passage and along the hall. Tradition says that he stumbled upstairs and into his room in a rather undignified way. He had recovered his self-possession, however, by the morning, when he sent for old Baldwin to speak to him alone, and told him the events of the night.

Of course one knows that in these days a magistrate would have walked coolly forward to the lady in white satin, and inquired judicially into her business there; but a hundred and fifty years ago there were still such things as ghosts; and, considering this, Mr. Woolner's prudence does not seem to me unnatural.

"Who is she, Baldwin?" he said, and his manner was much quieter and more becoming than it had been the night before. "I never heard that you had a ghost here."

"Oh, sir, she's very harmless," said Baldwin, gravely shaking his head. "It's bad news for the family, though, that you've seen her. She appears when any great misfortune is hanging over them. We don't know much more of her. But your honour need not be alarmed."

"I never saw a ghost before, though—and I never half believed in them," said Mr. Woolner. "She's right this time, I suspect. But, as soon as my affairs are in order, I shall call in the parson and have her laid. We shall manage to do without her at Roxley when her friends are gone."

"No doubt, sir. It's curious enough," said old Baldwin, thoughtfully; "but I should like to ask your honour a question. I never saw the lady myself—but would you please to come into the library with me?"

"Ay! what for? Stay a moment, though;" and Mr. Woolner turned back to snatch up his sword.

Then he followed Baldwin into the room, which in morning daylight and the white glare of snow looked cold, and dismal, and comfortless, without any sign of an inhabitant.

"She's gone now, at any rate," said Mr. Woolner. "And here's the table, as if it had never been touched."

"Yes, sir. Just please to look at that picture. Has it any likeness to what you saw last night?"

"By George!" said Mr. Woolner, after staring at it for a moment in bewildered silence, "'tis the lady herself—the very dress. I could swear to it anywhere."

"That is the lady, sir—so I have always heard," said Baldwin.

"And an uncommon ghostly-looking picture it is. Well painted, though. Some fools would give a round sum for that. We'll try them by-and-by; for I don't care to have pictures in my house that come out of their frames and walk about at night, disturbing honest people. Ay, the very same thing! I never met with anything so curious."

"These old families have their strange secrets," said old Baldwin, smiling a little as he turned away.

CHAPTER V

THE DEEDS

One set of shelves in the bookcase opposite the picture opened outwards with a spring, as I have told you before. Inside it there was a little narrow stone staircase, winding up in the thickness of the wall, leading to a small oblong room, with a matted floor and a low bed, and such few pieces of furniture as it would hold, warmed by its nearness to the hall-chimney, and lighted by a narrow slit in the wall between two roofs, not visible from outside, and further screened by the ivy which clustered over that side of the house. Such rooms as this seem to tell a story of adventures which would effectually shake the nerves of our contemporaries, if they were called upon to go through them.

Here Lady Lisle, after successfully acting ghost for the first time, sat down rejoicing, to look over the papers which she had snatched out of her husband's secret drawer. Just as Mr. Woolner opened the door, after half an hour more of vain endeavour, she had touched the spring, the small inner drawer had sprung open, and Dick's packet of letters lay before her. Yes, here they were, in the foolish fellow's wild, straggling hand, and as Lady Lisle looked into them, she saw enough to bring him and all his belongings twenty times over to the scaffold.

"If I had been Sir James, I'd have burnt these long ago,"

thought she. "However, here they are safe." And she locked them up in the leather box that was waiting for them.

The next day seemed very long and weary, though she slept through part of it, tired with anxiety and excitement. Late in the evening she ventured down, and found a little basket of food, and a small note from Baldwin, at the foot of the staircase.

"W. believes firmly in your ghostship," said the note. "Fright him as much as you will, but with care and caution. Make sure of the Roxley deeds, if you know where to lay hand upon them."

This word of warning was enough for Lady Lisle; it raised her impatience and daring to the highest pitch. She stopped a moment before the portrait, her inspiration, looking up into its dim features with a smile.

"Yes," she said, "I'll fright him. A ghost has no business with fear. What said Esther? 'If I perish, I perish!' She did it for her people; but I do it for Sir James, and little Harry, and Dick. Such an adventure would suit poor Dick's taste marvellously."

So she moralised, and, with her little lamp in her hand, went sweeping through the library, and along the passage to the door of the hall. There were voices talking inside. She paused, and gave three little taps on the door, which silenced them at once. She was not afraid of recognition; for she had painted and powdered her face, and drawn a white veil partly over it. She laid her hand on the latch, raised it gently, pushed the door slowly open, and glided in, her eyes bent on the ground, and her long train curling and sweeping after her.

The old oak of the hall was difficult to light up, and the lower part of the room, where she passed along, was in shadow. Two candles were burning on a table near the fire, where Mr. Woolner was sitting in one of the great chairs with a bowl of punch before him, and old Baldwin standing by, with one or two of the upper servants. All these people stared in blank silence at the apparition. Mr. Woolner dropped the spoon he had in his hand; it clanked and jingled on the hearth. The men stood with their mouths open, and old Baldwin shook his head and sighed deeply. Then Mrs. Farrer came in from the kitchen, carrying a dish, right in the ghost's path, started violently, but fortunately without dropping her dish, and fell heavily on her knees with a piteous groan.

"Saints protect us! Madam, whoever you be, have mercy upon us!"

The ghost moved her head gently from side to side, waved her hand, and went gliding on, passing between Mrs. Farrer and the company by the fire. The housekeeper, as she passed, caught up the hem of her gown and kissed it—a movement of daring affection which, fortunately, escaped Mr. Woolner. The lady was gone; she had glided out towards the staircase, and nobody seemed inclined to follow her. Mrs. Farrer crossed herself devoutly, got up from her knees, and came forward in a slow, shaky manner to the table. Mr. Woolner was the first to break the silence.

"Upon my life, these Lisles are in a bad way. Does that lady mean to walk the house every night till their heads are off? I vow I'll send for some of those fellows that don't believe in ghosts— they'll believe their own eyes, I suppose."

"Poor dear lady!" sighed Mrs. Farrer. "I wish she could rest quiet in her grave. How sad she looks, to be sure!"

"You may have your wish, dame, in a month or two's time," said Mr. Woolner. "She shall rest quiet enough, or I'll make bold to know the reason of it. There, you fellows, get you gone to the kitchen, and don't prate your tongues off—or do, if you like— they'd be no loss. Now, Baldwin, about these deeds. Where are they? I mean to have 'em, mind you; so the sooner you hunt 'em up the better."

"Deeds, bless your honour! There are whole bundles of deeds in the big carved chest in the lumber-room that's lost the key," said Mrs. Farrer.

"Then we'll have the lid off. First thing in the morning, Baldwin—d'ye hear? I wonder where the ghost is now!" said Mr. Woolner, thoughtfully. "She seems harmless enough, to be sure; but 'tis none so pleasant to have a thing like that walking to and fro in your house. I say, good woman, did you ever see it before?"

"Never, sir," said Mrs. Farrer solemnly.

"But you had heard of it?"

"Many and many a time. 'Tis a serious sign of misfortune to the family," and Mrs. Farrer sighed. "I am glad, to be sure, that my lady's not here to see it. Why, Mr. Baldwin, it would scare her out of all her pretty wits."

"So it would—so it would," agreed Baldwin.

And, with no wish to reflect on the discretion of these two good servants, I must say it was a mercy that Mr. Woolner did not catch sight of their faces just then, being absorbed in his punch.

In the meantime Lady Lisle, with all her pretty wits about her, was kneeling on the floor of the fireplace cupboard in Sir James's room, collecting a good roll of deeds, and smiling to herself as she glanced leisurely over them. It really was good sport outwitting Mr. Woolner in this wonderful way—such a sharp, clever man, as people called him, too! "There must be something in him very foolish," Lady Lisle decided. "Sir James would never be cheated so absurdly." She sat in the cupboard till the house was quite silent, and then stole back to her hiding-place. The only danger was that she might become foolhardy from success.

The next morning, when Mr. Woolner and his assistants were busy with the great chest in the lumber-loom, she actually went in broad daylight into the hall, and began to dive into the chest there, where certain precious deeds were hidden under the best tablecloths. An odd place, you will say; but in those uncertain times people thought it safer to have their valuable things scattered about in unlikely places. The bundle of parchments was safe in Lady Lisle's hands, and she had closed the lid, when a lad came running into the hall: it was Mr. Woolner's groom, a rather pert and forward boy. He stopped short when he saw the lady standing there. She fixed her eyes on him and stood perfectly still; but I suppose anything that falls short of the really supernatural is not so effective in the matter-of-fact light of day. The boy stared at her; he had not seen the ghost before, and this looked to him very like a real lady in a white satin gown.

"What's your will, madam? Shall I tell Mr. Woolner you're here?" said the boy, after a moment's silence.

There was no movement, and no answer; it certainly was strange.

"Nay, then I will," said young Tony, and away he scampered to the lumber-room, where the village blacksmith, with Mr. Woolner looking on, was working at the iron hinges of the great box.

"Please, sir, there's a lady in the hall. She wouldn't speak, but there she stands all in white. I thought I'd best tell you."

"Mum, you young fool!" answered his master. "I've seen enough of her. Shut the door: we don't want her here."

"What! was it the ghost then?" whispered Tony to the butler, who was standing by.

"Ay, booby! Couldn't you see that? Didn't you hear us tell how she came into the hall last night?"

"What, the same, all in white shiny stuff?" responded Tony in the same undertone. "Ghost! I thought ghosts were thin, so that you could see through them. This is a real lady, I tell you. Go and see for yourself. No more of a ghost than me."

"Hold your tongue, you stupid ape. You'll never be drowned, so take that for your comfort." And the butler went to help in raising the great heavy lid.

Tony was not satisfied to have all his former ideas of ghosts overthrown in this way, and presently slipped out, ran downstairs, and peeped cautiously round the corner into the hall. One thing was certain: whether she belonged to this world or the other, the lady in white satin was there no longer.

CHAPTER VI

THE LETTERS

After her encounter with the sceptical Tony, Lady Lisle became more cautious, and only ventured out when she was pretty sure not to be seen. The easiest part of her work was over. It was comparatively nothing to snatch a definite thing from a definite place; but Sir James had said that Dick had left his letters all about the house, and that among them there were three special letters from my Lord Derwentwater, which would of themselves cost Dick his head.

Every night for a week, when all the house was quiet, Lady Lisle stole from one to another of the old well-known rooms, along narrow panelled passages, up and down the mysterious little flights of steps that went winding and twisting about in the upper part of the house. It was often snowy and stormy; the wind was a friend to her, for she could move without so much fear of being heard; and all the world outside was a white waste, with great deep drifts here and there. Where was Sir James? she wondered. Across the sea by this time, perhaps; safe in France with King James the Third, who no doubt had welcomed him as he deserved. "He little knows what I am doing!" she thought. "We shall laugh over it when we meet again. O blessed Mary, that it may not be long!"

For after the first fun and novelty of ghostship had worn off, the poor ghost herself began to be sick of her masquerading. Cold shrinking feelings would come over her; she would start nervously sometimes as she passed before a mirror, or when her shadow came sweeping after her through some low dark doorway. Baldwin had warned her that Mr. Woolner had found nothing of any value in the great chest, and was sour and angry in consequence; she had better avoid him as much as possible for fear of his suspecting a trick. During these dismal December nights she turned out every drawer and desk in the house, and collected by degrees a packet of letters from Dick's friends, more or less dangerous, all of them; they would have borne serious witness against him and many others at the coming trials. But those three, the worst of all, which Lord Derwentwater had written to him before the fatal day at Preston, and which had overruled his brother's more prudent counsels, and carried him off to join the forlorn hope there—those three were nowhere to be found. Lady Lisle hunted for them till she began to despair.

In the meanwhile Baldwin had contrived one night to carry the box with all the other deeds and papers safely away to his house; and he began to give hints that it was time my lady and master Harry found their way into Derbyshire: Mr. Woolner might make up his mind to arrest them. At last, one evening, Lady Lisle had a few words with Baldwin at the foot of her little staircase.

"My lady," said the old man, "I'm in fear for Mr. Richard. Mr. Woolner has laid hands on a little valise of his with a few letters in it, and has them with him now in the parlour. I think—I think they must be——"

"Ah!" said Lady Lisle. It was a cry suddenly choked. Were her pains wasted then, after all?

"I dare not advise the risk. Mr. Woolner is asleep in his chair,"

Baldwin went on. "But listen to me, madam. You can do no more. Come away to my house to-night. You have done wonders, but there must somewhere be an end."

"If I do come to your house tonight," said Lady Lisle, "it will be with those letters in my hand. Courage, Baldwin! one more charge for the old name."

She looked at him and smiled. The old man took her hand and kissed it, for he could say no more. Lady Lisle glided off on her dangerous errand with a sudden recovery of all her old spirit.

The hall was empty; she met no one, but stole along the passages, and gently pushed open the door of the winter parlour. There, opposite to her, in the very place where she had listened that night for Sir James's return, sat Mr. Woolner fast asleep. On the table beside him lay three letters. Lady Lisle moved slowly round to his left side, half behind him, bent over the table, looked at them, and gathered them into her hand with a sudden movement. Then she looked up at him again, and saw that he was awake, staring at her with the confused uncertainty of a sudden return from dreams. Lady Lisle drew slowly back, crumpling the letters in her hand.

"I wish you a good-night, Mr. Woolner!" she said in a soft, quiet voice, curtseyed low and gracefully, glided to the door and was gone.

But he had recognised her: the eyes that, forgetting their character, had stared at him so naturally, the voice, the manner—he sprang up shouting from his chair.

"I'll be hanged if that's more of a ghost than I am. What infernal cheat is this? My Lady Lisle! hallo, where are you, my lady?"

But she was gone. An active, spirited young woman who had gained her object was not likely to stay and be caught at last. Baldwin heard the noise and prudently popped out at the back of the house. She flew, with the letters clasped in her hands and her train swimming after her, along two or three passages and straight out of the garden-door into the snow, plunging away into the shadows with her uncovered head, among the trees in the park where she could glide more ghostlike than ever from one dark mass of shade to another, and found her way at last to the house where little Harry was waiting for her. I do not think she felt cold or fright or loneliness, now that her work was done.

CHAPTER VII

AFTERWARDS

This is all the story, as far as it is connected with the picture in the Roxley library. But one more little scene comes to us over the long years that stretch themselves between now and then.

A summer evening: climbing roses hanging their pink heads and looking in at the narrow library windows; green and shade and flowers outside, a sleepy secure tranquillity inside the cool old house. A handsome sunburnt young man was leaning lazily back in the great chair opposite the picture, holding a boy of ten years old on his knees.

"But, Uncle Dick, why did the King pardon you?" said Harry Lisle.

"You seem to think I came off better than I deserved," said his uncle. "I tell you they had nothing to prove against me, except the fact that I was at Preston; and there were too many of us in that case to have all our heads cut off. You know all the rest. You know who collected heaps of letters and burnt them, so that there might be no witness against me or your father."

"Yes, I know!" cried Harry enthusiastically. "The bravest woman in the world—and that's my mother. But why did you go off to the East?"

"Because I wanted to see the world. Now all's quiet, and the Fifteen has blown over, here I am again, you see. Hallo, Harry, who comes here? A picture out of its frame."

Harry jumped away from his uncle and ran to meet the lady in white satin who was coming slowly along the room, followed by Sir James, whose grave face was smiling, and his manner quite lighthearted as he called out behind her, "Room for her ghost-ship, my Lady Lisle!"

Dick Lisle got up and went forward to meet his sister-in-law with a low bow, and bent to kiss her hand with a reverence which was not all assumed.

"Our dear and beautiful ghost!" he said, standing up and smiling as he looked at her. "And was it exactly in this dress? Why, where did you find it?"

"In your grandmother's wardrobe, Dick," said Lady Lisle.

She sat down, and the two looked at each other; the dim, soft-eyed lady in the picture, in her gleaming folds, and her wonderful likeness with the bright dark eyes and slight active figure, whose face was grave in her recovered happiness, and her lips a little tremulous, as she remembered that strange week in her life.

"She looks at me reproachfully," said Lady Lisle. "She says I need not figure any longer in this imitation of her."

"Not at all, Kate; you misjudge her," said Sir James. "She loves to look at you."

"And so do we all, bless your ladyship!" said the voice of Mrs. Farrer, who had come into the room on tiptoe, while all their eyes were bent on Lady Lisle and the portrait. "Here's Mr. Baldwin wants to know if he may have a look at you in the satin gown."

Old Baldwin came hobbling in; he was getting rather infirm now; and then Dick began to ask him questions, and so the whole story had to be told over again.

And still, when the servants were gone, and when the soft summer twilight had deepened in the room, so that the lady on the wall only looked out a faint grey shadow from her background, those four remained in her presence, till their talk dropped into a word now and then, and presently into silence. Little Harry had fallen asleep sitting on the ground by his mother's side, his head resting safely and peacefully on the white satin petticoat.

They are all gone now; and presently they will be forgotten, with the ruin of the old house that was so dear to them. Only the picture remains. The lady looks down still with a sweet solemnity, meeting our eyes as she did those of Kate, Lady Lisle, in her great trouble a hundred and fifty years ago. So it is: "the generations pass away;" and a picture here and there tells some story of the past. So it will be also with these lives of ours that are going on now.

Sir Henry talks of sending his Vandyck, one of these years, to the Exhibition of Old Masters at Burlington House. I hope he will carry out his intention, and I hope that any one who sees it there will recognise it, and remember my story of Lady Lisle.

Alfred Crowquill

NICODEMUS

Victorian Christmas ghost stories were often meant to frighten, but they were also sometimes meant simply to entertain, deliver a moral lesson, or, as in this case, to elicit a laugh. This story by "Alfred Crow-quill", pseudonym of ALFRED HENRY FORRESTER (1804-1872), *first appeared in Mary Elizabeth Braddon's popular illustrated monthly magazine* Belgravia's *Christmas annual in 1867. The story of a bibulous, reprobate monk who runs afoul of the spirit world, it ends in a punchline which that greatest of Victorian Christmas ghost story writers, Charles Dickens, would surely have appreciated.*

M Y UNCLE THE VICAR WAS A FACETIOUS MAN, with a good heart and a good cellar, who, when I first made his acquaintance, had two chins, which in course of time developed into three; but I must say, in justice to him, that he did not forget to fatten his parishioners at the same time, for no deserving person asked of him in vain, and his cook made the poor people soup of a charming consistency; so that, take him for all in all, my uncle was a very good vicar, and never bothered his simple flock with his college metaphysics. As I have written, my uncle was a facetious man, and loved to have a sly thrust at his predecessors the monks, whose fish-preserves were at the bottom of his garden— though not tenanted as formerly, but in the quiet possession of his choice brood of ducks; and the once noble abbey had resolved itself into a few cart-loads of rubble and limestone, glimmering through the trees like a ghost that cannot leave the spot of its ancient glories or troubles. Beneath this ruin my uncle, with a few old chums and us youngsters, would calmly smoke his pipe, and sound the depths of a magnum of his double-diamond port, in the cool of the evening. The spot always seemed to inspire him with a story-telling faculty, and the legends, more or less connected with late inhabitants of the locality, tinged with the mild sarcasm of his character, would run on, much to the delight of his audience. Upon one of these occasions he told us the following veracious legend of Father Nicodemus, not remembered by the oldest inhabitant.

THE LEGACY.

Father Nicodemus—an unpromising name for such a saint-like character—was celebrated for the strength of his lungs: the choir, in fact, would have been weak without his *basso profundo*. He was equally effective in the refectory, where his stomach evinced a profound depth that was quite as astonishing. His power of drinking was never correctly ascertained, as such indulgence was not permitted within the sacred walls; but, if you might judge by his nose, his out-door amusements could not have been quite so innocent. But this, perhaps, was only scandal, as anyone great in any way is sure to be pelted with the mud of the envious and grovelling; so I feel inclined not to dilate upon the colour of his nose, of which there was not the slightest sign in the statue erected to his memory.

Father Nicodemus did a great deal of out-door work. He was a kind of ecclesiastical whipper-in, and kept the idle and shirking up to their duties. He was particularly attentive to the old and the feeble who were without heirs. He always found excuses for their not attending chapel, when they paid someone else qualified to do all that was necessary for them; and even went so far as to see after the final disposition of their property, he always appointing himself the executor and curator; so that he was the cause of many beautiful decorations in the chapel of his abbey, much to the admiration of the abbot and the fraternity, and also to the future benefit of the departed—*whose heirs were never found.*

One old lady, who was the relict of a long-ago-departed miller of the Abbey Mills, knowing her husband's miller-like faculty of taking toll, most piously returned it tenfold through Father Nicodemus, who, good man, *never mentioned it to anyone;* and thereby the miller escaped much scandal.

With this old lady, then, Father Nicodemus was an especial

favourite, and the best of everything was saved for the happy occasions of his visits, which could not be too often; for if he received comfort, he brought comfort with him, and never departed empty-handed, for he always had a saint or two under expensive repair, and drew the old lady's purse-strings accordingly. Now this old lady, although she pooh-poohed the little peccadilloes of her late husband in the matter of toll, enjoyed without a twinge of remorse the ample proceeds thereof; and the mill being let to another, the temptation had departed with the tenancy, and she walked as uprightly as her age would allow her.

Father Nicodemus knew that she had what was facetiously called "a stocking" put by in some safe corner. Why a stocking, I have never been able to discover by the most unremitting antiquarian research; at all events the old lady was her own banker, and Father Nicodemus was her principal accountant and dispenser.

Gently and delicately did he handle the stocking, looking upon its contents as really his own, the possession being only delayed by the old woman's obstinate tenacity to life. At last she became so feeble that he looked upon her flickering lamp as at the last flash; and one eventful evening it flashed up indeed, to his astonishment, for the old lady, with a bright light in her eyes and power in her voice, gave him her last instructions clearly and distinctly, without hesitation or reservation, thus:

That all her property in money and otherwise should be given, after her decease and decent burial, to her husband's poor relations and a far-away niece of her own, equally divided, as he would find it written on the fly-leaf of an old account-book; reserving, as in duty bound, a certain sum, also therein specified, for the benefit of the prayers of the whole fraternity of the abbey, with all their power ecclesiastical.

Father Nicodemus, with a mental reservation, swore to perform all this; and the next morning at daybreak found him rummaging the old woman's eccentric hiding-places, and filling the pouch which hung under his cassock. He smiled as he patted the treasure, which materially interfered with his outline, and eventually interfered with his peace of mind and comfort. Thus it fell out:

The old lady being quietly disposed of, it struck Father Nicodemus that he might get permission to make a pilgrimage to some saint whose name has long been forgotten; thereby giving himself a better opportunity of enjoying the ill-gotten treasure, and escaping the whispers of the foolish and profane that were rife about the supposed rich old woman dying so poor, not even leaving a legacy to the church of her adoption to pass through the hands of her old chum Nicodemus. But as he never complained, what right had they? He shook his head, and said nothing; but being granted leave, the *basso profundo* departed on his way rejoicing.

But the old woman's spirit did not rest. She resisted the unfair advantage taken of her by her old ecclesiastical crony, and as they said in those days of superstition, "could not rest in her grave;" and she didn't.

Father Nicodemus had proceeded some miles on his way, strengthened by the good wine that hung at his girdle, once the private property of his dear old departed friend, when he found himself towards evening in the depths of a thick wood. Sombre and melancholy as such places are in the twilight, a slight moaning wind tended very much to increase the dreariness of this. He hurried on, but the night overtook him in the very midst; so that, like a blind man, he had to feel his way with his staff. The thick undergrowth twined round his legs, and precipitated him amidst the briars, and knocked his naked shins against the gnarled roots. He did not swear, but his deep bass voice growled forth his discontent in no very amiable manner—which, perhaps, after all, was his way of blessing himself.

In the midst of his misery, just as he had picked himself up after an unpleasant fall, a light, intensely bright, suddenly burst through the darkness. "The moon," said he, congratulating himself a little too soon. It was—what was it?

It was an unmistakable apparition *of a suit of clothes,* long worn by the deceased miller's wife. There stood her crutch-stick, but no hand leant upon it for support; there was her shoe, but no foot in it; there was her well-worn old velvet hood, but not—hold! was it her face? No, it was not that, but a refulgent light with a frightful — but I do not think it was ever clearly ascertained what he saw. Suffice it to say, that it was something very unpleasant, which made him tremble like a large blanc-mange. "His flesh crawled," and his marrow became like ice, when a voice sepulchrally solemn addressed him in the following unlady-like manner:

"You foresworn rascal! return the money that you have in your scrip, or I will never leave you, but throw a light phosphoric upon your path wherever you go; and I know now that your actions will not always bear the light. So refund, robber, before I strip you of your sanctimonious character, and leave you exposed to the sneers of the world, and expelled from the community you disgrace!"

As the—whatever it was—finished speaking, it faded from the old sinner's horror-stricken sight.

Father Nicodemus wouldn't believe it, yet his heart beat and the trembling had not left him. He sang no more, but hurried on until he tore his cassock and scratched his face most wofully. At last he gained a clearer path, and came in sight of a hostelry. He made towards it without the slightest hesitation, although it might be thought by straitlaced people that it was not exactly the place for a holy father; but his fear made him oblivious of trifles. But just as he sneaked into the porch a bright light was shed upon him, that made him as distinctly seen as at noonday. He turned and saw the horrid hood and phantom-beams. He uttered a groan and rushed in for companionship; and the ribald riot of the motley crew in possession was not hushed at his appearance, which was none of the most favourable.

When he issued from the hostelry again—it was deep in the night—there was an uncertainty in his gait that spoke of pottles deep. He felt his condition, and congratulated himself upon the favourable cover of the darkness; but whenever he approached a village the persevering hood appeared and lighted his path, much to his annoyance and the amusement of the villagers, who jumped out of their beds to see the cause of it, and beheld the worthy Father Nicodemus taking both sides of the way, for the simple reason that one of his legs would not stand by the other, the melancholy consequence of which was that he was brought to a standstill in the midst of a slough just deep enough to engulf him to his armpits. Here he lustily roared, whilst the hood shed its illumination round the spot, that the people, hurrying to the rescue, might see the convivial priest like a toad in a hole.

At the first blush of morning—which blushed more than usual as the dirty and draggled priest left the roof that had sheltered him for the night—poor Nicodemus turned his steps homeward, in hopes that the sanctity of its roof would defend him against the visitations of the horrid spectre, and that, with all his tools about him, he might be able to exorcise the troublesome spirit into the very depths of the Red Sea.

So, cheering up his drooping spirits, he proceeded homeward with the intention of reaching the abbey about nightfall, when he might gain his cell and a clean dress without being observed by the brotherhood, as he knew a very convenient corner whereby he might scale the wall, and which he had often used to elude the vigilance of watchers when he had been out beyond canonical hours.

Footsore, chagrined, and terrified, he dragged his body along, which had never undergone such a penance before; for truly his flesh had been mortified in all his mishaps and misadventures.

He smiled to himself as he thought how he should circumvent his ghostly tormentor when he got within the protection of the holy walls. This thought caused him to step out boldly, and reach the outward boundary of the abbey-grounds as the twilight darkened into night. He soon found the dilapidated buttress, the inequalities of which gave him a sure foothold, and had often answered his purpose on a less pressing occasion.

Unfortunately for him, the abbot that night was rather dyspeptic, therefore was indulging himself with a cool walk in the grounds, and heard the sound of some falling stones caused by the ascent of Nicodemus. He stood still and listened; during which pause the unfortunate climber had reached the summit of the wall, and was just preparing to descend when the spectre appeared upon the ground, and threw the full power of its light upon the descending figure. The abbot, startled by the sight of Nicodemus, whom he recognised, as well as by the supernatural light, rang the alarm-bell, which soon brought to his aid a pious, brawny throng, who quickly laid hands on the suspected culprit.

He was dragged before the authorities of the convent; but his rapid ideality stood his friend, and he made up so pretty a drama of the miracle kind as established him ever after as a particularly favoured individual; all of which was emblazoned in missals in the artistic department, and Nicodemus became glorified.

This was all very well, but the old woman was not to be cheated; for wherever he did not wish to be seen, the light would discover him, until his life became one scene of terror and apprehension. So at last he made an appointment with the ghost in his cell, where he took nothing but holy water, for he wouldn't give a chance away.

True to its appointment, the ghost, with its light a little turned down, made its appearance. Bowing politely to Nicodemus, it stood waiting patiently to hear his proposal. Refusing to take a chair, the clothes hung themselves on a peg usually appropriated to wet umbrellas, and, as he presumed, listened.

"Now, my good old friend," said Nicodemus, beginning with a friendly and confidential style, although, to tell the truth, his teeth chattered, "it pains me to see you in that uncomfortable position. I wish I could persuade you to take a chair, so that you might discuss this matter more at your ease."

"Nonsense," said the spirit, "it's only my clothes."

"Ah, well, as you like," continued he; "but now to business. Could not we come to some amicable arrangement? Can you not allow me to pay a dividend, and be quit of you? Come, don't be hard."

The hood slightly quivered, and said in a sharp decisive tone, "I'll see you hanged first."

"Then I'll drown you in holy water," cried he, starting up, with his ruby gills much redder than usual.

"Pooh!" said the hood; "water can't put out spirits."

"You're an obstinate old fool," said he; "and pray tell me, if I hold tight, what power have you to get it?"

"How, knave?—since you are not choice in your epithets, I'll tell you how. In the next grave to me lies a chatty old lawyer. I have stated my case to him, and his advice is, throw it *into Chancery*, and then the fiend himself can't get it."

Grant Allen

WOLVERDEN TOWER

GRANT ALLEN (1848-1899) *was a popular Victorian author and probably the best known of the writers in this volume. During his lifetime he was famous for his controversial novel* The Woman Who Did (1895), *the story of an independent woman who defies convention by living with her lover and having a child out of wedlock. He is also remembered today for his detective fiction, including* Miss Cayley's Adventures (1899), *one of the earliest works to feature a female detective and which has been reprinted by Valancourt. "Wolverden Tower" first appeared in the* Illustrated London News Christmas Number *in 1896.*

I

MAISIE LLEWELYN HAD NEVER BEEN ASKED TO WOLVERDEN before; therefore, she was not a little elated at Mrs. West's invitation. For Wolverden Hall, one of the loveliest Elizabethan manor-houses in the Weald of Kent, had been bought and fitted up in appropriate style (the phrase is the upholsterer's) by Colonel West, the famous millionaire from South Australia. The Colonel had lavished upon it untold wealth, fleeced from the backs of ten thousand sheep and an equal number of his fellow-countrymen; and Wolverden was now, if not the most beautiful, at least the most opulent country-house within easy reach of London.

Mrs. West was waiting at the station to meet Maisie. The house was full of Christmas guests already, it is true; but Mrs. West was a model of stately, old-fashioned courtesy: she would not have omitted meeting one among the number on any less excuse than a royal command to appear at Windsor. She kissed Maisie on both cheeks—she had always been fond of Maisie—and, leaving two haughty young aristocrats (in powdered hair and blue-and-gold livery) to hunt up her luggage by the light of nature, sailed forth with her through the door to the obsequious carriage.

The drive up the avenue to Wolverden Hall Maisie found quite delicious. Even in their leafless winter condition the great limes looked so noble; and the ivy-covered hall at the end, with its mullioned windows, its Inigo Jones porch, and its creeper-clad gables, was as picturesque a building as the ideals one sees in Mr. Abbey's sketches. If only Arthur Hume had been one of the party now, Maisie's joy would have been complete. But what was the use of thinking so much about Arthur Hume, when she didn't even know whether Arthur Hume cared for her?

A tall, slim girl, Maisie Llewelyn, with rich black hair, and ethereal features, as became a descendant of Llewelyn ap Iorwerth —the sort of girl we none of us would have called anything more than "interesting" till Rossetti and Burne-Jones found eyes for us to see that the type is beautiful with a deeper beauty than that of your obvious pink-and-white prettiness. Her eyes, in particular, had a lustrous depth that was almost superhuman, and her fingers and nails were strangely transparent in their waxen softness.

"You won't mind my having put you in a ground-floor room in the new wing, my dear, will you?" Mrs. West inquired, as she led Maisie personally to the quarters chosen for her. "You see, we're so unusually full, because of these tableaux!"

Maisie gazed round the ground-floor room in the new wing with eyes of mute wonder. If *this* was the kind of lodging for which Mrs. West thought it necessary to apologise, Maisie wondered of what sort were those better rooms which she gave to the guests she delighted to honour. It was a large and exquisitely decorated chamber, with the softest and deepest Oriental carpet Maisie's feet had ever felt, and the daintiest curtains her eyes had ever lighted upon. True, it opened by French windows on to what was nominally the ground in front; but as the Italian terrace, with its formal balustrade and its great stone balls, was raised several feet above the level of the sloping garden below, the room was really on the first floor for all practical purposes. Indeed, Maisie rather liked the unwonted sense of space and freedom which was given by this easy access to the world without; and, as the windows were secured by great shutters and fasteners, she had no counterbalancing fear lest a nightly burglar should attempt to carry off her little pearl necklet or her amethyst brooch, instead of directing his whole attention to Mrs. West's famous diamond tiara.

She moved naturally to the window. She was fond of nature. The view it disclosed over the Weald at her feet was wide and varied. Misty range lay behind misty range, in a faint December haze, receding and receding, till away to the south, half hidden by vapour, the Sussex downs loomed vague in the distance. The village church, as happens so often in the case of old lordly manors, stood within the grounds of the Hall, and close by the house. It had been built, her hostess said, in the days of the Edwards, but had portions of an older Saxon edifice still enclosed in the chancel. The one eyesore in the view was its new white tower, recently restored (or rather, rebuilt), which contrasted most painfully with the mellow grey stone and mouldering corbels of the nave and transept.

"What a pity it's been so spoiled!" Maisie exclaimed, looking across at the tower. Coming straight as she did from a Merioneth rectory, she took an ancestral interest in all that concerned churches.

"Oh, my dear!" Mrs. West cried, *"please* don't say that, I beg of you, to the Colonel. If you were to murmur 'spoiled' to him you'd wreck his digestion. He's spent ever so much money over securing the foundations and reproducing the sculpture on the old tower we took down, and it breaks his dear heart when anybody disapproves of it. For *some* people, you know, are so absurdly opposed to reasonable restoration."

"Oh, but this isn't even restoration, you know," Maisie said; with the frankness of twenty, and the specialist interest of an antiquary's daughter. "This is pure reconstruction."

"Perhaps so," Mrs. West answered. "But if you think so, my dear, don't breathe it at Wolverden."

A fire, of ostentatiously wealthy dimensions, and of the best glowing coal, burned bright on the hearth; but the day was mild, and hardly more than autumnal. Maisie found the room quite unpleasantly hot. She opened the windows and stepped out on the terrace. Mrs. West followed her. They paced up and down the broad gravelled platform for a while—Maisie had not yet taken off her travelling-cloak and hat—and then strolled half unconsciously towards the gate of the church. The churchyard, to hide the tombstones of which the parapet had been erected, was full of quaint old monuments, with broken-nosed cherubs, some of them dating from a comparatively early period. The porch, with its sculptured niches deprived of their saints by puritan hands, was still rich and beautiful in its carved detail. On the seat inside an old woman was sitting. She did not rise as the lady of the manor approached, but went on mumbling and muttering inarticulately to herself in a sulky undertone. Still, Maisie was aware, none the less, that the moment she came near a strange light gleamed suddenly in the old woman's eyes, and that her glance was fixed upon her. A faint thrill of recognition seemed to pass like a flash through her palsied body. Maisie knew not why, but she was dimly afraid of the old woman's gaze upon her.

"It's a lovely old church!" Maisie said, looking up at the trefoil finials on the porch—"all, except the tower."

"We *had* to reconstruct it," Mrs. West answered apologetically—Mrs. West's general attitude in life was apologetic, as though she felt she had no right to so much more money than her fellow-creatures. "It would have fallen if we hadn't done something to buttress it up. It was really in a most dangerous and critical condition."

"Lies! lies! lies!" the old woman burst out suddenly, though in a strange, low tone, as if speaking to herself. "It would *not* have fallen—they knew it would not. It could not have fallen. It would never have fallen if they had not destroyed it. And even then—I was there when they pulled it down—each stone clung to each, with arms and legs and hands and claws, till they burst them asunder by main force with their new-fangled stuff—I don't know what they call it—dynamite, or something. It was all of it done for one man's vainglory!"

"Come away, dear," Mrs. West whispered. But Maisie loitered.

"Wolverden Tower was fasted thrice," the old woman continued, in a sing-song quaver. "It was fasted thrice with souls of

maids against every assault of man or devil. It was fasted at the
foundation against earthquake and ruin. It was fasted at the top
against thunder and lightning. It was fasted in the middle against
storm and battle. And there it would have stood for a thousand
years if a wicked man had not raised a vainglorious hand against
it. For that's what the rhyme says—

> "Fasted thrice with souls of men,
> Stands the tower of Wolverden;
> Fasted thrice with maidens' blood,
> A thousand years of fire and flood
> Shall see it stand as erst it stood."

She paused a moment, then, raising one skinny hand towards
the brand-new stone, she went on in the same voice, but with
malignant fervour—

> "A thousand years the tower shall stand
> Till ill assailed by evil hand;
> By evil hand in evil hour,
> Fasted thrice with warlock's power,
> Shall fall the stanes of Wulfhere's tower."

She tottered off as she ended, and took her seat on the edge of
a depressed vault in the churchyard close by, still eyeing Maisie
Llewelyn with a weird and curious glance, almost like the look
which a famishing man casts upon the food in a shop-window.

"Who is she?" Maisie asked, shrinking away in undefined
terror.

"Oh, old Bessie," Mrs. West answered, looking more apologetic (for the parish) than ever. "She's always hanging about here.
She has nothing else to do, and she's an outdoor pauper. You see,
that's the worst of having the church in one's grounds, which is
otherwise picturesque and romantic and baronial; the road to it's
public; you must admit all the world; and old Bessie *will* come
here. The servants are afraid of her. They say she's a witch. She
has the evil eye, and she drives girls to suicide. But they cross her
hand with silver all the same, and she tells them their fortunes—
gives them each a butler. She's full of dreadful stories about Wol-

verden Church—stories to make your blood run cold, my dear, compact with old superstitions and murders, and so forth. And they're true, too, that's the worst of them. She's quite a character. Mr. Blaydes, the antiquary, is really attached to her; he says she's now the sole living repository of the traditional folklore and history of the parish. But I don't care for it myself. It 'gars one greet,' as we say in Scotland. Too much burying alive in it, don't you know, my dear, to quite suit *my* fancy."

They turned back as she spoke towards the carved wooden lych-gate, one of the oldest and most exquisite of its class in England. When they reached the vault by whose doors old Bessie was seated, Maisie turned once more to gaze at the pointed lancet windows of the Early English choir, and the still more ancient dog-tooth ornament of the ruined Norman Lady Chapel.

"How solidly it's built!" she exclaimed, looking up at the arches which alone survived the fury of the Puritan. "It really looks as if it would last for ever."

Old Bessie had bent her head, and seemed to be whispering something at the door of the vault. But at the sound she raised her eyes, and, turning her wizened face towards the lady of the manor, mumbled through her few remaining fang-like teeth an old local saying, "Bradbury for length, Wolverden for strength, and Church Hatton for beauty!

> "Three brothers builded churches three;
> And fasted thrice each church shall be:
> Fasted thrice with maidens' blood,
> To make them safe from fire and flood;
> Fasted thrice with souls of men,
> Hatton, Bradbury, Wolverden!"

"Come away," Maisie said, shuddering. "I'm afraid of that woman. Why was she whispering at the doors of the vault down there? I don't like the look of her."

"My dear," Mrs. West answered, in no less terrified a tone, "I will confess I don't like the look of her myself. I wish she'd leave the place. I've tried to make her. The Colonel offered her fifty pounds down and a nice cottage in Surrey if only she'd go—she frightens me so much; but she wouldn't hear of it. She said she must stop by the bodies of her dead—that's her style, don't you see: a sort of modern ghoul, a degenerate vampire—and from the bodies of her dead in Wolverden Church no living soul should ever move her."

II

For dinner Maisie wore her white satin Empire dress, high-waisted, low-necked, and cut in the bodice with a certain baby-like simplicity of style which exactly suited her strange and uncanny type of beauty. She was very much admired. She felt it, and it pleased her. The young man who took her in, a subaltern of engineers, had no eyes for any one else; while old Admiral Wade, who sat opposite her with a plain and skinny dowager, made her positively uncomfortable by the persistent way in which he stared at her simple pearl necklet.

After dinner, the tableaux. They had been designed and managed by a famous Royal Academician, and were mostly got up by the members of the house-party. But two or three actresses from London had been specially invited to help in a few of the more mythological scenes; for, indeed, Mrs. West had prepared the entire entertainment with that topsy-turvy conscientiousness and scrupulous sense of responsibility to society which pervaded her view of millionaire morality. Having once decided to offer the county a set of tableaux, she felt that millionaire morality absolutely demanded of her the sacrifice of three weeks' time and several hundred pounds money in order to discharge her obligations to the county with becoming magnificence.

The first tableau, Maisie learned from the gorgeous programme, was "Jephthah's Daughter." The subject was represented at the pathetic moment when the doomed virgin goes forth from her father's house with her attendant maidens to bewail her virginity for two months upon the mountains, before the fulfilment of the awful vow which bound her father to offer her up for a burnt offering. Maisie thought it too solemn and tragic a scene for a festive occasion. But the famous R.A. had a taste for such themes, and his grouping was certainly most effectively dramatic.

"A perfect symphony in white and grey," said Mr. Wills, the art critic.

"How awfully affecting!" said most of the young girls.

"Reminds me a little too much, my dear, of old Bessie's stories," Mrs. West whispered low, leaning from her seat across two rows to Maisie.

A piano stood a little on one side of the platform, just in front of the curtain. The intervals between the pieces were filled up with songs, which, however, had been evidently arranged in keeping with the solemn and half-mystical tone of the tableaux. It is the habit of amateurs to take a long time in getting their scenes in order, so the interposition of the music was a happy thought as far as its prime intention went. But Maisie wondered they could not have chosen some livelier song for Christmas Eve than "Oh, Mary, go and call the cattle home, and call the cattle home, and call the cattle home, across the sands of Dee." Her own name was Mary when she signed it officially, and the sad lilt of the last line, "But never home came she," rang unpleasantly in her ear through the rest of the evening.

The second tableau was the "Sacrifice of Iphigenia." It was admirably rendered. The cold and dignified father, standing, apparently unmoved, by the pyre; the cruel faces of the attendant priests; the shrinking form of the immolated princess; the mere blank curiosity and inquiring interest of the helmeted heroes looking on, to whom this slaughter of a virgin victim was but an ordinary incident of the Achæan religion—all these had been arranged by the Academical director with consummate skill and pictorial cleverness. But the group that attracted Maisie most among the components of the scene was that of the attendant maidens, more conspicuous here in their flowing white chitons than even they had been when posed as companions of the beautiful and ill-fated Hebrew victim. Two in particular excited her close attention—two very graceful and spiritual-looking girls, in long white robes of no particular age or country, who stood at the very end near the right edge of the picture. "How lovely they are, the two last on the right!" Maisie whispered to her neighbour—an Oxford undergraduate with a budding moustache. "I do so admire them!"

"Do you?" he answered, fondling the moustache with one dubious finger. "Well, now, do you know, I don't think I do. They're rather coarse-looking. And besides, I don't quite like the way they've got their hair done up in bunches; too fashionable, isn't it?—too much of the present day? I don't care to see a girl in a Greek costume, with her coiffure so evidently turned out by Truefitt's!"

"Oh, I don't mean those two," Maisie answered, a little shocked he should think she had picked out such meretricious faces; "I mean the two beyond them again—the two with their hair so simply and sweetly done—the ethereal-looking dark girls."

The undergraduate opened his mouth, and stared at her in blank amazement for a moment. "Well, I don't see——" he began, and broke off suddenly. Something in Maisie's eye seemed to give him pause. He fondled his moustache, hesitated, and was silent.

"How nice to have read the Greek and know what it all means!" Maisie went on, after a minute. "It's a human sacrifice, of course; but, please, what is the story?"

The undergraduate hummed and hawed. "Well, it's in Euripides, you know," he said, trying to look impressive, "and—er—and I haven't taken up Euripides for my next examination. But I *think* it's like this. Iphigenia was a daughter of Agamemnon's, don't you know, and he had offended Artemis or somebody— some other goddess; and he vowed to offer up to her the most beautiful thing that should be born that year, by way of reparation—just like Jephthah. Well, Iphigenia was considered the most beautiful product of the particular twelvemonth—don't look at me like that, please! you—you make me nervous—and so, when the young woman grew up—well, I don't quite recollect the ins and outs of the details, but it's a human sacrifice business, don't you see; and they're just going to kill her, though I *believe* a hind was finally substituted for the girl, like the ram for Isaac; but I must confess I've a very vague recollection of it." He rose from his seat uneasily. "I'm afraid," he went on, shuffling about for an excuse to move, "these chairs are too close. I seem to be incommoding you."

He moved away with a furtive air. At the end of the tableau one or two of the characters who were not needed in succeeding pieces came down from the stage and joined the body of spectators, as they often do, in their character-dresses—a good opportunity, in point of fact, for retaining through the evening the advantages conferred by theatrical costume, rouge, and pearl-powder. Among them the two girls Maisie had admired so much glided quietly toward her and took the two vacant seats on either side, one of which had just been quitted by the awkward undergraduate. They were not only beautiful in face and figure, on a closer view, but Maisie found them from the first extremely sympathetic. They burst into talk with her, frankly and at once, with charming ease and grace of manner. They were ladies in the grain, in instinct and breeding. The taller of the two, whom the other addressed as Yolande, seemed particularly pleasing. The very name charmed Maisie. She was friends with them at once. They both possessed a certain nameless attraction that constitutes in itself the best possible introduction. Maisie hesitated to ask them whence they came, but it was clear from their talk they knew Wolverden intimately.

After a minute the piano struck up once more. A famous Scotch vocalist, in a diamond necklet and a dress to match, took her place on the stage, just in front of the footlights. As chance would have it, she began singing the song Maisie most of all hated. It was Scott's ballad of "Proud Maisie," set to music by Carlo Ludovici—

> "Proud Maisie is in the wood,
> Walking so early;
> Sweet Robin sits on the bush,
> Singing so rarely.
>
> 'Tell me, thou bonny bird,
> When shall I marry me?'
> 'When six braw gentlemen
> Kirkward shall carry ye.'
>
> 'Who makes the bridal bed,
> Birdie, say truly?'

'The grey-headed sexton
That delves the grave duly.

'The glow-worm o'er grave and stone
Shall light thee steady;
The owl from the steeple sing,
"Welcome, proud lady." ' "

Maisie listened to the song with grave discomfort. She had never liked it, and to-night it appalled her. She did not know that just at that moment Mrs. West was whispering in a perfect fever of apology to a lady by her side, "Oh dear! oh dear! what a dreadful thing of me ever to have permitted that song to be sung here to-night! It was horribly thoughtless! Why, now I remember, Miss Llewelyn's name, you know, is Maisie!—and there she is listening to it with a face like a sheet! I shall never forgive myself!"

The tall, dark girl by Maisie's side, whom the other called Yolande, leaned across to her sympathetically. "You don't like that song?" she said, with just a tinge of reproach in her voice as she said it.

"I hate it!" Maisie answered, trying hard to compose herself.

"Why so?" the tall, dark girl asked, in a tone of calm and singular sweetness. "It is sad, perhaps; but it's lovely—and natural!"

"My own name is Maisie," her new friend replied, with an ill-repressed shudder. "And somehow that song pursues me through life. I seem always to hear the horrid ring of the words, 'When six braw gentlemen kirkward shall carry ye.' I wish to Heaven my people had never called me Maisie!"

"And yet *why*?" the tall, dark girl asked again, with a sad, mysterious air. "Why this clinging to life—this terror of death—this inexplicable attachment to a world of misery? And with such eyes as yours, too! Your eyes are like mine"—which was a compliment, certainly, for the dark girl's own pair were strangely deep and lustrous. "People with eyes such as those, that can look into futurity, ought not surely to shrink from a mere gate like death! For death is but a gate—the gate of life in its fullest beauty. It is written over the door, 'Mors janua vitae.' "

"What door?" Maisie asked—for she remembered having read

those selfsame words, and tried in vain to translate them, that very day, though the meaning was now clear to her.

The answer electrified her: "The gate of the vault in Wolverden churchyard."

She said it very low, but with pregnant expression.

"Oh, how dreadful!" Maisie exclaimed, drawing back. The tall, dark girl half frightened her.

"Not at all," the girl answered. "This life is so short, so vain, so transitory! And beyond it is peace—eternal peace—the calm of rest—the joy of the spirit."

"You come to anchor at last," her companion added.

"But if—one has somebody one would not wish to leave behind?" Maisie suggested timidly.

"He will follow before long," the dark girl replied with quiet decision, interpreting rightly the sex of the indefinite substantive. "Time passes so quickly. And if time passes quickly in time, how much more, then, in eternity!"

"Hush, Yolande," the other dark girl put in, with a warning glance; "there's a new tableau coming. Let me see, is this 'The Death of Ophelia'? No, that's number four; this is number three, 'The Martyrdom of St. Agnes.'"

III

"My dear," Mrs. West said, positively oozing apology, when she met Maisie in the supper-room, "I'm afraid you've been left in a corner by yourself almost all the evening!"

"Oh dear, no," Maisie answered with a quiet smile. "I had that Oxford undergraduate at my elbow at first; and afterwards those two nice girls, with the flowing white dresses and the beautiful eyes, came and sat beside me. What's their name, I wonder?"

"Which girls?" Mrs. West asked, with a little surprise in her tone, for her impression was rather that Maisie had been sitting between two empty chairs for the greater part of the evening, muttering at times to herself in the most uncanny way, but not talking to anybody.

Maisie glanced round the room in search of her new friends,

and for some time could not see them. At last, she observed them in a remote alcove, drinking red wine by themselves out of Venetian-glass beakers. "Those two," she said, pointing towards them. "They're such charming girls! Can you tell me who they are? I've quite taken a fancy to them."

Mrs. West gazed at them for a second—or rather, at the recess towards which Maisie pointed—and then turned to Maisie with much the same oddly embarrassed look and manner as the undergraduate's. "Oh, *those!*" she said slowly, peering through and through her, Maisie thought. "Those—must be some of the professionals from London. At any rate—I'm not sure which you mean—over there by the curtain, in the Moorish nook, you say— well, I can't tell you their names! So they *must* be professionals."

She went off with a singularly frightened manner. Maisie noticed it and wondered at it. But it made no great or lasting impression.

When the party broke up, about midnight or a little later, Maisie went along the corridor to her own bedroom. At the end, by the door, the two other girls happened to be standing, apparently gossiping.

"Oh, you've not gone home yet?" Maisie said, as she passed, to Yolande.

"No, we're stopping here," the dark girl with the speaking eyes answered.

Maisie paused for a second. Then an impulse burst over her. "Will you come and see my room?" she asked, a little timidly.

"Shall we go, Hedda?" Yolande said, with an inquiring glance at her companion.

Her friend nodded assent. Maisie opened the door, and ushered them into her bedroom.

The ostentatiously opulent fire was still burning brightly, the electric light flooded the room with its brilliancy, the curtains were drawn, and the shutters fastened. For a while the three girls sat together by the hearth and gossiped quietly. Maisie liked her new friends—their voices were so gentle, soft, and sympathetic, while for face and figure they might have sat as models to Burne-Jones or Botticelli. Their dresses, too, took her delicate Welsh fancy; they were so dainty, yet so simple. The soft silk fell in natural folds and dimples. The only ornaments they wore were two curious brooches of very antique workmanship—as Maisie supposed—somewhat Celtic in design, and enamelled in blood-red on a gold background. Each carried a flower laid loosely in her bosom. Yolande's was an orchid with long, floating streamers, in colour and shape recalling some Southern lizard; dark purple spots dappled its lip and petals. Hedda's was a flower of a sort Maisie had never before seen—the stem spotted like a viper's skin, green flecked with russet-brown, and uncanny to look upon; on either side, great twisted spirals of red-and-blue blossoms, each curled after the fashion of a scorpion's tail, very strange and lurid. Something weird and witch-like about flowers and dresses rather attracted Maisie; they affected her with the half-repellent fascination of a snake for a bird; she felt such blossoms were fit for incantations and sorceries. But a lily-of-the-valley in Yolande's dark hair gave a sense of purity which assorted better with the girl's exquisitely calm and nun-like beauty.

After a while Hedda rose. "This air is close," she said. "It ought to be warm outside to-night, if one may judge by the sunset. May I open the window?"

"Oh, certainly, if you like," Maisie answered, a vague foreboding now struggling within her against innate politeness.

Hedda drew back the curtains and unfastened the shutters. It was a moonlit evening. The breeze hardly stirred the bare boughs of the silver birches. A sprinkling of soft snow on the terrace and the hills just whitened the ground. The moon lighted it up, falling full upon the Hall; the church and tower below stood silhouetted in dark against a cloudless expanse of starry sky in the background. Hedda opened the window. Cool, fresh air blew in, very soft and genial, in spite of the snow and the lateness of the season. "What a glorious night!" she said, looking up at Orion overhead. "Shall we stroll out for a while in it?"

If the suggestion had not thus been thrust upon her from outside, it would never have occurred to Maisie to walk abroad in a strange place, in evening dress, on a winter's night, with snow whitening the ground; but Hedda's voice sounded so sweetly persuasive, and the idea itself seemed so natural now she had once proposed it, that Maisie followed her two new friends on to the moonlit terrace without a moment's hesitation.

They paced once or twice up and down the gravelled walks. Strange to say, though a sprinkling of dry snow powdered the ground under foot, the air itself was soft and balmy. Stranger still, Maisie noticed, almost without noticing it, that though they walked three abreast, only one pair of footprints—her own— lay impressed on the snow in a long trail when they turned at either end and re-paced the platform. Yolande and Hedda must step lightly indeed; or perhaps her own feet might be warmer or thinner shod, so as to melt the light layer of snow more readily.

The girls slipped their arms through hers. A little thrill coursed through her. Then, after three or four turns up and down the terrace, Yolande led the way quietly down the broad flight of steps in the direction of the church on the lower level. In that bright, broad moonlight Maisie went with them undeterred; the Hall was still alive with the glare of electric lights in bedroom windows; and the presence of the other girls, both wholly free from any signs of fear, took off all sense of terror or loneliness. They strolled on into the churchyard. Maisie's eyes were now fixed on the new white tower, which merged in the silhouette against the starry sky into much the same grey and indefinite hue as the older parts of the building. Before she quite knew where she was, she found herself at the head of the worn stone steps which led into the vault by whose doors she had seen old Bessie sitting. In the pallid moonlight, with the aid of the greenish reflection from the snow, she could just read the words inscribed over the portal, the words that Yolande had repeated in the drawing-room, "Mors janua vitae."

Yolande moved down one step. Maisie drew back for the first time with a faint access of alarm. "You're—you're not *going down* there!" she exclaimed, catching her breath for a second.

"Yes, I am," her new friend answered in a calmly quiet voice. "Why not? We live here."

"You live here?" Maisie echoed, freeing her arms by a sudden movement and standing away from her mysterious friends with a tremulous shudder.

"Yes, we live here," Hedda broke in, without the slightest emotion. She said it in a voice of perfect calm, as one might say it of any house in a street in London.

Maisie was far less terrified than she might have imagined beforehand would be the case under such unexpected conditions. The two girls were so simple, so natural, so strangely like herself, that she could not say she was really afraid of them. She shrank, it is true, from the nature of the door at which they stood, but she received the unearthly announcement that they lived there with scarcely more than a slight tremor of surprise and astonishment.

"You will come in with us?" Hedda said in a gently enticing tone. "We went into your bedroom."

Maisie hardly liked to say no. They seemed so anxious to show her their home. With trembling feet she moved down the first step, and then the second. Yolande kept ever one pace in front of her. As Maisie reached the third step, the two girls, as if moved by one design, took her wrists in their hands, not unkindly, but coaxingly. They reached the actual doors of the vault itself—two heavy bronze valves, meeting in the centre. Each bore a ring for a handle, pierced through a Gorgon's head embossed upon the surface. Yolande pushed them with her hand. They yielded instantly to her light touch, and opened *inward*. Yolande, still in front, passed from the glow of the moon to the gloom of the vault, which a ray of moonlight just descended obliquely. As she passed, for a second, a weird sight met Maisie's eyes. Her face and hands and dress became momentarily self-luminous; but through them, as they glowed, she could descry within every bone and joint of her living skeleton, dimly shadowed in dark through the luminous haze that marked her body.

Maisie drew back once more, terrified. Yet her terror was not quite what one could describe as fear: it was rather a vague sense of the profoundly mystical. "I can't! I can't!" she cried, with an appealing glance. "Hedda! Yolande! I cannot go with you."

Hedda held her hand tight, and almost seemed to force her. But Yolande, in front, like a mother with her child, turned round with a grave smile, "No, no," she said reprovingly. "Let her come if she will, Hedda, of her own accord, not otherwise. The tower demands a willing victim."

Her hand on Maisie's wrist was strong but persuasive. It drew her without exercising the faintest compulsion. "Will you come with us, dear?" she said, in that winning silvery tone which had captivated Maisie's fancy from the very first moment they spoke together. Maisie gazed into her eyes. They were deep and tender. A strange resolution seemed to nerve her for the effort. "Yes, yes—I—will—come—with you," she answered slowly.

Hedda on one side, Yolande on the other, now went before her, holding her wrists in their grasp, but rather enticing than drawing her. As each reached the gloom, the same luminous appearance which Maisie had noticed before spread over their bodies, and the same weird skeleton shape showed faintly through their limbs in darker shadow. Maisie crossed the threshold with a convulsive gasp. As she crossed it she looked down at her own dress and body. They were semi-transparent, like the others', though not quite so self-luminous; the framework of her limbs appeared within in less certain outline, yet quite dark and distinguishable.

The doors swung to of themselves behind her. Those three stood alone in the vault of Wolverden.

Alone, for a minute or two; and then, as her eyes grew accustomed to the grey dusk of the interior, Maisie began to perceive that the vault opened out into a large and beautiful hall or crypt, dimly lighted at first, but becoming each moment more vaguely clear and more dreamily definite. Gradually she could make out great rock-hewn pillars, Romanesque in their outline or dimly Oriental, like the sculptured columns in the caves of Ellora, supporting a roof of vague and uncertain dimensions, more or less strangely dome-shaped. The effect on the whole was like that of the second impression produced by some dim cathedral, such as Chartres or Milan, after the eyes have grown accustomed to the mellow light from the stained-glass windows, and have recovered from the blinding glare of the outer sunlight. But the architecture, if one may call it so, was more mosquelike and magical. She turned to her companions. Yolande and Hedda stood still by her side; their bodies were now self-luminous to a greater degree than even at the threshold; but the terrible transparency had disappeared altogether; they were once more but beautiful though strangely transfigured and more than mortal women.

Then Maisie understood in her own soul, dimly, the meaning of those mystic words written over the portal—"Mors janua vitæ"—Death is the gate of life; and also the interpretation of that awful vision of death dwelling within them as they crossed the threshold; for through that gate they had passed to this underground palace.

Her two guides still held her hands, one on either side. But they seemed rather to lead her on now, seductively and resistlessly, than to draw or compel her. As she moved in through the hall, with its endless vistas of shadowy pillars, seen now behind, now in dim perspective, she was gradually aware that many other people crowded its aisles and corridors. Slowly they took shape as forms more or less clad, mysterious, varied, and of many ages. Some of them wore flowing robes, half mediæval in shape, like the two friends who had brought her there. They looked like the saints on a stained-glass window. Others were girt merely with a light and floating Coan sash; while some stood dimly nude in the darker recesses of the temple or palace. All leaned eagerly forward with one mind as she approached, and regarded her with deep and sympathetic interest. A few of them murmured words—mere cabalistic sounds which at first she could not understand; but as she moved further into the hall, and saw at each step more clearly into the gloom, they began to have a meaning for her. Before long, she was aware that she understood the mute tumult of voices at once by some internal instinct. The Shades addressed her; she answered them. She knew by intuition what tongue they spoke; it was the Language of the Dead; and, by passing that portal with her two companions, she had herself become enabled both to speak and understand it.

A soft and flowing tongue, this speech of the Nether World— all vowels it seemed, without distinguishable consonants; yet dimly recalling every other tongue, and compounded, as it were, of what was common to all of them. It flowed from those shadowy lips as clouds issue inchoate from a mountain valley; it was formless, uncertain, vague, but yet beautiful. She hardly knew, indeed, as it fell upon her senses, if it were sound or perfume.

Through this tenuous world Maisie moved as in a dream, her two companions still cheering and guiding her. When they reached an inner shrine or chantry of the temple she was dimly conscious of more terrible forms pervading the background than any of those that had yet appeared to her. This was a more austere and antique apartment than the rest; a shadowy cloister, prehistoric in its severity; it recalled to her mind something indefinitely intermediate between the huge unwrought trilithons of Stonehenge and the massive granite pillars of Philae and Luxor. At the further end of the sanctuary a sort of Sphinx looked down on her, smiling mysteriously. At its base, on a rude megalithic throne, in solitary state, a High Priest was seated. He bore in his hand a wand or sceptre. All round, a strange court of half-unseen acolytes and shadowy hierophants stood attentive. They were girt, as she fancied, in what looked like leopards' skins, or in the fells of some earlier prehistoric lion. These wore sabre-shaped teeth suspended by a string round their dusky necks; others had ornaments of uncut amber, or hatchets of jade threaded as collars on a cord of sinew. A few, more barbaric than savage in type, flaunted torques of gold as armlets and necklets.

The High Priest rose slowly and held out his two hands, just level with his head, the palms turned outward. "You have brought a willing victim as Guardian of the Tower?" he asked, in that mystic tongue, of Yolande and Hedda.

"We have brought a willing victim," the two girls answered.

The High Priest gazed at her. His glance was piercing. Maisie trembled less with fear than with a sense of strangeness, such as a neophyte might feel on being first presented at some courtly pageant. "You come of your own accord?" the Priest inquired of her in solemn accents.

"I come of my own accord," Maisie answered, with an inner consciousness that she was bearing her part in some immemorial ritual. Ancestral memories seemed to stir within her.

"It is well," the Priest murmured. Then he turned to her guides. "She is of royal lineage?" he inquired, taking his wand in his hand again.

"She is a Llewelyn," Yolande answered, "of royal lineage, and of the race that, after your own, earliest bore sway in this land of Britain. She has in her veins the blood of Arthur, of Ambrosius, and of Vortigern."

"It is well," the Priest said again. "I know these princes." Then he turned to Maisie. "This is the ritual of those who build," he said, in a very deep voice. "It has been the ritual of those who build from the days of the builders of Lokmariaker and Avebury. Every building man makes shall have its human soul, the soul of a virgin to guard and protect it. Three souls it requires as a living talisman against chance and change. One soul is the soul of the human victim slain beneath the foundation-stone; she is the guardian spirit against earthquake and ruin. One soul is the soul of the human victim slain when the building is half built up; she is the guardian spirit against battle and tempest. One soul is the soul of the human victim who flings herself of her own free will off tower or gable when the building is complete; she is the guardian spirit against thunder and lightning. Unless a building be duly fasted with these three, how can it hope to stand against the hostile powers of fire and flood and storm and earthquake?"

An assessor at his side, unnoticed till then, took up the parable. He had a stern Roman face, and bore a shadowy suit of Roman armour. "In times of old," he said, with iron austerity, "all men knew well these rules of building. They built in solid stone to endure for ever: the works they erected have lasted to this day, in this land and others. So built we the amphitheatres of Rome and Verona; so built we the walls of Lincoln, York, and London. In the blood of a king's son laid we the foundation-stone: in the blood of a king's son laid we the coping-stone: in the blood of a maiden of royal line fasted we the bastions against fire and lightning. But in these latter days, since faith grows dim, men build with burnt brick and rubble of plaster; no foundation spirit or guardian soul do they give to their bridges, their walls, or their towers: so bridges break, and walls fall in, and towers crumble, and the art and mystery of building aright have perished from among you."

He ceased. The High Priest held out his wand and spoke again. "We are the Assembly of Dead Builders and Dead Victims," he said, "for this mark of Wolverden; all of whom have built or been built upon in this holy site of immemorial sanctity. We are the stones of a living fabric. Before this place was a Christian church, it was a temple of Woden. And before it was a temple of Woden, it was a shrine of Hercules. And before it was a shrine of Hercules, it was a grove of Nodens. And before it was a grove of Nodens, it was a Stone Circle of the Host of Heaven. And before it was a Stone Circle of the Host of Heaven, it was the grave and tumulus and underground palace of Me, who am the earliest builder of all in this place; and my name in my ancient tongue is Wolf, and I laid and hallowed it. And after me, Wolf, and my namesake Wulfhere, was this barrow called Ad Lupum and Wolverden. And all these that are here with me have built and been built upon in this holy site for all generations. And *you* are the last who come to join us."

Maisie felt a cold thrill course down her spine as he spoke these words; but courage did not fail her. She was dimly aware that those who offer themselves as victims for service must offer themselves willingly; for the gods demand a voluntary victim; no beast can be slain unless it nod assent; and none can be made a guardian spirit who takes not the post upon him of his own free will. She turned meekly to Hedda. "Who are you?" she asked, trembling.

"I am Hedda," the girl answered, in the same soft sweet voice and winning tone as before; "Hedda, the daughter of Gorm, the chief of the Northmen who settled in East Anglia. And I was a worshipper of Thor and Odin. And when my father, Gorm, fought against Alfred, King of Wessex, was I taken prisoner. And Wulfhere, the Kenting, was then building the first church and tower of Wolverden. And they baptized me, and shrived me, and I consented of my own free will to be built under the foundation-stone. And there my body lies built up to this day; and *I* am the guardian spirit against earthquake and ruin."

"And who are you?" Maisie asked, turning again to Yolande.

"I am Yolande Fitz-Aylwin," the tall dark girl answered; "a royal maiden too, sprung from the blood of Henry Plantagenet. And when Roland Fitz-Stephen was building anew the choir and chancel of Wulfhere's minster, I chose to be immured in the fabric of the wall, for love of the Church and all holy saints; and there my body lies built up to this day; and *I* am the guardian against battle and tempest."

Maisie held her friend's hand tight. Her voice hardly trembled. "And I?" she asked once more. "What fate for me? Tell me!"

"Your task is easier far," Yolande answered gently. "For *you* shall be the guardian of the new tower against thunder and lightning. Now, those who guard against earthquake and battle are buried alive under the foundation-stone or in the wall of the building; there they die a slow death of starvation and choking. But those who guard against thunder and lightning cast themselves alive of their own free will from the battlements of the tower, and die in the air before they reach the ground; so their fate is the easiest and the lightest of all who would serve mankind; and thenceforth they live with us here in our palace."

Maisie clung to her hand still tighter. "Must I do it?" she asked, pleading.

"It is not *must*," Yolande replied in the same caressing tone, yet with a calmness as of one in whom earthly desires and earthly passions are quenched for ever. "It is as you choose yourself. None but a willing victim may be a guardian spirit. This glorious privilege comes but to the purest and best amongst us. Yet what better end can you ask for your soul than to dwell here in our midst as our comrade for ever, where all is peace, and to preserve the tower whose guardian you are from evil assaults of lightning and thunderbolt?"

Maisie flung her arms round her friend's neck. "But—I am afraid," she murmured. Why she should even wish to consent she knew not, yet the strange serene peace in these strange girls' eyes made her mysteriously in love with them and with the fate they offered her. They seemed to move like the stars in their orbits. "How shall I leap from the top?" she cried. "How shall I have courage to mount the stairs alone, and fling myself off from the lonely battlement?"

Yolande unwound her arms with a gentle forbearance. She coaxed her as one coaxes an unwilling child. "You will *not* be alone," she said, with a tender pressure. "We will all go with you. We will help you and encourage you. We will sing our sweet songs of life-in-death to you. Why should you draw back? All we have faced it in ten thousand ages, and we tell you with one voice, you need not fear it. 'Tis life you should fear—life, with its dangers, its toils, its heartbreakings. Here we dwell for ever in unbroken peace. Come, come, and join us!"

She held out her arms with an enticing gesture. Maisie sprang into them, sobbing. "Yes, I will come," she cried in an access of hysterical fervour. "These are the arms of Death—I embrace them. These are the lips of Death—I kiss them. Yolande, Yolande, I will do as you ask me!"

The tall dark girl in the luminous white robe stooped down and kissed her twice on the forehead in return. Then she looked at the High Priest. "We are ready," she murmured in a low, grave voice. "The Victim consents. The Virgin will die. Lead on to the tower. We are ready! We are ready!"

IV

From the recesses of the temple—if temple it were—from the inmost shrines of the shrouded cavern, unearthly music began to sound of itself, with wild modulation, on strange reeds and tabors. It swept through the aisles like a rushing wind on an Æolian harp; at times it wailed with a voice like a woman's; at times it rose loud in an organ-note of triumph; at times it sank low into a pensive and melancholy flute-like symphony. It waxed and waned; it swelled and died away again; but no man saw how or whence it proceeded. Wizard echoes issued from the crannies and vents in the invisible walls; they sighed from the ghostly interspaces of the pillars; they keened and moaned from the vast overhanging dome of the palace. Gradually the song shaped itself by weird stages into a processional measure. At its sound the High Priest rose slowly from his immemorial seat on the mighty cromlech which formed his throne. The Shades in leopards' skins ranged themselves in bodiless rows on either hand; the ghostly wearers of the sabre-toothed lions' fangs followed like ministrants in the footsteps of their hierarch.

Hedda and Yolande took their places in the procession. Maisie stood between the two, with hair floating on the air; she looked like a novice who goes up to take the veil, accompanied and cheered by two elder sisters.

The ghostly pageant began to move. Unseen music followed it with fitful gusts of melody. They passed down the main corridor, between shadowy Doric or Ionic pillars which grew dimmer and ever dimmer again in the distance as they approached, with slow steps, the earthward portal.

At the gate, the High Priest pushed against the valves with his hand. They opened *outward*.

He passed into the moonlight. The attendants thronged after him. As each wild figure crossed the threshold the same strange sight as before met Maisie's eyes. For a second of time each ghostly body became self-luminous, as with some curious phosphorescence; and through each, at the moment of passing the portal, the dim outline of a skeleton loomed briefly visible. Next instant it had clothed itself as with earthly members.

Maisie reached the outer air. As she did so, she gasped. For a second, its chilliness and freshness almost choked her. She was conscious now that the atmosphere of the vault, though pleasant in its way, and warm and dry, had been loaded with fumes as of burning incense, and with somnolent vapours of poppy and mandragora. Its drowsy ether had cast her into a lethargy. But after the first minute in the outer world, the keen night air revived her. Snow lay still on the ground a little deeper than when she first came out, and the moon rode lower; otherwise, all was as before, save that only one or two lights still burned here and there in the great house on the terrace. Among them she could recognise her own room, on the ground floor in the new wing, by its open window.

The procession made its way across the churchyard towards the tower. As it wound among the graves an owl hooted. All at once Maisie remembered the lines that had so chilled her a few short hours before in the drawing-room—

> "The glow-worm o'er grave and stone
> Shall light thee steady;
> The owl from the steeple sing,
> 'Welcome, proud lady!'"

But, marvellous to relate, they no longer alarmed her. She felt rather that a friend was welcoming her home; she clung to Yolande's hand with a gentle pressure.

As they passed in front of the porch, with its ancient yew-tree, a stealthy figure glided out like a ghost from the darkling shadow. It was a woman, bent and bowed, with quivering limbs that shook half palsied. Maisie recognised old Bessie. "I knew she would come!" the old hag muttered between her toothless jaws. "I knew Wolverden Tower would yet be duly fasted!"

She put herself, as of right, at the head of the procession. They moved on to the tower, rather gliding than walking. Old Bessie drew a rusty key from her pocket, and fitted it with a twist into the brand-new lock. "What turned the old will turn the new," she murmured, looking round and grinning. Maisie shrank from her as she shrank from not one of the Dead; but she followed on still into the ringers' room at the base of the tower.

Thence a staircase in the corner led up to the summit. The High Priest mounted the stair, chanting a mystic refrain, whose runic sounds were no longer intelligible to Maisie. As she reached the outer air, the Tongue of the Dead seemed to have become a mere blank of mingled odours and murmurs to her. It was like a summer breeze, sighing through warm and resinous pine woods. But Yolande and Hedda spoke to her yet, to cheer her, in the language of the living. She recognised that as *revenants* they were still in touch with the upper air and the world of the embodied.

They tempted her up the stair with encouraging fingers. Maisie followed them like a child, in implicit confidence. The steps wound round and round, spirally, and the staircase was dim; but a supernatural light seemed to fill the tower, diffused from the bodies or souls of its occupants. At the head of all, the High Priest still chanted as he went his unearthly litany; magic sounds of chimes seemed to swim in unison with his tune as they mounted. Were those floating notes material or spiritual? They passed the belfry; no tongue of metal wagged; but the rims of the great bells resounded and reverberated to the ghostly symphony with sympathetic music. Still they passed on and on, upward and upward. They reached the ladder that alone gave access to the final story. Dust and cobwebs already clung to it. Once more Maisie drew back. It was dark overhead, and the luminous haze began to fail them. Her friends held her hands with the same kindly persuasive touch as ever. "I cannot!" she cried, shrinking away from the tall, steep ladder. "Oh, Yolande, I cannot!"

"Yes, dear," Yolande whispered in a soothing voice. "You can.

It is but ten steps, and I will hold your hand tight. Be brave and mount them!"

The sweet voice encouraged her. It was like heavenly music. She knew not why she should submit, or, rather, consent; but none the less she consented. Some spell seemed cast over her. With tremulous feet, scarcely realising what she did, she mounted the ladder and went up four steps of it.

Then she turned and looked down again. Old Bessie's wrinkled face met her frightened eyes. It was smiling horribly. She shrank back once more, terrified. "I can't do it," she cried, "if that woman comes up! I'm not afraid of *you*, dear"—she pressed Yolande's hand—"but she, she is too terrible!"

Hedda looked back and raised a warning finger. "Let the woman stop below," she said; "she savours too much of the evil world. We must do nothing to frighten the willing victim."

The High Priest by this time, with his ghostly fingers, had opened the trap-door that gave access to the summit. A ray of moonlight slanted through the aperture. The breeze blew down with it. Once more Maisie felt the stimulating and reviving effect of the open air. Vivified by its freshness, she struggled up to the top, passed out through the trap, and found herself standing on the open platform at the summit of the tower.

The moon had not yet quite set. The light on the snow shone pale green and mysterious. For miles and miles around she could just make out, by its aid, the dim contour of the downs, with their thin white mantle, in the solemn silence. Range behind range rose faintly shimmering. The chant had now ceased; the High Priest and his acolytes were mingling strange herbs in a mazar-bowl or chalice. Stray perfumes of myrrh and of cardamoms were wafted towards her. The men in leopards' skins burnt smouldering sticks of spikenard. Then Yolande led the postulant forward again, and placed her close up to the new white parapet. Stone heads of virgins smiled on her from the angles. "She must front the east," Hedda said in a tone of authority: and Yolande turned her face towards the rising sun accordingly. Then she opened her lips and spoke in a very solemn voice. "From this new-built tower you fling yourself," she said, or rather intoned, "that you may serve mankind, and all the powers that be, as its guardian spirit against thunder and lightning. Judged a virgin, pure and unsullied in deed and word and thought, of royal race and ancient lineage—a Cymry of the Cymry—you are found worthy to be intrusted with this charge and this honour. Take care that never shall dart or thunderbolt assault this tower, as She that is below you takes care to preserve it from earthquake and ruin, and She that is midway takes care to preserve it from battle and tempest. This is your charge. See well that you keep it.'

She took her by both hands. "Mary Llewelyn," she said, "you willing victim, step on to the battlement."

Maisie knew not why, but with very little shrinking she stepped as she was told, by the aid of a wooden footstool, on to the eastward-looking parapet. There, in her loose white robe, with her arms spread abroad, and her hair flying free, she poised herself for a second, as if about to shake out some unseen wings and throw herself on the air like a swift or a swallow.

"Mary Llewelyn," Yolande said once more, in a still deeper tone, with ineffable earnestness, "cast yourself down, a willing sacrifice, for the service of man, and the security of this tower against thunderbolt and lightning."

Maisie stretched her arms wider, and leaned forward in act to leap, from the edge of the parapet, on to the snow-clad churchyard.

V

One second more and the sacrifice would have been complete. But before she could launch herself from the tower, she felt suddenly a hand laid upon her shoulder from behind to restrain her. Even in her existing state of nervous exaltation she was aware at once that it was the hand of a living and solid mortal, not that of a soul or guardian spirit. It lay heavier upon her than Hedda's or Yolande's. It seemed to clog and burden her. With a violent effort she strove to shake herself free, and carry out her now fixed intention of self-immolation, for the safety of the tower. But the hand was too strong for her. She could not shake it off. It gripped and held her.

She yielded, and, reeling, fell back with a gasp on to the platform of the tower. At the selfsame moment a strange terror and commotion seemed to seize all at once on the assembled spirits. A weird cry rang voiceless through the shadowy company. Maisie heard it as in a dream, very dim and distant. It was thin as a bat's note; almost inaudible to the ear, yet perceived by the brain or at least by the spirit. It was a cry of alarm, of fright, of warning. With one accord, all the host of phantoms rushed hurriedly forward to the battlements and pinnacles. The ghostly High Priest went first, with his wand held downward; the men in leopards' skins and other assistants followed in confusion. Theirs was a reckless rout. They flung themselves from the top, like fugitives from a cliff, and floated fast through the air on invisible pinions. Hedda and Yolande, ambassadresses and intermediaries with the upper air, were the last to fly from the living presence. They clasped her hand silently, and looked deep into her eyes. There was something in that calm yet regretful look that seemed to say, "Farewell! We have tried in vain to save you, sister, from the terrors of living."

The horde of spirits floated away on the air, as in a witches' Sabbath, to the vault whence it issued. The doors swung on their rusty hinges, and closed behind them. Maisie stood alone with the hand that grasped her on the tower.

The shock of the grasp, and the sudden departure of the ghostly band in such wild dismay, threw Maisie for a while into a state of semi-unconsciousness. Her head reeled round; her brain swam faintly. She clutched for support at the parapet of the tower. But the hand that held her sustained her still. She felt herself gently drawn down with quiet mastery, and laid on the stone floor close by the trap-door that led to the ladder.

The next thing of which she could feel sure was the voice of the Oxford undergraduate. He was distinctly frightened and not a little tremulous. "I think," he said very softly, laying her head on his lap, "you had better rest a while, Miss Llewelyn, before you try to get down again. I hope I didn't catch you and disturb you too hastily. But one step more, and you would have been over the edge. I really couldn't help it."

"Let me go," Maisie moaned, trying to raise herself again, but feeling too faint and ill to make the necessary effort to recover the power of motion. "I *want* to go with them! I *want* to join them!"

"Some of the others will be up before long," the undergraduate said, supporting her head in his hands; "and they'll help me to get you down again. Mr. Yates is in the belfry. Meanwhile, if I were you, I'd lie quite still, and take a drop or two of this brandy."

He held it to her lips. Maisie drank a mouthful, hardly knowing what she did. Then she lay quiet where he placed her for some minutes. How they lifted her down and conveyed her to her bed she scarcely knew. She was dazed and terrified. She could only remember afterward that three or four gentlemen in roughly huddled clothes had carried or handed her down the ladder between them. The spiral stair and all the rest were a blank to her.

VI

When she next awoke she was lying in her bed in the same room at the Hall, with Mrs. West by her side, leaning over her tenderly.

Maisie looked up through her closed eyes and just saw the motherly face and grey hair bending above her. Then voices came to her from the mist, vaguely: "Yesterday was so hot for the time of year, you see!" "Very unusual weather, of course, for Christmas." "But a thunderstorm! So strange! I put it down to that. The electrical disturbance must have affected the poor child's head." Then it dawned upon her that the conversation she heard was passing between Mrs. West and a doctor.

She raised herself suddenly and wildly on her arms. The bed faced the windows. She looked out and beheld—the tower of Wolverden church, rent from top to bottom with a mighty rent, while half its height lay tossed in fragments on the ground in the churchyard.

"What is it?" she cried wildly, with a flush as of shame.

"Hush, hush!" the doctor said. "Don't trouble! Don't look at it!"

"Was it—after I came down?" Maisie moaned in vague terror.

The doctor nodded. "An hour after you were brought down,"

he said, "a thunderstorm broke over it. The lightning struck and shattered the tower. They had not yet put up the lightning-conductor. It was to have been done on Boxing Day."

A weird remorse possessed Maisie's soul. "My fault!" she cried, starting up. "My fault, my fault! I have neglected my duty!"

"Don't talk," the doctor answered, looking hard at her. "It is always dangerous to be too suddenly aroused from these curious overwrought sleeps and trances."

"And old Bessie?" Maisie exclaimed, trembling with an eerie presentiment.

The doctor glanced at Mrs. West. "How did she know?" he whispered. Then he turned to Maisie. "You may as well be told the truth as suspect it," he said slowly. "Old Bessie must have been watching there. She was crushed and half buried beneath the falling tower."

"One more question, Mrs. West," Maisie murmured, growing faint with an access of supernatural fear. "Those two nice girls who sat on the chairs at each side of me through the tableaux— are they hurt? Were they in it?"

Mrs. West soothed her hand. "My dear child," she said gravely, with quiet emphasis, "there were *no* other girls. This is mere hallucination. You sat alone by yourself through the whole of the evening."

Eliza Lynn Linton

CHRISTMAS EVE IN BEACH HOUSE

ELIZA LYNN LINTON (1822-1898) *provides an interesting juxtapo-sition with the author of the previous story: while Grant Allen wrote in support of feminism, many of Linton's writings took a strongly anti-feminist slant. A* New York Times *article in 1898 termed her "vixenish," writing, "Her dislikes were many . . . toward modern society ways, thoughts, and manners . . . It is difficult to understand how a sweet-faced old lady with white locks, gold spectacles, and a placid manner wrote such sharp, incisive words." Linton was the author of a number of novels, none of which were very successful, and she supported herself by writing hundreds of stories and articles for various periodicals, including this rare venture into horror fiction published in* Routledge's Christmas Annual *in 1870.*

IT SEEMED AS IF THE MACKENZIES WERE UNDER A SPELL, and that none of the men were ever destined to die in their beds. We sometimes see this strange law of persistent accident run through a family, and generation after generation fulfils what looks like the ordained decree, either of violent death or loss by fire, either of shipwreck or that mysterious and sudden disap-pearance when a person "goes under" like a stone in the water, and is never heard of again. I, who write this, know of a family where the law of "running away" has been in force for four gen-erations; one or more lads of each brood having run away from home, school, or legal master as the case might be—some turn-ing up again after a season of wild-oat sowing, perhaps all the better for the process, but others gone for ever, and their ultimate fate a mystery never cleared up.

The law of the Mackenzies was, as I have said, a violent end. Old Zachary the grandfather, and Michael the father, of Captain Charles, had both died of their sins, or as the traditional phrase

went "died standing;" and Captain Charles himself had disappeared. He was a married man, but a wild one, according to the
way of the Mackenzies; and ten years ago had been serving with
his regiment in Cornwall, while his wife and two children were
left behind in London. No one ever knew more of him than that
he was reported absent when he should have returned to his
quarters at Truro, after a week's leave; and that from that time to
this he was missing, and had left no trace behind. Every effort had
been made to find him, but without success; and his family had
by now almost given up the hope not only of seeing him again
but of knowing what his end had been; though indeed his widow,
poor soul, who loved him as certain women do love scampish
men, handsome, affectionate, generous, and unfaithful, still
clung to hope against hope, and refused to wear the conventional
weeds, or do more than "provisionally" administer to his effects.
Still, there the mystery of his fate remained, and it looked likely
enough to remain a mystery to the end of time. Meanwhile the
son grew up, and went out into the world; and now the daughter
Alice had just married Walter Garwood, a young man of some
means and roving habits, and so had begun life on her own
account when this story opens.

Walter Garwood, an artist by temperament and a *rentier* by
profession—which means of no profession at all—had one
absorbing passion, namely, a love for the wild sea-coast, which
he must enjoy in the most absolute solitude if he would enjoy it
at all. So he took Alice down for their honeymoon to Cornwall,
a country which he knew by heart so far as its coast line went,
though he was not a Cornish man by birth; and the fair delicate
young London girl was soon initiated into the mysteries of loveliness to be found in rolling seas and weather-beaten crags, with a
solitude almost as deep as death.

At first they lived in small towns and villages, wandering from
place to place as the fancy took them, and moving always farther
away from anything like "centres," till at last the proximity of
a mere village seemed too close a contact with humanity, and
nothing but the completest isolation would content the eremiti-
cal young artist. When therefore he heard that Beach House was
vacant—a lone place among rocks and cliffs, miles away from

any town, and not within call of any other gentleman's house,
the nearest neighbours of which were half a dozen fishermen in
a hamlet some two miles off—he resolved at once upon taking
it, as a man who knows his own mind and who has found what
he wants. It was in a dilapidated state enough. The garden, or
what had once been the garden, was a mere tangled wilderness
of weeds; the house wanted all sorts of repairs; but money and
taste can do a great deal even when far removed from "centres;"
and Alice was as yet too young a girl, and too fond a bride, to have
a will of her own or to find a flaw in her husband's. To be sure
she was a little shocked when she saw the barren, deserted, God-
forgotten ruin out of which Walter meant to build her a home
that was to be the most beautiful thing in England; but if he said it
would be beautiful she was sure it would be so, and in her simple
faith began to take a profound interest in everything about the
place, and to enjoy going over to superintend with her husband
the alterations and improvements he was making. In time the
work was done, though it had been a weary time about; but then,
Cornish workmen are not the quickest in England; and just as
October set in, the young people took possession, and began
their home life in earnest.

It was indeed a wild and lonesome home that Walter had
chosen for his wife! Sea-fowl screamed about it, and the angry
waves beat up on the iron-bound coast, and every now and then a
vessel, mastered by the wind, drifted close upon the rocks where
lay the doom of many men; but the scene in general was of nothing but a wild waste of waters, with the bold headlands to the
side running far out into the sea, and the sunset flooding the sky
with gold or bathing it in blood. The house itself was set on a
secondary height overshadowed by a huge cliff; so that it was
just out of the reach of the highest tides, though it was drenched
with the spray flung up by the storms that break so often on that
fierce northern Cornish coast. The rugged cliff that rose above
seemed to shut off all access to the upper world, and the wild
rough shore below was no pathway to civilization. The only road
that led to or from the house was a steep winding way but little
used; indeed it had been totally unused by all wheeled vehicles
for the last six or seven years, during which time the place had

been empty; consequently it had become overgrown with weeds, rutted and channelled with winter rains, and in parts as unsafe as it was everywhere unsightly.

Truth to tell, Beach House had always been a difficult property to let. About eight years ago a family had taken it, after about the same length of time of desertion, but they had left it after a short term of uneasy occupation; since when it had got a bad name among the fishermen of the little hamlet, for more than the traditional shelter it afforded to smugglers and wreckers—which indeed would not have much daunted them—and he would have been a bold man who would have denied the report that it was haunted—the fishermen said, with ghosts—the landsmen added, smugglers. Be that as it may, both fishermen and landsmen were shy of passing it any time after sundown; and more than one belated sinner had been scared into sobriety and religion for the rest of his life, by the nameless horror of what he had seen or heard at Beach House, somewhere about midnight.

But the Thing haunting the place was not always equally terrible. It was only about Christmas-time that the worst and most deadly things happened—though indeed when you came to inquire closely, and probe deep, as to what those things were, you could find nothing more definite than, "I was skeared," and "I dunno what it were, but there was a summit;" and "I heerd a grane and a sigh, and a patter patter of feet, and I rin."

The only man who was not afraid was Jem Penreath; and he had volunteered to take charge of the place while it was empty, and had therefore made it his home, and had always kept about it. When asked if he had ever heard or seen anything, he would laugh—and his laugh was not pleasant to hear—and say, "Nay, nay, the ghosts knows me, and I know un, and they know better nor to trouble me with their nonsense, that do un!"

We may be very sure that nothing of all this was told to the new-comer, Walter Garwood; and when he bought and took possession he was as innocent as a child that the place had a bad name, or that it was supposed to be haunted with ghosts or with smugglers, with the disembodied or the embodied.

This Jem Penreath was a man whose character fitted in with

the house he chose to guard, and whose appearance fitted in with his character. Yet he was handsome in a way: a tall, brawny, broad-shouldered man, with a reddish-brown beard; long, thick, tangled locks also reddish-brown; dark, deep-set, fiery, eyes; and an expression of lawless daring, that, taken in connection with his tremendous strength, made one shudder. He was known as the most reckless and defying savage of the whole district, and the strongest. Smuggling, drinking, wrecking, or work that would knock up any other man—all came alike to him. He did not seem to value his life more than a rat's or a crow's, and no one's else more than his own. Every one was afraid of him; every one fought shy of him; yet no one knew anything definite against him, or if they did they kept it to themselves. Folks said he had been much worse in these latter times, since Mary Mainfote so strangely disappeared some ten years ago. He had loved Mary all his life, but she had never said the word, and often told her friends she never would. She did not favour Jem Penreath's addresses, and used to say, tossing her fair head with its wealth of golden hair, that for her own part when she had a man at all she would have one she was not afraid of, and knew the life of.

"I do not take with dark ways," she would add; and Jem Penreath's ways were unquestionably dark.

Jem swore, many a time, that if she would not be his she should be no other man's; for that he would "scat the head on un," if any one dared to take what he desired. And this threat seemed to have frightened his mates; for though Mary was the prettiest girl of the fishing hamlet to which Jem belonged by birth, no man had yet made her his wife, and she was past twenty when she disappeared.

The last known or seen of her was on Christmas Eve—a wild one—after she had returned from Truro, where she had been staying with an aunt. An old man—he was dead now—said he saw her walking down the rough road which led to Beach House, with a stranger and a gentleman. He was not one of them, nor one he had ever seen before, nor a working man in his Sunday best; he was a gentleman, with black beard and curly hair, and he stood very upright, and they were walking down the road and talking—leastways he was talking to her as if he had summut to say very pressing—and as they got on he put his arm round her waist, and she didn't seem to say him nay.

No one else had seen them; at least no one who told anything; but there had been a pair of eyes watching them as well as old David's, only he who saw them coming down that steep rough road said less than David, and kept his own counsel—as perhaps not being able to share it.

David's tale was accepted as final; and after Mary's disappearance it was set down as a fact that she had gone off with the strange gentleman who was not known in these parts, and had come to no good, poor lass! But ever since her loss, Jem Penreath, savage as he always was, had become more savage still, more reckless, more Godless, more dangerous every way; till more than once the elders of the hamlet spoke about him among themselves, and said he would do his-self or some on un a mischief afore he was under grass.

For his strength was something almost terrifying; and he knew, as well as any of them, that he was master of them all when he chose to exert his authority and put out his power.

He was terribly annoyed when Beach House was sold to young Walter Garwood. It was turning him out of his home, he said, with many a bitter oath; and he prophesied but a short term of ownership for the new-comer.

"The ghostes would do for un," he said, with a short laugh. "Them and me bin old friends, but they do take on against new folk. Iss, sure enough the ghostes will do for un!"

But though the Garwoods had been in possession from October until now, near Christmas time, their home had as yet been very quiet, and they had heard nothing of either ghosts or smugglers. To be sure there were odd noises every now and again in the house, and queer things occurred about the place that could not be accounted for; but "rats" have broad shoulders, and bear heavy weights in country places. Alice, in her secret heart, added smugglers; but she thought that even if they were in the immediate neighbourhood—in some cave, maybe, among the rocks hard by, of which she and Walter knew nothing—yet so long as she and her husband did not pry, and did not discover, they were safe, and perhaps more than safe; the very fact of their living there—

two young, innocent people, who did not smuggle on their own account, who had no connection with smugglers any way, who would not know how to set about smuggling if they tried, or what to do with the things if they had them—being so much of a guarantee for the respectability of the immediate beach, would be justly so much of a protection to their less reputable neighbours: which was not bad reasoning on the part of that young and timid London girl.

There was one thing however that she did not like—the persistency with which Jem Penreath used to come about the place. From the first she had taken one of those strong, shuddering dislikes to him, not rare with a certain kind of nervous organization. She could not explain why, but his presence filled her with an infinite undefinable dread, and she could never meet his eyes. But she did not say anything to her husband beyond her first expression of dislike, which had not touched Walter very deeply. And he, a born artist, cared more for the man's picturesque magnificence of build and face than he cared for the evil spirit lurking behind those deep-set flaming eyes; and because he made a striking accessory to the scenes he was so fond of painting, encouraged him to come as often as he liked, and went into raptures over the tones of his grey jersey which the red rays of the setting sun turned to purple, or the value of his scarlet cap among the bleached old rocks, or against the slaty background of the sea. Encouraged then as he was by the master, Jem had no cause to stay away, and every day he came to Beach House on one or other pretext—but as all, save Walter, saw for the main reason of keeping an eye on what was doing there—though neither maid nor man, still less the young mistress, who kept close to her own room when he was about, could divine what it was he wanted to watch, what it was he feared would be found out.

Surely something in the place did not agree with Alice! She had grown thin, and pale, and melancholy, and was quite unlike the fresh, if delicate, young bride who had come over in October to take possession of the new home. Yet this was only a fortnight before Christmas, and the change which had been wrought was painfully great and sudden. At last Walter saw the pallor and depression which had stolen like a shadow over the sweet, fair face. Dreamy and abstracted as he was, absorbed in his poetry or his art, it was really a strong proof of love that he noticed anything at all, that he saw any change, short of death itself, in his wife.

It was about a fortnight before Christmas, when the days were at their shortest and darkest. Alice was sitting in the bay of the window, gazing into the garden, and looking across the wide sea, where not a living thing was in sight save the wild birds that wheeled and circled in the waning light, and beat their white wings upon the waters and against the dull background of the heavy clouds. There was neither colour nor savagery enough to make a picture or a poem; it was just a uniform cold grey throughout; and Walter, wearied with the book he had been reading alone in the study, threw it down on the table, and sauntered into the drawing-room where his young wife was sitting, also alone, in the deep bay-window looking over the wild sea.

"My darling! how pale and ill you are looking!" said Walter fondly, as the light fell on her upturned face. His eyes were suddenly opened, as is often the way with unobservant people; and for the first time he noticed what the very servants had seen and commented on for weeks. "Are you ill, Alice?" he continued, drawing her close to him. "What is the matter with you, darling?"

"I don't know, dear," she answered, with a heavy sigh; "nothing, so far as I can tell; I only feel weak, and so stupidly nervous! I cannot tell you what a coward I have become, Wally; I could scream if a bird flies suddenly before me, and I am afraid of my own shadow. And then I have such dreadful dreams; or they are scarcely dreams—they are like visions more than dreams, for I seem to myself to be wide awake all the time."

"What dreams, dear?—you darling little coward! Why, I never imagined you were such a little faint-heart, I am afraid our lonely life is too much for you, dear. If you are going to have all these fancies, I don't know what I must do with you; send you back to London, I think." He spoke tenderly for all the lightness of his words, smoothing her fair hair and kissing her forehead at every pause. "Now, come, bring these dark things of yours into the light, darling, and tell me what your dreams are like. There is nothing like telling a thing of this kind to get rid of it. The mind falls into tricks just as the body does, and bad dreams and ghostly visions are its commonest tricks. What is it, my own?"

The girl shuddered, and pressed a little closer to his bosom. "It is of poor papa," she half whispered. "I have such dreadful dreams or visions—I don't know what they are—about him, Wally. Night after night he seems to come to my bedside, so pale, and with all the blood streaming from his bead. And he looks at me so sorrowfully; it is the sadness of his face that makes me so wretched, far more than the horror of even the blood about him. And sometimes I see what looks like a woman's head, with a quantity of fair hair, near him, but I cannot see her face; and sometimes"—here she shivered, and drew her breath, as she sank her voice so low that Walter could hardly hear her,—"I see a man like that Penreath, standing by them, with such a scowl, such a terrible expression on his face! Oh, Walter, dear," she went on, weeping now, "you know that poor papa was lost in Cornwall when he was quartered at Truro. I do so fear that something bad happened to him—something worse than being drowned, or lost in an old mine, which I remember our friends used to tell poor mamma was the most likely thing. Oh, Walter, what shall I do?— it is killing me!"

"Poor, sweet child! what can I do for you?" said her husband tenderly. "Shall I send you away for a while? No? Shall mamma, then, come and stay with you?"

"Yes, yes!" she cried. "I did not like to ask you, darling, for it looked as if I was discontented, but I should like to see mamma again; and, oh, I should like to have her here! She won't mind the loneliness and wildness, I am sure, and I shall be so much happier when she is with us again. But, Walter," and again that shiver passed over her, "she will not *see* anything, as I do, will she?"

"My dear!" he said, in a deprecating voice, "what would become of the world if we were all as sensitive and imaginative as you? No; I should think that mamma would sleep quietly enough, and not have the same bad dreams as her restless little daughter."

"But why do I dream so much, and so continually the same thing?" persisted Alice. "Oh, Walter, if you could only see him— poor, dear, handsome papa—with that great wound in his head, and that sad, sad face! And he looks at me so pitifully! and then the woman's yellow hair seems to fall across his breast, and that dreadful man's face comes in, oh, so horrible, so fierce! Walter!" she cried, her passion rising and overmastering her caution, "I am sure he has had a hand in something bad! I am sure he has done something wrong to papa. Oh!" she shrieked, clinging to her husband nervously, as a heavy step ground on the gravel walk before the windows, and Jem Penreath, in a red cap and jersey, stood dark against the dusky sky, holding in his hand a batch of fish, which was his excuse for his evening's visit to the house.

Walter dashed out, and for the first time spoke to him angrily, and ordered him out of the garden.

"What business had he," said the young man haughtily, "to come before the drawing-room windows in that rude manner? Did he think the place was his own, that he had so little respect for any one in it?" with more to the same purpose, angrily, intemperately said.

Jem made no answer. It would have been better, perhaps, if he had; for even Walter was startled, and for an instant almost terrified, at the sudden savageness, the fiendish fury that came into his face. He compressed his lips as if with an effort, then in a hoarse voice, but a quiet manner, said, "I brought un these fish, mayster. Fish do be scarce just now, and I thought as the young mistress ud like un."

But Walter, though a trifle scared, was not to be "got over," and went on rating him as young men will when they have a grievance, and the offender is beneath them in social circumstances.

To all of which Jem Penreath answered not a word, but stood with his eyes bent to the ground; once, and once only, lifting them, as he said, with a forced voice of patience, and a terrible look to belie it, "Then, may be, the young mistress do not want the fish, and I be losing my time, and yours, mayster?"

And when he had said this he turned away, and disappeared behind the rocks.

"Yes, Alice is right," thought Walter, as he went back into the house. "That Penreath *is* a dangerous fellow. I wonder I never saw it before!"

Of course Mrs. Mackenzie accepted the invitation to that wild Cornish home, where her darling daughter was, as she termed it, "buried alive;" and a few days saw her safely housed, too happy in her girl's society to feel at first the full force of the wildness, the desolateness of the scene, and entering into all the small domestic details of household arrangements as only a mother can.

Among other things—it was only a trivial matter, perhaps—she urged on Alice to make a laundry of a certain outhouse not far from the kitchen, and which at present was a mere stick and lumber place. "The washing" was one of the grievances of the young wife's life as it stood, and a good laundry would make this little hitch run smooth. So mamma proposed, and Alice requested, and Walter gave the order, that the outhouse should be cleared and set to rights, and made into a laundry with all despatch. They sent over to the nearest town for the proper work-men to see to the copper, the flue, the ironing-board, and all fit appliances; but first the place had to be cleared, and some of the men in the fishing hamlet—times being bad, and neither fish nor wrecks on hand—volunteered to help the town workmen, and save their time and the master's by clearing the place for them.

Since his fall-out with the master, Jem Penreath had been less than usual about the place, so that he did not quite know what was going on; and when he heard down in the village that the young master of Beach House was going to fit up a fine new wash-house out of the stack-house at the back, even his mates were astonished at the ferocity with which he swore he should not do it.

"A fool!" he said, with an oath; "a wandering, idle fool! Can he not let un alone?—if he can't he must learn, and I be the one for to teach him!"

On saying which he strode out of the beer-shop where he was sitting, and darted off to Beach House as if life and death depended on his speed.

"Where's the young master?" he asked, as he flung himself into the kitchen.

"Law, Jem, an' you do skear me!" cried the servant, letting the jug she was carrying fall from her hands. "Master?—he be out," she answered after a pause, during which Jem's roving blood-shot eyes seemed, as she said afterwards, "like swords."

"And the young mistress?" said Jem, in his hoarse harsh voice, that had almost the effect of an animal's growl.

"She?—she be in the drawing-room," replied the girl.

And Jem Penreath, without another word, passed through the kitchen and shouldered his way to the drawing-room where Alice and her mother were sitting.

He knocked at the door, perhaps a little roughly, and a startled voice said, "Come in," with an accent of terror that was almost a scream.

Jem opened the door, and came forward.

"Ye be a-thinking of that stack-house?" he said, touching his cap, which he kept on his head.

"We are clearing it out," Alice answered with a visible shudder, as the man pressed forward.

"Ye do foolishly," Jem said; "I know the place, and ye do know nothing of it. That stack-house, it will tumble down about your heads if ye do touch it. It is all rot—beam and rafter. Be warned by me, miss, and leave un alone."

"I do not interfere in my husband's arrangements," Alice answered, with a fair amount of dignity. "If you have any advice to give about the house you had better give it to him."

"But the boys are at work in it now, miss; and I must speak to you, because I do not know where the young master be; and you would be skeared, and more than skeared, if you heard the place a-banging down like a cannon-ball about un's head; and it will, I tell ye. Be warned, I do say to you again!"

In his eagerness, Jem pressed still nearer to the table by which the two ladies were sitting. In the middle was a large painted miniature of her husband, the handsome captain, which poor Mrs. Mackenzie always carried about with her. It was her fancy to have this beloved face for ever before her, and she had brought it with her to Beach House, where it stood on Alice's table as she had remembered it, for more than ten years now, standing always on the table at home. It had been taken just before Captain Mackenzie had gone into Cornwall—that fatal sojourn from which he had never returned; and it was a wonderful likeness. It caught Jem Penreath's eye; and Alice's blood froze in her veins at the strange, only half-checked, groan, mingled with a curse, which the man uttered as his eyes fell on it.

"Who's he?" he said abruptly, and he touched the picture with his hand.

The girl snatched it up and pressed it to her bosom, as if to protect it.

"My father!" she cried, standing up, white and trembling, but meeting Jem's fierce look with the courage of desperation.

"My husband!" broke out the poor widow, laying her hand on the man's arm. "Did you know him? Can you tell me anything of him?"

"I didn't know him, and I cannot tell you of him," said Jem, speaking slowly and as if with difficulty; but by this time he had restrained himself, and had lowered his eyes to the ground.

Then he said no more, but, still never raising his eyes, turned round and left the room, and they heard his heavy tread echo through the passage.

A sudden fear possessed Alice. "Where is Walter?" she cried. "Mamma! come with me! that man will kill Walter! I saw it in his eyes; he means to kill him as he killed papa!"

"My child—Alice—you are raving, darling!" said her mother, soothingly; but she too was trembling.

The whole scene, strange, unintelligible, harrowing as it was, had shaken her nerves, and while trying to restrain, even to support, her daughter, she needed comfort for herself.

"I know what I am saying, mamma—come with me! come!" Her voice had risen now to a shrill scream, as she caught her mother by the arm and dragged her with her through the passage to the kitchen, and so on to the stack-house which the men were clearing.

It was a wild dark evening, and the wind was sobbing round the house in fitful gusts that told of a rising storm for the morrow. Yet to-morrow would be Christmas Day,—that day of joy to thousands, of peace, and love, and pleasant knitting-up of home-ties, of tender regrets for the past, though dead not buried nor yet forgotten, of loveliest hopes for the future,—that day associated with all that is best in the heart and the life of England,—the first Christmas Day that Alice had ever spent away from her mother's home. But what a Christmas Eve was this! Dread and nameless anguish within doors—without, gloom, desolation, and the awful signs of a coming storm. The wind was moaning across the tossing stretch of waters; the sea-birds wheeled low, and shrieked and screamed as if in pain; the wild waves dashed against the sounding beach, and tore down the shingles as they were sucked back into the vast world of seething waters; the heavy sky hung low and lowering—ah! it was, indeed, a threatening Christmas Eve on that wild Cornish coast, and even the hardy fishermen themselves felt the foreboding influences, and were saddened though they did not tremble.

Within the stack-house the men were working by the fitful light of a few lanterns set on the floor, and the candles which, miner-like, some carried in their caps. There were three sturdy fellows from the hamlet; the master workman from the neighbouring town, come to take measurements when the place should be cleared; and Jem Penreath, haggard, anxious, desperate-looking, facing Walter Garwood who stood with his hands in the pockets of his shooting-jacket looking on, every now and then pausing in his work to gaze full at the young master, with something in his face not pleasant to behold. He had tried to persuade him to leave the work alone, but Walter would not, and all the more because the man was so strange and so persistent. It was noticed at the time, and spoken much of afterwards, how Jem stood doggedly to one side of the house where the heaviest stakes were:—why did he look so often at Walter, balancing that heavy club across his palm, and with a kind of speculation in his eyes, a kind of preparatory spring in his feet?—and how he wrought there, not so diligently as noisily, moving about the logs and stakes and brushwood piled up in that corner with a great show of exertion, but doing so little that the other men had turned out all the rest whilst his part was still unfinished. And it was noticed too, how fierce he looked towards the young master, and how, once or twice, still balancing that heavy stake across his palm, he had edged a step or two nearer. And yet, what ill had the young man done? and what cause had they to be afraid that Jem would do him a mischief? But one of them, somehow or another, always managed to get between Walter and Penreath; and just as they came up to his side of the place, and began to clear away the rubbish thence, Alice, wild and white, stood in the doorway, and calling his name aloud, rushed forward to her husband.

He turned at the beat of her hurrying feet, at the sound of her frightened voice, and the turn saved him; for as he stepped aside, a heavy beam came down on the very spot where he had stood, and at the same moment a loud exclamation broke from one of the men. A loose board had rotted, and the heavy fall of the beam broke through the crumbling wood—broke through on to a battered mass of earth, which it stirred and scattered, showing the handle of something that looked like a cutlass, and a stiffened end of darkened cloth—some parts a lightish grey, others a blackened red.

"Why, what's this?" said the master workman from the town, stooping down.

"Leave un alone," hissed Jem, laying his broad hand on the man's shoulder; "leave un alone, I say, or it may be the worse for ye!"

"Hey, man! what's this ye say? It do look like knowing more about a dark job than ought to be," answered the townsman, thrusting him back, while at the same time he pulled at the handle, and brought out a rusty cutlass, with one deep hack in the blade. "There's more where that came from," he shouted; for he was excited, and the find was suggestive.

"Lower the lights, men, and work away!" cried Walter. "Mother, look to Alice," he added, he too pressing forward with the rest.

But Alice was not to be kept back. Her eyes wild, her lips apart, her young face blanched, and strangely stiffened in all her limbs, she stood close by Jem Penreath, despite her horror of the man, holding her mother by the wrist, and forcing her to look too. Spadeful by spadeful they uncovered what was lying under the earth—slowly as it seemed to those who, excited, strained, half-maddened, according to their degree, waited for that which was to be revealed. And then they uncovered—what? The crumbling bodies of a man with short, dark, curly locks, and of a woman down to whose waist fell a mass of golden hair. Across the man's breast hung a thick gold chain of a peculiar pattern, to which was attached a locket that had been forced open, and the locket held the miniature likeness of Mrs. Mackenzie, and on the fleshless hand glittered a diamond ring.

A piercing shriek burst from the poor widow. It needed no second glance to tell her who and what she saw. "My husband! Charles! Oh, Charles!" she sobbed, flinging herself on her knees by the terrible grave.

"And this is his murderer!" cried Alice, as she clutched Jem Penreath by the arm, and held him.

Strong man as he was—none stronger in all the country round—that slight girl's touch held him. He stood for a moment paralyzed and lost. His memory went back to this very day ten years ago—almost at this same hour—when he had stolen on the traces of Mary Mainfote and her gallant lover from Truro, as they took shelter in this deserted out-house from the storm, and ended both their lives together. There had been no struggle, no outcry, no pleading for life—only a woman's hand had grasped his arm, scarcely knowing what it did in the terrible suspense of the moment. Quietly, as they sat there in the deepening gloom, he had stolen upon them from the other side, and one blow had struck the life out of him who had gained what he had been refused, another had finished the work on her, and had avenged his denial in blood. The whole scene, so swift and bloody as it had been, wrought itself again before his eyes, so that he had not felt the tight hand which grasped his own with fingers braced to slender bars of steel as *hers* had been.

But when the men came forward, his senses were aroused. The touch of the woman's hand had been only a continuance, a part of the vision that had been conjured up again before him; but when the men's rough grasp seized him, he woke back to himself, to his manhood, to his strength, and with a laugh of contempt he shook them off, and stood at bay.

"Ay, boys, it's come at last!" he said, "and ye see it before ye. I swore it, she should never be living man's if not mine; and I kept my oath; and I kept it well. She and him, they lie there where they courted, and where I watched them, boys, and went mad; but not so mad that I could not strike—that I could not end it all before the day came when she was to go with him—to her shame. Now, ye have it all; and do your worst."

Swift steps pressed forward, sturdy hands were thrust out, but, swifter and stronger than any, Jem Penreath thrust them all aside, then sprang through the doorway, and was down the steep rocks before they could tell which way he had gone; and, search as they might, he never was seen in the place again, and never a sign, never a trace of him was found.

Days after, drifting with the current, washed up by the tide, a dreadful human corpse was flung on the shore of a lonely French village. It was buried in the small churchyard, and masses for the dead were said in its behalf; and some pitiful little maiden flung a crown of *immortelles* on the nameless sod; and kind souls sorrowed, thinking of the friends and lovers of the unknown—parents may be, may be children, wife, or lover—who would watch and wait through days and weeks of agony and hope deferred, till perhaps the poor burdened hearts could bear no more, but would break under their weight of misery. So they made up tender and pathetic stories over the corpse that had floated to their shores; and none dreamt of that bloody scene which one Christmas Eve saw enacted, and another revealed.

Beach House was soon deserted again after this, and the Garwoods' short occupancy seemed to be the end of its life as a dwelling-place. It fell into ruins, and got a worse name than ever, being said to be accursed, and to bring ill luck on any one possessing or occupying it. And when the news came down that way that the poor young lady had gone clean out of her mind since that awful night, and the doctors said she would never be herself again, Beach House was blamed for it all, and the curse was held undoubted. But Alice was not in quite such a hopeless state as report made out. She did certainly for a time lose her reason, but she rallied again, and threw off her malady before it had struck too deeply. And by care, and the kindly agency of time, she lost the vividness of the horror that had overtaken her, and remembered that terrible evening only as one remembers a bad dream— a dream that may darken, shadow, sadden our day, but that does not destroy the years, nor extend into the future.

Isabella F. Romer

THE NECROMANCER;
or, GHOST *versus* GRAMARYE

ISABELLA FRANCES ROMER (1798-1852) *was known mainly as a writer of travel volumes, a number of which appeared in the 1840s, and also as the author of the novel* Sturmer: A Tale of Mesmerism (1841), *an early example of the fascination exercised on the Victorian imagination by mesmerism, or hypnotism. In this story, which appeared in* Bentley's Miscellany *in January 1842, Romer's necromancer is a sort of mesmerist or charlatan who perhaps gets more than he bargained for when he attempts a phony ceremony to invoke the dead.*

"Is not this something more than phantasy?"—HAMLET.

"THEN I AM TO INFER, FROM ALL THAT YOU HAVE JUST advanced, that you really believe in ghosts?"

"Stop, my dear friend! I did not go quite so far, although I will admit that a belief in supernatural visitations does not appear to me to be incompatible with the exercise of reason; nor ought it to be advanced as a proof of ignorant credulity or vulgar superstition in those persons who own their credence in them. Everything is possible with the Allwise Being, whose ways are inscrutable to our limited comprehensions. The traditions of all nations and all religions contain accounts of apparitions, ghostly warnings, and revelations, mysteriously connected with the world of spirits; and I myself have seen—"

"My dear Baron, if *you* assure me that in your sober senses, and in a waking mood, you have seen a spirit, my incredulity will certainly be greatly staggered, and I shall almost be prepared to admit that such things may be; for I know you to be the soul of truth."

"Softly, softly! Had you not interrupted me, you would already be aware that I meant only to tell you that I had seen, and been well acquainted with, a person who had witnessed a supernatural appearance of so awful a nature, that he would have discarded it from his mind as the coinage of an over-excited imagination, had not other persons been present at the time, to whose senses the shadowy visitant was equally apparent, and had not circumstances borne out the strange and fearful mystery developed by it."

The preceding conversation took place one winter's evening, in the dark oak-panelled hall of an antique castle, on the German border of the Boden See (Lake of Constance), not far from the little peninsula which is occupied by the fortified town of Lindau, and commanding a view across the broad expanse of waters of the opposite shores of Thurgau, and of the snow-covered Alps of St. Gall and Appenzell, which form its magnificent back-ground. The interlocutors were an old Bavarian nobleman, proprietor of the mansion, and a Tyrolese gentleman, who was his guest.

"For Heaven's sake," resumed the latter, "let me hear your story: I have a passion for these sort of horrors; and the time, the season, and the place we are in, are all admirably suited for a narrative of the supernatural school. I think, however, it will go hard with me if I do not account for your marvels by natural causes."

"You shall judge," rejoined the noble *châtelain*. "All I ask is, that you do not interrupt me in my recital. The story was related to me very many years ago; and I have not alluded to it for such a length of time, that it will be necessary for me to concentrate my recollections of its various details in order to render them intelligible to you."

Then passing his hand over his forehead, and silently collecting his thoughts for a few moments, he thus proceeded:—

"The person from whose lips I received the details I am now about to relate to you was a countryman of my own, named Waldkirch, and a disciple of the famous Cagliostro. He had passed part of his youth in Paris at the period when that extraordinary empiric was the lion of the day, and had become deeply imbued with the mystical arts with which he inthralled the imaginations of the lovers of the wild and marvellous. Every one who has heard of Cagliostro has heard of the startling revelations which he made to various persons respecting future events of their lives, through the medium of magic mirrors. My friend Waldkirch had applied himself so successfully to this peculiar branch of the *black art*, that he had become nearly as great an adept in phantasmagoria as his celebrated master, or even as that prince of necromancers, Cornelius Agrippa."

"Pardon me for this once interrupting you," said the Tyrolian. "I thought it was of real *bonâ fide* phantoms you were to discourse, and not of optical delusions such as come under the denomination of phantasmagoria, and the shadowy deceptions conjured up by such a charlatan as Cagliostro."

"And so it is," returned the old Bavarian; "and my phantom will appear in the proper place, if you will allow me to proceed uninterruptedly in a narrative, the interest of which I should be unwilling to mar by confused or broken details. Waldkirch travelled for some time through the southern states of Europe, after his departure from Paris, and during his stay in Sicily became acquainted with the Conte Felice Sammartino, a young nobleman of the greatest promise, the only surviving child of the Duke Sammartino, who was himself the representative of one of the wealthiest and most ancient families in the island. This young man became so interested in the occult sciences, which formed the favourite pursuit of Waldkirch, that he passed much of his time in his society, and finally induced him to visit his father, the Duke, at a magnificent villa which he possessed on the sea coast, about five leagues from Palermo, where he had lived in almost monastic seclusion, since the loss of his eldest son, who had been torn from the bosom of his family in the most afflicting and inexplicable manner.

"The Duke Sammartino's family had consisted of two sons, the youngest of whom (the Conte Felice) had originally been destined for the ecclesiastical state, in order that the undivided wealth and estates of that noble house might be settled upon his elder brother, the Marchese Gaetano Sammartino; that being one of the conditions upon which depended his marriage with the Marchesina Lucrezia Parisio, an orphan heiress, to whom he had been betrothed while they were both children. Although their projected union had originated in family conventions, which had decided that the riches of the Sammartini and the Parisii should form one *apanage*,—and although, as is generally the case in such arrangements, the inclinations of the young people had been the last thing taken into consideration by the directing elders,—yet, by a happy chance, so strong a sympathy sprung up between Lucrezia and Gaetano, that they were lovers while they were yet children, and would mutually have chosen each other as the partner of their future existence, even if their parents had not already decided upon their union. Three years' absence from Sicily made by Gaetano, during which period he visited the principal courts of Europe, instead of diminishing the ardent affection they had so early evinced for each other, appeared to impart to it increased intensity; and no sooner had the young Marchese returned to Palermo than preparations for the solemnization of their nuptials were forthwith commenced with extraordinary magnificence. All that was noblest in Palermo had been invited to assist at the ceremony, and a succession of fêtes to be given by the different connexions of the youthful bride and bridegroom were to follow it; when, the day but one before that appointed for the marriage, Gaetano suddenly disappeared, and was seen no more!

"Since his return to Palermo, he had been in the habit of going almost every evening to the villa I have already alluded to, (the one inhabited by the Duke Sammartino when Waldkirch first became acquainted with the family,) that he might superintend the preparations that were in progress for the reception of his bride, who was to pass the first days of their marriage in that beautiful retreat with him. On the evening of his disappearance, he had proceeded thither as usual; but the night passed away, and he did not return to Palermo,—the morning came, and still he was absent. Expresses were sent in all directions in search of him, but in vain. None of his attendants had accompanied him to the villa; those of the Duke who remained in permanence there had beheld him depart as usual; and this is all that was ever known on the subject.

"To describe the consternation and despair into which the fair young bride and the whole of the Sammartino family were plunged, when hour after hour passed away, and no trace could be discovered of the lost Gaetano, would be impossible. On the day following his disappearance, it became known that an Algerine corsair had been seen off the coast on the fatal evening, and that some of the crew had landed in a boat, and carried off several of the inhabitants of those shores. The Duke immediately ordered two of the fast-sailing vessels called *speronari* to be equipped and sent in pursuit of the pirates, and Felice insisted upon embarking in one of them. But a violent gale of wind dispersed the little squadron off Trapani; one of the *speronari* became disabled, and was obliged to return to Palermo; the other one, containing Felice, with difficulty entered the port of Trapani, where they heard that a Barbary corsair had been seen to founder the preceding day, and all on board perished. This intelligence was but too well calculated to extinguish all rational hopes of Gaetano's still surviving, which had been connected with the supposition of his capture by the Algerines; yet so unwilling were the bereaved family to give themselves up to despair, that they still clung to the possibility that the vessel which had been seen to go down at sea might not have been the one in which the unfortunate youth had been carried off; and the Duke, accordingly, instituted inquiries all along the Barbary coast, tending to ascertain whether Gaetano had been carried into slavery thither, and in that case offering an immense ransom for his liberation.

"Nearly three years were thus spent in unavailing researches, and they were at length forced to resign themselves to the belief, that if the ocean had not buried in its unfathomable depths the object of their painful solicitude, he must have fallen a victim to the barbarous treatment of the pirates, and perished at their hands. And could anything have embittered the utter despair which succeeded to the clinging tenacity of their long-cherished hopes, it must have been the cruel uncertainty in which they remained concerning the catastrophe which had deprived them of one so amiable and so beloved.

"The destinies of Felice, however, were materially altered by the death of his brother; for, as he by that event became sole heir of the Sammartino family, he was emancipated from the life of celibacy to which the ecclesiastical profession would have doomed him, and it became the absorbing wish of the Duke that the hand of Lucrezia should be transferred to his surviving son, and that the union of the two families, which had been decided upon for so many years, should be thus ratified. One person alone obstinately objected to this substitution; and that person was the fair young mourner, whose widowed heart recoiled with horror from the idea of breaking its faith to the lost Gaetano.

"Felice, although captivated by the beauty and virtues of the young heiress, and sensitively alive to all the advantages of such an alliance, refused, with a noble generosity which did honour to his feelings, to press his suit with her as soon as he became aware of her strong objections to another marriage; he even carried his disinterestedness so far as to advocate her cause *against himself* with his family, and with her guardians (of whom his father was one), and generously protected her against the solicitations with which they persecuted her. 'Lucrezia is right!' he would often say; 'who knows but that my brother still lives? and would it not be dreadful to take advantage of the uncertainty that involves that question, in order to deprive him for ever of that which was dearest to him in the world! Could I, after co-operating in so culpable an action, dare to raise my voice to Heaven, and supplicate for his restoration to us? And, *if*, indeed, he no longer exists, how can we better honour his memory than by abstaining from filling up the void which his death has left amongst us—by sacrificing all our hopes upon his tomb,—by respecting as sacred all that ever belonged to him?'

"This exaltation of sentiment, however, did not coincide with the Duke's feelings and wishes, and all that Felice could obtain from him was, that he should refrain from molesting Lucrezia for another year, during which time he continued his researches for his lost brother with unabated ardour, but with no happy result. As for Lucrezia, touched by the delicacy of Felice's conduct towards her, she felt herself constrained to respect and admire the man she could not love, and insensibly a tender pity succeeded in her bosom to the profound indifference she had previously evinced for him. She could not remain blind to the extent of his passion for her, nor insensible to the magnanimity with which he protected her from the importunities of his family; every new victory that he obtained over himself rendered him more estimable in her eyes; every fresh sacrifice of his dearest wishes to her peace of mind was eagerly advanced by the Duke as a motive for softening the inflexibility of her resolves.

"It was at this particular stage of the affair that Waldkirch appeared at Palermo, and was invited by Felice to visit the Duke at his villa. The presence of the German stranger there formed an interesting epoch in the existence of the melancholy circle; his acquirements were varied and captivating; the exaltation of his ideas; the mysticism with which his conversation was tinged, and vague hints, darkly thrown out, of supernatural powers exercised by him—powers that could bring him into communion with beings of another world,—invested him with a sort of solemn interest in their eyes. He soon divined their characters,—entered into their individual feelings,—became the confidant of each,—and gradually acquired a dominion over the minds of all, for which it would have been difficult for them to account. The Duke especially, whose mental powers had become weakened by grief, succumbed to the influence exercised by this extraordinary man, and unresistingly admitted the mysterious inferences thrown out by him of an intercourse with supernatural agencies; Waldkirch became his oracle,—and the heart of the bereaved father thrilled with an awful hope that, through his ministry, the fate of his lost son might be revealed to him.

"At last he ventured to give utterance to those hopes, and one day throwing himself into the arms of his new friend, besought him to exert his powers in order to throw some light upon the inexplicable disappearance of Gaetano.

"'My friend,' he said, 'although the Church of Rome brands with the epithets of *sorcery* and *malefice* the science you have mastered, and threatens with excommunication not only those who practise it, but those who have recourse to it, yet I cannot resist the impulse which drives me to brave that contingent penalty, that, through your exertions, I may obtain some certain insight into a mystery which has desolated my domestic happiness. You see the wretched state of mind into which we are all plunged: Lucrezia's grief for the loss of my poor Gaetano has so far yielded to the influence of time, that it has softened into a calm and tender regret, which would ultimately leave her willing to favour the addresses of Felice, could her conscience be satisfied as to the certainty of his brother's death. Felice, on his part, is consuming away,—his health and courage sinking under the perpetual struggle to which his feelings are exposed by the intensity of his passion for Lucrezia, and his respect for her scruples. As for myself, you behold an unfortunate father, the representative of a noble and time-honoured race, who sees his name about to be extinguished,—his hopes of living in the children of his children sacrificed to the dreadful doubt that hangs like a cloud over the fate of one of them! Could that doubt be but dispelled, all would be well. Waldkirch, you understand me! have you the power of raising the veil which conceals the secrets of the world of spirits from the uninitiated? does your science embrace the possibility of ascertaining whether Gaetano be alive or dead? and, if so, can you bring conviction home to the minds of those so deeply interested in knowing the truth?'

Waldkirch fearlessly assured him that he could.

"Scarcely was this interview over, when Felice, unconscious of the conversation that had just passed, sought his friend, and flinging himself into an arm-chair with every demonstration of despair, exclaimed,

" 'Waldkirch, I can bear this no longer! I must quit this spot,—I must leave my country.'

" 'Gracious Heaven!' exclaimed Waldkirch, 'what has happened?'

" 'My friend—my dear friend!' replied the young man, 'in vain have I struggled against my love for Lucrezia! it has overcome my firmest resolution to smother it within my own bosom; every day increases the intensity of my feelings; and if I remain longer here, I shall not be able to resist persecuting her with the expression of them.'

" 'Be assured,' said Waldkirch, 'that the heart of the Marchesina will at last pronounce itself in your favour; and that she will yield to the wishes of her friends, and bestow her hand upon you.'

" 'Never!' cried Felice,—'never, as long as she retains a vestige of hope that Gaetano still lives!'

" 'You believe, then, that an awful certainty would decide her?'

inquired Waldkirch; 'and, what if I tell you that it would be possible for me to bring that certainty home to her conviction?'

" 'What do you mean?' exclaimed Felice hastily, and fixing his eyes with terrified surprise upon the countenance of his friend.

" 'I mean,' was the answer, 'that it is possible to compel the disembodied spirit to appear once more upon earth; and, if ever terrestrial interests could warrant the peace of the tomb being thus invaded, it would be in a case like the present, where the tranquillity of so many persons depends upon the truth being incontrovertibly established.'

" 'No, no!' exclaimed Felice, shuddering, and turning to a deathlike paleness, 'I cannot countenance so impious a measure! In the name of Heaven, say no more of it, Waldkirch! Let me still be the victim. Destined from my earliest infancy to be sacrificed to my brother's aggrandisement and happiness, let me to the last fulfil my melancholy doom!' And, hiding his face in his hands, he wept bitterly.

"Waldkirch reasoned long and eloquently with Felice upon his scruples; and, giving him at last to understand that the experiment which he proposed would be merely a pious fraud, intended to bring certainty to the minds of the Duke and Lucrezia, (by convincing them through an optical delusion, of the reality of that melancholy termination to Gaetano's existence, which had long since ceased to be a doubt to all but to those two persons,) he succeeded in obtaining his adhesion to the plan he meditated. But it was necessary also to obtain that of Lucrezia; and Waldkirch found that to be the most difficult part of his undertaking. At last, upon receiving from him a solemn assurance that, if her betrothed lover still lived, the conjuration would produce no result, a reluctant assent was wrung from her, and only granted in the lingering hope that the failure of Waldkirch's experiment would give weight to her fond expectation of once more beholding the living Gaetano, and authorise her to persist in preserving inviolate the faith she had plighted to her first and only love.

"As soon as the unanimous consent of the family had been obtained, Waldkirch required that a delay of several days should be granted to him, in order to prepare, by reference to his books of gramarye, for the great undertaking. During his *séjour* at the

Duke's, he had had ample opportunity of making himself master of every detail relative to the appearance and manner of the unfortunate Gaetano; a full-length portrait of him, which had been terminated but a few days previous to his disappearance, enabled the adept to impart to the shadowy vision which he was preparing the closest resemblance to the ill-fated youth; and the supposed manner of his death decided him as to the way in which he should represent that catastrophe to have happened.

"At the expiration of ten days Waldkirch's preparations were terminated, and he announced that in the evening the mysterious question was to be resolved. Fasting, prayers, and vigils, added to the mystical communications of the German necromancer, had produced the desired effect upon the minds of his friends; wound up to a state of fanatical credulity in his powers, the emotions they evinced ended by inflaming his own imagination; and the state of nervous excitement to which he was raised contributed powerfully to the illusion which he wished to produce. In the dimly-lighted chamber of their guest, the lower end of which was buried in shadow, the Sammartino family were assembled: Waldkirch had neglected nothing that was likely to add to the mysterious horror of the scene that was to be enacted; an Æolian harp (an invention then unknown in that part of the world, and specially reserved by him for his exhibitions of magic,) had been placed outside of one of the windows, and the wild, unearthly tones it gave forth as the night-wind swept across its strings, seemed to the trembling listeners to be the wailings of a spirit in purgatory. They drew more closely together, and Waldkirch, stepping forth from the group, in a solemn voice adjured the spirit of the departed Gaetano to appear to them, and reveal the manner in which death had overtaken him.

"Scarcely had the words been pronounced when a blue and ghastly light partially illuminated the obscure end of the chamber, and discovered a large mirror, from the surface of which a dense mist slowly rolled away, and revealed to the astonished gazers the form of Gaetano Sammartino, clothed in the identical dress which he had worn on the night of his disappearance, his hands heavily fettered, and water streaming from his hair and garments, as he lay stretched in utter lifelessness upon the sea shore!

While their eyes, as though fascinated with horror, remained fixed upon the apparition, the surge appeared to roll slowly over it, and bear it away to its ocean grave. The mist again spread over the surface of the mirror, and all was shrouded in darkness. Not a word had been uttered during this strange scene; breathless silence had attested to the awe with which it had pervaded the minds of the excited family; but at the termination of it, a cry of anguish burst from the lips of the heart-stricken Lucrezia, and she fell fainting into the arms of the venerable Duke.

"A dangerous illness was the consequence of the painful emotions she had endured on the evening of Waldkirch's exhibition of his supposed unearthly powers; but from that date no further doubt remained upon her mind as to the fate of her lover; and to the fluctuating hopes which had so long tortured her, succeeded a calm resignation which betokened, at no very distant period, a still happier and brighter state of feeling—so true it is that the worst certainty is less intolerable than a state of suspense.

"Meanwhile the Sammartino family publicly attested to their belief in the death of Gaetano by going into mourning for him; masses were said for the repose of his soul; a monument erected to his memory in the chapel belonging to the family in the church of La Martorana, in Palermo; and finally, Felice assumed his brother's title, and from thenceforth became the Marchese Sammartino. Waldkirch had quitted Sicily shortly after his successful stratagem, and, after having passed some months at Naples was preparing to leave it for Rome, when he received a letter from Felice, announcing to him that his fondest hopes were about to be realized, and inviting him to return immediately to Palermo, that he might be present at his marriage with Lucrezia, and witness an event which he had been so instrumental in bringing to pass.

"Waldkirch lost no time in obeying the summons; he embarked for Sicily, but, the wind being contrary, the vessel did not reach Palermo until the eve of the day on which the nuptials were to take place; and, as Lucrezia had expressed a desire that the ceremony should be solemnized in the chapel of the Duke's villa, in the presence only of the nearest relations of the two families,—and that it should be followed by no rejoicings save a *fête-*

champêtre given to the tenantry, in order to distinguish it from the courtly splendours that had been prepared for her first bridal,—Waldkirch proceeded direct to the villa, and arrived there just in time to accompany his friend to the altar.

"The noble pleasure-grounds and gardens had been thrown open to the numerous peasantry belonging to the Duke's estates; and the lovely young bride, leaning upon the arm of the happy Felice, whose countenance was radiant with an expression of triumphant love, mingled with the gay throng, receiving their respectful felicitations, and acknowledging them with graceful affability. After the *bal champêtre* (which commenced on the smooth lawn at sunset) had terminated, a plentiful repast was served in the great hall of the villa, to which all the rustic guests were indiscriminately admitted, as well as the various strangers who had gathered together from the neighbouring *paesi* to witness the rejoicings. Among these latter, the noble hosts had remarked a person whose presence seemed ill suited to the joyful occasion; for he wore a dress peculiar to one of those confraternities which abound in the southern states of Italy, and whose members, in observance of a vow, devote themselves to attending condemned malefactors to the place of execution;—a dress which not only effectually conceals the countenance of the individual wearing it, but imposes a solemn prohibition against his being spoken to,—I mean the habit of a Grey Penitent. The ghastly fashion of the garb, the long shapeless robe of livid grey loosely shrouding a form of almost shadowy thinness,—the close capuchon covering the head and face, with two holes cut for the eyes, which invested it with the character of a death's head,—contrasted strangely with the gay holiday dresses of the Sicilian peasants, and the more costly elegance of the bridal party, and forcing upon the imagination images of suffering and death, caused the hearts of all who had remarked the unseasonable guest to sink with undefined apprehension. This vague terror was more particularly experienced by Lucrezia and Felice, whose glances were, in despite of themselves, strangely fascinated towards the unwelcome visitant; and each time that they gazed upon him they beheld his lack-lustre eyes intently fixed upon them.

"At last, towards midnight, the crowd dispersed, the orchestra became silent, the tables in the banqueting-hall were abandoned by their late noisy occupants, and nobody remained there but the immediate family of the bride and bridegroom, Waldkirch, and the Grey Penitent (who had remained immoveably fixed in the recess of a window, having by signs declined sharing in the banquet).

" 'My children,' said the Duke, looking at the young couple with glistening eyes, 'the fondest wish of my heart is realized by your union, and my grey hairs will now descend with satisfaction to the grave. May my blessing rest upon your heads, and prosper you! My friends,' he continued, turning to his few remaining guests, 'before we retire, let us drink to the happiness of Felice and Lucrezia!'

"At these words the Grey Penitent emerged from the recess where he had remained half concealed by the draperies of the window-curtain, and advancing with measured, noiseless steps towards the table, seized upon one of the flowing goblets that had just been filled out, and raised it to a level with his lips.

" 'Have you no other name to pledge?' said he, in hollow accents. 'And *Gaetano*, where is he?'

"The Duke started at this abrupt allusion to his dead son, and an expression of sadness overclouded his countenance as he replied, 'Alas! my beloved Gaetano is lost to us for ever on earth. You do not seem to be aware, reverend stranger, that he has been taken from us to that world from whence there is no return.'

" 'And yet,' continued the stranger, in the same accents, 'if the last voice that vibrated on his ear could *now* be heard, he would not remain deaf to the call! Old man!' he continued, turning to the Duke, 'bid thy son, Felice, call upon his brother's name!'

" 'What does he mean?' murmured the affrighted group; while Felice, pale as death, grasped the arm of Waldkirch for support, and Lucrezia leaned half fainting upon the shoulder of her father-in-law.

" 'Who pledges me?' resumed the terrible stranger, looking around. 'To the memory of Gaetano! and let all those who loved him follow my example.' And he raised the goblet to his lips.

" 'Whoever you may be, reverend penitent,' said the Duke in a tremulous voice, 'you have pronounced a name which has insured you a welcome here. Approach, my friends! let us not be outdone by a stranger; let us all drink to the memory of our beloved Gaetano!' And at this appeal, the glasses were raised with trembling hands to the lips of all present, with *one* exception, and replaced empty upon the table.

" 'There still remains one full goblet,' said the penitent; ' 'tis that of Felice! wherefore does he not drink to the memory of his brother?'

"He held the wine-cup towards him; Felice shrunk back from the invitation, pale and trembling, his forehead covered with cold drops of agony, his eyes wildly distended; but a gesture of entreaty from his father seemed to overcome his repugnance, and seizing the goblet from the hand of the Grey Penitent, he stammered forth, 'To the memory of my dear Gaetano!' and replaced it upon the table untouched.

" *'Tis the voice of my assassin!'* exclaimed the Grey Penitent, in an accent which thrilled all present with horror; and, tearing open his garments, the cowl fell back from his head, and revealed the well-remembered lineaments of the unfortunate Gaetano, stumped with the ghastly characteristics of death, the breast and throat perforated with gaping wounds!

"At this horrid spectacle, all those whom terror had not trans-fixed to the spot, fled shrieking from the hall; and Waldkirch, who for the first time beheld the realisation of that which his arts had so often simulated, fell to the ground in a swoon.

"When he recovered his senses, the phantom had disappeared, the guests had dispersed, and he found himself stretched upon a couch in his own room, with his servant watching beside him."

Here the Tyrolian, who had during the preceding recital been smoking very assiduously, laid down his *meerschaum*, and inter-rupted his friend.

"Do you not think it possible," he inquired, "that your nec-romancer, Monsieur de Waldkirch, might have exceeded the bounds of temperance at the wedding-supper, and that the appa-rition of the Grey Penitent was conjured up by the fumes of the libations he had poured out to the black-eyed Sicilian girls?"

"He would fain have believed so," replied the Bavarian, "and have contemplated the whole occurrence as nothing more than a distempered dream; but the state into which the unfortunate Felice had been thrown, deprived him of the possibility of a doubt. A prey to the most horrible convulsions, the unhappy bridegroom only recovered his consciousness to ask for a confessor, with whom he remained shut up for several hours. What passed between them never transpired, for the seal of confession is sacred; and Felice, who never arose from the bed to which he had been carried from the banqueting-hall on that fatal night, expired without proffering a word to any other human being. The Duke did not long survive him, and bequeathed the whole of his possessions to the virgin bride of his two sons."

"And, what became of her?" interrupted the Tyrolian.

"She founded a convent on the site of the villa where the strange events I have just related had occurred, and, taking the veil, ended her days there. In laying the foundations of a magnificent chapel, which she caused to be built in expiation of the horrible crime which had involved the extinction of the Sammartino family, an old dry well, the entrance of which had apparently been bricked up for several years, and covered over with brushwood, was discovered, and from its depths was drawn forth the skeleton of a man, bearing upon the third finger of his left hand the gold *alliance* with which Gaetano Sammartino had been betrothed to Lucrezia Parisio!"

"Umph!" ejaculated the Tyrolian, with a most provoking expression of incredulity. "Take notice, my dear Baron, that I do not attempt to dispute the fact of the murder, but I take up my position against the genuineness of the ghost; and now I will tell you what my actual impressions are. That Felice murdered his brother, I look upon as an undisputed fact; two strong motives impelled him to that horrid deed,—first, to save himself from becoming a priest, and lastly, that he might marry a beautiful young heiress, with whom he had fallen in love. It is natural to suppose that he confessed his crime to his spiritual director; and my opinion is that that reverend personage, disapproving of the marriage, and not daring to prevent it by betraying the secrets of confession to the family of the delinquent, enacted the part of the ghost, that he might terrify the conscience of the murderer into an avowal of his crime. Did this supposition never present itself to the mind of your friend, Waldkirch, who himself was such an adept in practising upon the credulity of his dupes by presenting to them ghosts and goblins of his own manufacture?"

"I fancy not," replied the old Bavarian gravely, "for I know it to be a truth that so *serious* an impression did it produce upon his mind, that from that day Waldkirch abjured the black art, and everything connected with the delusions of necromancy, and that, like Prospero, he broke his wand, and buried his book in the sea, 'deeper than did plummet ever sound!'"

James Grant

THE VEILED PORTRAIT

JAMES GRANT (1822-1887) *turned to writing after his military career, publishing over seventy novels, many of them adventure stories for boys. As its title suggests, "The Veiled Portrait" is one of many Gothic or ghostly tales that draw on the unsettling effect the image of someone dead, captured in a painting and seemingly looking down on us from a wall, can have upon us. As with Ellen Wood's "A Mysterious Visitor" in Valancourt's first collection of Christmas ghost stories, Grant's tale concerns the Indian Mutiny of 1857, during which Indian soldiers rebelled against the British, leading to acts of extreme violence and cruelty on both sides, including the massacre of British women and children by the Indians. Grant's story first appeared in the* London Society *Christmas Number in 1874.*

I T HAS BEEN ASSERTED THAT ONE CANNOT HOLD INTERCOURSE with that which is generally called the Unseen World, or behold anything supernatural, and live; but these ideas, from my own experience, I am inclined to doubt.

In the year subsequent to the great Bengal mutiny, I found myself at home on sick leave. My health had been injured by service in India, and by our sufferings consequent on the revolt; while my nervous system had been so seriously shaken by a grape-shot wound received at Lucknow, that it was completely changed, and I became cognisant of many things so utterly new to me, and so bewildering, that until I read Baron Reichenbach's work on magnetism and crystalism, I feared that I was becoming insane. I was sensible of the power of a magnet over me, though it might be three rooms distant, and twice, in darkness which seemed perfect to others, my room became filled with light; but the Baron holds that darkness is full of light, and that to increase the sensitiveness of the visual organs is to render that rare and dissipated light susceptible, with all that it may *contain*.

I was now compelled to acknowledge the existence of that new power in nature which the Baron calls the Odic Light, and of many other phenomena that are described in "Der Geist in der Natur," of Christian Oersted—the understanding that pervades all things.

But to my story.

Nearly a year had elapsed since the mutiny. The massacres at Delhi, Lucknow, Cawnpore, and elsewhere had been fearfully avenged by that army of retribution which marched from Umballah, and I found myself in London, enfeebled, enervated, and, as the saying is, "weak as a child." The bustle of the great capital stunned and bewildered me; thus I gladly accepted a hearty invitation which I received from Sidney Warren, one of "ours," but latterly of the Staff Corps, to spend a few weeks—months if I chose—at his place in Herts; a fine old house of the Tudor times, approached from the London road by an avenue that was a grand triumphal arch of nature's own creation, with lofty interlacing boughs and hanging foliage.

Who, thought I, that was lord of such a place could dream of broiling in India—of sweltering in the white-washed barrack at Dumdum, or the thatched cantonments of Delhi or Meerut!

My friend came hurrying forth to meet me.

"How goes it, old fellow? Welcome to my new quarters," he exclaimed.

"Well, Sidney, old man, how are you?"

Then we grasped each other's hands as only brother soldiers do.

I found Warren, whom I had not seen since the commencement of the revolt, nearly as much changed and shattered in constitution as myself; but I knew that he had lost those whom he loved most in the world amid the massacre at Meerut. He received me, however, with all the warmth of an old comrade, for we had a thousand topics in common to con over; while the regiment, which neither of us might ever see again—he certainly not, as he had sold out—would prove an endless source of conversation.

Sidney Warren was in his fortieth year, but looked considerably older. His once dark hair and coal-black moustache were quite grizzled now. The expression of his face was one of intense sadness, as if some secret grief consumed him; while there was a weird and far-seeing expression that led me to fear he was not fated to be long in this world. Yet he had gone through the storm of the Indian war without receiving even a scratch! Why was this?

Before I had spent two days with Sidney, he had shown me all the objects of interest around the Warren and in it—the portrait gallery, with its courtiers in high ruffs, and dames in the long stomachers of one period and *décolletée* dresses of another; his collection of Indian antiquities, amassed at the plundering of Delhi; and those which were more interesting to me, ponderous suits of mail which had been hacked and battered in the wars of the Roses, and a torn pennon unfurled by Warren's troop of horse, "for God and the King," at Naseby.

But there was one object which he would neither show nor permit me to look upon, and which seemed to make him shiver or shudder whenever it caught his eye, and this was a picture of some kind in the library—a room he very rarely entered. It was the size of a life-portrait, but covered closely by a green-baize hanging. Good taste compelled me to desist from talking to him on the subject, but I resolved to gratify my curiosity on the first convenient occasion; so one day when he was absent at the stable court I drew back the hanging of this mysterious picture.

It proved to be the full-length portrait of a very beautiful girl—a proud and stately one, too—bordering on blooming womanhood. Her features were clearly cut and classic; she had an olive-coloured complexion, that seemed to tell of another land than England, yet the type of her rare beauty was purely English. Her forehead was broad and low; her dark eyes, that seemed to haunt and follow me, were deeply set, with black brows well defined; her chin was rather massive, as if indicating resolution of character, yet the soft, ripe lips were full of sweetness; while the gorgeous coils of her dark hair were crisp and wavy. Her attire was a green riding-habit, the skirt of which was gathered in her left hand, while the right grasped the bridle of her horse.

It was *not* a portrait of his wife, whom I remember to have been a fair-haired little woman; so *who* was this mysterious lady? I cannot describe the emotion this portrait excited within me;

but I started and let fall the curtain, with a distinct sensation of some one, or *something* I could not see, being close beside me; so I hurried from the shady library into the sunshine. Lovely though the face—I can see it yet in all its details—it haunted me with an unpleasant pertinacity, impossible either to analyse or portray. But I was a creature of fancies then.

"Herein," thought I, "lurks some mystery, which may never be cleared up to me." But in this surmise I was wrong, for one night—the night of Sunday, the 10th May, *the first anniversary* of the outbreak at Meerut, after we had discussed an excellent dinner, with a bottle or two of Moselle, and betaken us to iced brandy *pawnee* (for so we still loved to call it), and to the "soothing weed," on the sofas of the smoking-room, Warren became suddenly seized by one of those confidential fits which many men unaccountably have at such times, and, while he unsparingly and bitterly reproached himself for the part he had acted in it, I drew from him, little by little, the secret story of his life.

Some ten years before those days of which I write, when in the Guards, and deeply dipped in debt by extravagance, he had, unknown to his family, married secretly a beautiful girl who was penniless, at the very time his friends were seeking to retrieve his fortune by a wealthy alliance. An exchange into the Line—"the sliding scale"—became necessary, thus he was gazetted to our regiment in India, at a period when his young wife was in extremely delicate health; so much so that the idea of her voyaging round the Cape—there were no P. and O. Liners then—was not to be thought of, as it was expressly forbidden by the medical men; so they were to be separated for a time; and that time of parting, so dreaded by Constance, came inexorably.

The last fatal evening came—the last Sidney was to spend with her. His strapped overlands and bullock-trunks, his sword and cap, both cased, were already in the entrance hall; the morrow's morning would see him off by the train for Southampton, and his place would be vacant; and she should see his fond hazel eyes no more.

"Tears again!" said he, almost impatiently, while tenderly caressing the dark and glossy hair of his girl-wife; "why on earth are you so sad, Conny, about this temporary separation?"

"Would that I could be certain it is only such!" she exclaimed. "Sad; oh, can you ask me, Sidney, darling? The presentiment of a great sorrow to come is hanging over me."

"A presentiment, Constance! Do not indulge in this folly."

"If I did not love you dearly, Sidney, would such a painful emotion rack my heart?"

"It is the merest superstition, darling, and you will get over it when I am fairly away."

Her tender eyes regarded him wistfully for a moment, and then her tears fell faster at the contemplation of the coming loneliness.

After a pause, she asked:

"Are there many passengers going out with you?"

"A few—in the cuddy," he replied carelessly.

"Do you know any of them?"

"Yes; one or two fellows on the staff."

"And the ladies?" she asked, after another pause.

"I don't know, Conny dear; what do they matter to me?"

"I heard incidentally that—that Miss Dashwood was going out in your vessel."

"Indeed; I believe she will."

Constance shivered, for with the name of this finished flirt that of her husband had been more than once linked, and his change of colour was unseen by her as he turned to manipulate a cigar. So for four, perhaps six months, these two would be together upon the sea.

Constance knew too well the irritable nature of her husband's temper to say more on the subject of her secret thoughts; and deeply loth was she that such ideas should embitter the few brief hours they were to be together now; so a silence ensued, which, after a time, she broke, while taking between her slender fingers a hand of Sidney, who was leaning half moodily, half listlessly against the mantelpiece, twisting his moustache with a somewhat mingled expression of face.

"Sidney, darling," said she entreatingly, "do forgive me if I am dull and sad—so *triste*—this evening."

"I do forgive you, little one."

"You know, Sidney, that I would die for you!"

"Yes; but don't, Conny—for I hate scenes," said he, playfully kissing her sweetly sad, upturned face; and the poor girl was forced to be contented with this matter-of-fact kind of tenderness.

So the dreaded morrow came with its sad moment of parting.

To muffle the sound of the departing wheels she buried her head, with all its wealth of dark, dishevelled hair, among the pillows of her bed, and some weeks—weeks of the most utter loneliness, elapsed, ere she left it, with the keen and ardent desire to recover health and strength, to the end that she might follow her husband over the world of waters and rejoin him; but the strength and health, so necessary for the journey, were long of coming back to her.

She had hoped he would write her before sailing from Southampton—a single line would have satisfied the hungry cravings of her heart; but, as he did not do so, she supposed there was not time; yet the transport lay three days in the docks after the troops were on board. He would write by some passing ship, he had said, and one letter, dated from Ascension, reached her; but its cold and careless tone struck a mortal chill to the sensitive heart of Constance, and one or two terms of endearment it contained were manifestly forced and ill-expressed.

"He writes me thus," she muttered, with her hand pressed upon her heaving bosom; "thus—and with that woman, perhaps, by his side!"

She consulted the map, and saw how far, far away on the lonely ocean was that island speck. Months had elapsed since *he* had been there; so she knew that he must be in India now, and she had the regular mails to look to with confidence—a confidence, alas! that soon faded away. Long, tender, and passionate was the letter she wrote in reply; she fondly fixed the time when she proposed to leave England and rejoin him, if he sent her the necessary remittances; but mail after mail came in without any tidings from Sidney, and she felt all the unspeakable misery of watching the postman for letters that never, never came!

Yet she never ceased to write, entreating him for answers and assuring him of unswerving affection.

Slowly, heavily, and imperceptibly a year passed away—a whole year—to her now a black eternity of time!

"Could Sidney be dead?" she asked herself with terror; but she knew that his family (who were all unaware of *her* existence) had never been in mourning, as they must infallibly have been in the event of such a calamity; and in her simplicity she never thought of applying to the Horse Guards for information concerning him—more information than she might quite have cared to learn.

Her old thoughts concerning Miss Dashwood took a strange hold of her imagination now; a hundred "trifles light as air" came back most gallingly to memory and took coherent and tangible shapes; but a stray number of the "Indian Mail" informed her of the marriage of Miss Dashwood—her *bête-noire*—to a Major Milton; and also that the regiment to which Sidney belonged "was moving up country," a phrase to her perplexing and vague.

Her funds were gone—her friends were few and poor. Her jewels—his treasured presents—were first turned into cash; then the furniture of her pretty villa, and next the villa itself with its sweet rose-garden, had to be exchanged for humbler apartments in a meaner street; and, ere long, Constance Warren found, that if she was to live, it must be by her own unaided efforts; and for five years she maintained a desperate struggle for existence—five years!

A lady going to India "wanted a young person as a governess and companion."

To India—*to India!* On her knees Constance prayed that her application might prove successful; and her prayer was heard, for out of some hundred letters—from a few which were selected— the tenor of hers suited best the taste of the lady in question. She said nothing of her marriage or of her apparent desertion; but as her wedding ring, which, with a fond superstition of the heart, she never drew from her finger, told a tale, she had to pass for a widow.

So in the fulness of time she found herself far away from England, and duly installed with an Anglo-Indian family in one of the stately villas of the European quarter of Calcutta—a veritable palace in the city of palaces, overlooking the esplanade before Fort William—in charge of one sickly, but gentle little pale-faced girl.

She had been a month there when her employer's family proposed to visit some relatives at Meerut, where she heard that Sidney's regiment was cantoned! To her it seemed as if the hand of Fate was in all this. Oh the joy of such tidings! Some one there must be able to unravel the horrible mystery involving his fate; for by this time she had ascertained that his name was out of the corps; but her heart suggested that he might have exchanged into another.

"If alive, is he worth caring for?" She often asked this of herself, but thrust aside the idea, and pursued with joy the long journey up country by river steamers, dawk-boats, and otherwise, on the Ganges to Jehangeerabad, from whence they were to travel by carriages to the place of their destination, some fifty miles distant.

On the way Constance had an addition to her charge in the person of a little boy, who, with his *ayah*, was going to join his parents at Meerut. This little boy was more than usually beautiful, with round and dimpled cheeks, dark hazel eyes, curly golden hair, and a sweet and winning smile. Something in the child's face or its expression attracted deeply the attention of Constance, and seemed to stir some memory in her heart. Where had she seen those eyes before?

She drew the boy caressingly towards her, and when kissing his fair and open forehead, her eyes fell involuntarily on a ring that secured his necktie, a mere blue riband. It was of gold, and on it were graven the initials C. and S. with a lover's knot between. These were those of herself and her husband, and the ring was one she had seen him wear daily. Constance trembled in every limb; she felt a deadly paleness overspread her face, and the room in which she sat swam round her; but on recovering her self-possession, she said:

"Child, let me look at this ring."

The wondering boy placed in her hand the trinket, which she had not the slightest doubt of having seen years before in London.

"Who gave you this, my child?" she asked.

"My papa."

"Your papa!—what is your name?"

"Sidney."

"What else?" she asked impetuously.

"Sidney Warren Milton."

"Thank God! But how came you to be named so? There is some mystery in this—a mystery that must soon be solved now. Where were you born, dear little Sidney?"

"In Calcutta."

"What is your age, child?"

"Next year, I shall be seven years old."

"Seven—how strange it is that you have the name you bear!"

"It is my papa's," said the boy, with a little proud irritability of manner.

"Where did your papa live before he came to Calcutta?"

"I don't know—in many places—soldiers always do."

"He is a soldier?"

"My papa is Major Milton, and lives in the cantonments at Meerut."

"A little time, and I shall know all," replied poor Constance, caressing the boy with great tenderness.

On arriving at Meerut, however, she found herself ill—faint and feverish, so that for days she was confined to her bed, where she lay wakeful by night, watching the red fire-flies flashing about the green jalousies, and full of strange, wild dreams by day. She had but one keen and burning desire—to see Major Milton, and to learn from his lips the fate of her husband. On the evening of the fifth day—the evening of the 10th of May—she was lying on her pillow, watching the red sunshine fading on the ruined mosques, and Abu's stately tomb, when just as the sunset gun pealed over the cantonments, the *ayah* brought her a card, inscribed, "Major Milton—Staff Corps."

"Desire the Major to come to me!" said Constance in a broken voice, and terribly convulsed by emotion; for now she was on the eve of knowing all.

"Here to the *mehm sahib*'s bedside?" asked the astonished *ayah*.

"Here instantly—go—go!"

Endued with new strength, as the woman withdrew, she sprang from her bed, put on her slippers, threw round her an ample cashmere dressing robe, and seated herself in a bamboo chair, trembling in every fibre. In a mirror opposite she could see that her face was as white as snow. The door was opened.

"Major Milton," said a voice that made her tremble, and attired in undress uniform, pith-helmet in hand, her husband, looking scarcely a day older, stood gazing at her in utter bewilderment. He gave one convulsive start, and then stood rooted to the spot; but no expression or glance of tenderness escaped him. His whole aspect bore the impress of terror.

Years had elapsed as a dream, and they were again face to face, those two, whom no man might put asunder. Softness, sorrow, and reproach faded from the face of Constance. Her broad, low forehead became stern; her deep-set, dark eyes sparkled perilously, her full lips became set, and her chin seemed to express more than ever, resolution.

"Oh, Constance—Constance," he faltered, "I know not what to say!"

"It may well be so, Sidney" (and at the utterance of his name her lips quivered). "So *you* are Major Milton, and the supposed husband of Miss Dashwood?"

There was a long pause, after which she said:

"I ask not the cause of your most cruel desertion; but whence this name of Milton?"

"A property was left me—and—but of course, you have long since ceased to love me, Constance?"

"*You* actually dare to take an upbraiding tone to me!" she exclaimed, her dark eyes flashing fire. Then looking upward appealingly, she wailed, "Oh, my God! my God! and *this* is the man for whom, during these bitter years, I have been eating my own heart!"

"Pardon me, Constance; you may now learn that there is no gauge to measure the treachery of which the human heart in its weakness is capable. Yet there has been a worm in mine that has never died."

She wrung her hands, and then said, with something of her old softness of manner:

"You surely loved me once, Sidney?"

"I did." He drew nearer, but she recoiled from him.

"Then whence this cruel change?"

"Does not some one write, that we love, and think we love truly, and yet find another to whom one will cling as if it required these two hearts to make a perfect whole?"

"Most accursed sophistry! But if you have no pity, have you not fear?"

"I have great fear," said he in a broken voice; "thus, Constance, by the love you once bore me, I beseech you to have pity, not on me, but on my little boy, and his poor mother—preserve their happiness——"

"And sacrifice my own?" said she in a hollow voice.

"Spare, and do not expose me—my commission—my position here——"

"Neither shall be lost through me," she replied, in a voice that grew more and more weak; "but leave me—leave me—the air is suffocating—the light has left my eyes. Farewell, Sidney—kiss your child, for my sake."

He drew near to take her hand, but she repulsed him with a wild gesture of despair, and throwing up her arms, fell back in her seat, with a gurgle in her throat, her head on one side and her jaw fallen.

"Dead—quite dead!" was his first exclamation, and with his terror was blended a certain selfish emotion of satisfaction and relief at his escape. The blood again flowed freely in his veins, and he was roused by the cantonment *ghurries* clanging the hour of *nine*.

"Help—help!" cried he; but no help came, and as he hurried away, the sudden din of musket-shots, of shrieks and yells, announced that the great revolt had begun at Meerut, and that the expected massacre of the Europeans had commenced. In that butchery, those he loved most on earth perished, and midnight saw him, wifeless and childless, lurking in misery and alone in a mango tope, on the road to Kurnaul.

While listening to the narrative of my friend Sidney, whom I had always known as Warren, rather than Milton, the clock on the mantelpiece struck *nine*, and he said in a broken voice:

"It was at this very hour, twelve months ago, that my boy and his mother were murdered by the 3rd Cavalry, at the moment that Constance was dying!"

As he spoke, a strange white light suddenly filled one end of the smoking-room, and amid it there came gradually, but distinctly to view, two figures, one was a little boy with golden hair, the other a woman whose left arm was around him—a beautiful woman, with clearly-cut features, masses of dark hair curling over a low, broad forehead, lips full and handsome, with a massive chin and classic throat—the woman of the veiled picture, line for line, but to all appearance living and breathing, with a beautiful smile in her eyes, and wearing, not the riding-habit, but a floating crapelike white garment, impossible to describe. There was a strange weird brightness in her face—the transfigured brightness of great joy and greater love.

"Constance—Constance and my child!" cried Sidney, in a voice that rose to a shriek; and like a dissolving view, the light, and all we looked on with eyes transfixed, faded away!

I was aware of an excess of sensitiveness, and that my heart was beating with painful rapidity. I did not become insensible, but some time elapsed before I became aware that lights were in the room, and that several servants, whom my friend's cry had summoned in haste and alarm, were endeavouring to rouse him to consciousness from a fit that had seized him; but from that fit he never recovered. His heavy stertorous breathing gradually grew less and less, and ere a doctor came, he had ceased to respire.

His death—sudden as hers on that eventful night, but a retributive one—was declared to be apoplexy; but I knew otherwise. Since then, though the effect of the grape-shot wound on my nervous system has quite passed away, I feel myself compelled to agree with the hackneyed remark of Hamlet, that "there are more things in heaven and earth, than are dreamt of in our philosophy."

Anonymous

THE GHOST CHAMBER

This atmospheric short tale, a somewhat different kind of "ghost story," first appeared anonymously in Ainsworth's Magazine *in January 1853.*

THERE! IT RISES BEFORE ME AS I WRITE. A long, low room, wainscoted and tapestried, the windows hung with yellow curtains, through which the daylight enters gorgeously; and the floor shining and black with its polished oak boardings. What strange gleams of light fall across the counterpane from the coloured glass, and outside there is an old rookery, the perpetual cawing of whose inhabitants would fain persuade us that already a whisper of Spring has got abroad upon the air. It has been the state-room of the family, but I see it now as when I sat in it during the long, lonely evening, when the firelight leapt and sparkled on the hearth, and strange smiles flitting over the pictured faces looked down upon me from the walls, when sounding but invisible footsteps ran creaking along the boards, and knowledge-like, a guest visited me, whispering "the chamber is haunted!" Yes, haunted, truly! but only by old spirit memories.

The old people who inhabited this room have long since been gathered to their fathers, and it is now their second son who inherits the property. Their portraits hang upon the walls, and look down upon us with something of a life presence still upon them. With stately carriage, and hand placed within his vest, eagle eye, and stern brow, the old man still seems keeping watch over his household. Opposite to him, in hat and feathers, white satin gown, low neck and arms, and all the acknowledged beauty of a past century, sits smiling his wife.

There is a history connected with these portraits. I think of them in the ghost chamber, where I have been placed by my own desire, and wonder if they ever descended from their grand state-liness to the little familiarities—the sweet social endearments—that twine so lovingly around the intercourse of life. There is an old Judge, with powdered wig, white cravat, and long waistcoat, who frowns down at me from over the mantel-piece; as this question suggests itself mentally, and as I glance across at the family heiress, in all the dignity of shepherdess attire, her crook seems to tremble in her hands, and the very folds of her dress to stand upright with horror.

But in the ghost chamber I still linger, haunted ever by these memories of the dead. I cannot sleep, so from between the tape-stried folds of the bed hanging I still look forth, and behold the heavy chairs cast shadows on the shining boards, and something glides in between them and the firelight, and the seats are occupied. What do I see? Nothing! I only heard the creaking of boards and rustling of garments, but is not that all-sufficient? Do I not know, as plainly as my imagination tells me that it is so, that the figure with the powdered hair, stern brow, and benevolent smile, even now loosening the cravat from his throat, is, in fact, the very owner of the ghost chamber? Does not the lady of the hat and feathers again sit before me? only now she has her hair rolled back off her brow in pyramids of curls, and her stiff silk dress seems to quiver with importance.

You tell me it is the wind that I hear in the chimneys, shadows from the moonlight, creakings from the old boards. Very good, we can both hold our own opinions. But I sleep—yes, even in the ghost chamber! and now the old family histories come sweeping like a strong tide in upon me. I see the household growing up around the old parent stock, and their eldest born, the prodigal, with his dear, warm heart, and ill-advised judgment. There is an old grandmother who is always supplying him with money, ever against the consent, often without the knowledge, of his parents. A stern-looking old lady she seems, with an upright carriage, and a gold-headed cane. The villagers call her "Madam Talbot," and bring all grievances and party quarrels before her. She holds a small court of justice, against which there is no appeal. The village urchins tremble at her anger. Her justice is summary, and she has been known to chain the offender caught stealing apples in the orchard to the bars of the gate—a kind of human scarecrow to trembling brethren! But the one weak spot in her heart is for this grandson. No one may blame him; she sees all the noble, generous points in his character; she is quite deaf and blind to his defects. So they grow up. Here is the second brother, the supplanter, wise, correct, calculating, too weak for virtue, and too cold for vice; ever stepping in between his eldest brother and his father. How the breach widens! I seem to see the crust thicken round the hearts of these his kindred; they are, as it were, poisoned, alienated from him, and he is too proud to sue for that pardon he thinks should be his of right. Reckless in his expenditure, careless in his profession, yet so kind, generous, and loving—not even understanding coldness in others. Now the shadow of that second brother falls again across me. I see him taking, as it were, the servant's place in the house, being all things to please all men; such an old-hearted head on such young shoulders. He gives false meanings to the faults of his eldest brother, so that they stand forward in unfavourable light; he implies, suggests—wounded feelings are made rankling sores by the force of his covert insinuations; and so the breach widens.

Now the eldest son has taken to himself a wife—fair, gentle, loving; but, alas! he has consulted but his own pleasure, and has looked for no dowry beyond the single one of virtue. How should he be forgiven? How can he who errs against his own interest ever expect the compassion of others? and, in a world where Mammon is worshipped, how think to live independent? And this, too, must be placed against him. He must not bring his wife to his father's hearth; his hasty choice is to be visited on her, as having entered the family on false pretensions; and the jealous pride of his wounded heart shall be accounted to him as an evil thing. No wonder that the breach widens! We see the second brother becoming everything to his father; he has all the guile of another Esau, so plausible is he with his regrets under the surface of fraternal sorrow; so fair an aspect bears he with so foul a soul! Now he sighs in his superior righteousness over the faults of the prodigal; now he winds himself with unseen coils into the old man's confidence; he has become, as it were, his right hand; he, the stern, proud father, is a slave to his child, and so unconscious a one, that though he cannot do without him, yet he still deludes himself that he possesses ever the same dominant power of old.

There comes a day, however, when the old man is struck with death. It is an awful time. The family crowd round him weeping, wailing, and lamenting; and there he lies, helpless like a little child, unnerved, palsied, trembling in the grasp of the great destroyer. Then better thoughts, old, long crushed affections return to him; standing, as it were, on the verge of the grave, he sees, as with different eyes, old things are fallen off from him, all things are become new. His hand wanders towards his prodigal son, kneeling at the foot of his bed, weeping hot, burning, passionate tears; he hears the prayer of his spirit poured out for forgiveness, and resting there he bows himself towards him, and with faultering voice blesses him aloud; he tells him that he has disinherited him, that he has bestowed all upon his brother; with feeble motion he points towards his will. But his son, heart-broken, agonised, still kneels before him; he offers no complaint, utters no murmur; only with choked voice he sobs forth, "Oh! let his brother keep all so that he may have his father's forgiveness." And the old man gives it to him. Solemn and slow on the shadowy twilight come forth those words of peace, and in the falling darkness of the ghost chamber there is only heard the strong man's sobs, and that death-bed blessing.

Now the room is again in stillness, the old man sleeps; and through the long night watches there only remains his daughter, seated patiently by his side; she stoops to screen the lamp-light from his eyes, and suddenly he calls upon her. She starts, for in his face there is an expression all unknown before; his voice is low and faint, but each word, as she catches it, seems to fall upon her ear with solemn meaning. He tells her how, laying there in the long night hours, a voice spoke to him; how men's eyes are opened at the portals of death; and how it was given him to see that far beyond the gains and honours of life, far beyond all its wealth and pleasure, there rests still Heaven's blessing on the large loving heart and liberal spirit; how all things fall off from men in death, but love still lingers. Then he spoke of how he had wronged her brother, passing through life without understanding him—putting forth the angel spirit that had been given him as a blessing. "But mark me, child," he said, and now his voice, before broken, became loud and clear; "I will yet, if God spares me, make restitution. I take you to witness of my purpose, and I lay it on you as my command to bring your brother to me with the daylight that justice may be restored," and with this he moved upon his pillow, turning his face towards the wall, and, as she thought, slept quietly.

But when the morning light came in, flooding the room, the sunbeams fell full on the face of the calm dead; and the daughter's cry of horror gathered in to her all the household. There were voices of lamentation—low dirges—weeping of women—and, with the sound of hushed feet, the dead passed onwards to his long home. The second son inherited the property, for there was none to dispute the will; but the returned prodigal, kneeling in the ghost chamber, offered thanks to God for that his father's heart had been restored to him, and then with a softened heart and a mind at peace, returned again to share the poverty of her who had chosen him for himself.

Am I dreaming in the ghost chamber? I seem to see still the son reconciled, visiting, as he does yet, sometimes at the house of his brother, the usurper. The ghost chamber is given up to him; he sleeps better in it, he says, than elsewhere; he has always pleasant dreams here. I do not wonder at it; for I know how, when he sleeps, the spirits of the old people still watch over him. I see them in my imagination (you will not allow me sight) putting aside the tapestried curtains, looking down upon him tenderly. The father has still his smile of benevolence, but his brow has lost all its sternness; he lays his hand upon him and blesses him, and the mother's face is irradiated with gladness! So, even in my dreams, these forms fall off from me, and I wake once more in the ghost chamber to the young day's sunshine, to the cheerful cawing of the rooks at work outside my window; and musing, as I lay, let the sounds of life flood in upon me till my heart is filled with their music, and the spirits of the ghost chamber pass from me to return again with the firelight, on the black boards, and the moonbeams stealing in fantastically through the stained windows.

"A. S."

A TERRIBLE RETRIBUTION;
or, SQUIRE ORTON'S GHOST

Rounding out our volume of Christmas ghost stories is this fine tale of a violent murder and retribution from beyond the grave with an ending that we think closes out the book on the right note. Anonymously published in the weekly periodical Bow Bells *in December 1871, this rare tale does not appear ever to have been previously reprinted.*

THE ASPECT OF THE DRAWING-ROOM OF IVY LODGE was ever bright and cheerful, but on this particular day, Christmas Eve, with the snow without, and the crackling logs within, it was more than usually so. It seemed scarcely the right place for a man to have all his best hopes crushed—to hear his doom of endless misery pronounced. Yet thus it was with me, rich Squire Orton's nephew—Parsimonious Squire Orton, as he was frequently termed.

For long I had loved Florence Bradlaw, adoring her with the blind affection of a man—the devotion of a dog—bearing her wilful caprices—content, rather than risk losing her, to be in favour one moment, only to be slighted the next; never, however, wholly despairing, for I was possessed by a secret consciousness, skilfully created by Florence herself, that, notwithstanding all her coquetries—charming enough in my eyes—in heart, I was her chosen lover.

But a man cannot dangle about a woman's skirts for months, without a desire to assure himself of what is to be his real fate. Dreading rejection—hoping an acceptance—he rushes forward; and I, Squire Orton's only heir, had, at beautiful Florence Bradlaw's feet, that Christmas Eve, besought her promise to be mine.

The declaration had not taken long to speak—nor the answer.

The result was the following tableau. I was standing, with gloomy, angry, despairing brow, near the table; Florence a few paces off by the fire, calm, though her colour was heightened, her head slightly bent, and her fingers plucked, unconsciously, to pieces some winter flowers I had brought her.

"This, then, is your final reply, Florence?" I exclaimed huskily, after a moment's silence. "After all, you do not love me—you will not marry me?"

"I did not say I did not love you, Sydney," she answered, quietly, without any agitation, glancing up. "I said I could not, under the circumstances, marry you."

"And those circumstances?"

"Your utter dependence on your uncle, Squire Orton. He is, if report speaks true, very—pardon my saying it—fond of his wealth and Miss Mayfield. Supposing, were you to offend him, he were to disinherit you? You would be penniless! What should we do?—I, who hate, abhor poverty!"

"Florence!" I cried earnestly, "you should not feel it; I would work day and night that you should not." Then I could not refrain from adding, rather bitterly, "But this is scarcely a proof of real love."

"Excuse me," she said; "it is, in my eyes, the truest, being destitute of all folly of romance, which ever leads to misery and discontent. Better in marriage, as other matters, to look well into the future, than leap blindly."

I was silent; her words cut me to the heart; but I loved her. After a space, I said, "Why should he disinherit me—I am his heir?"

"A fact a dash of his pen can alter," she rejoined, her cheek flushing with passionate indignation, as she continued, "Why would he disinherit you? For wedding *me,* whom he hates equally as he loves his gold."

I did not refute it; I knew well enough what she said was true. My uncle was never flattering in the terms he applied to Florence. "Heartless!" "Extravagant coquette!" "Selfish flirt!" were among the mildest. Thus her supposition of my disinheritance was not improbable. Did he imagine the gold he held so carefully would be squandered by my wife, I felt he would cut me off with a shilling. To prevent the chance of this, no doubt, was the reason that, though over twenty-one, he yet treated me as a boy. My allowance was large, but entirely dependent on his will.

"I have received your answer; I accept it, Florence," I said, coldly. "I suppose it is farewell with us for ever?"

"*I* do not say so!" And lifting her dark, brilliant eyes, she shot at me a glance that thrilled through every nerve, causing them to throb with the fever of my passion. "There is no hurry to decide yet, Sydney. Let us think the words just spoken were never uttered. Let us be the same as before, and wait. Who knows what may happen even in a few weeks?"

She extended her hand, and as I took it, her unpronounced thought seemed to communicate itself to me. My uncle was old—the winter was a severe one—he might die.

"Florence," I said, a tremor running through my frame, "tell me, if I were master of Orton Hall, would you be mine?"

She drooped her eyes, hesitated, and murmured, "Yes; if you were master of Orton, Sydney, this hand should be yours at once."

"Then, heaven forgive me! but I wish this day I were, for my love is more than I can bear."

I drew her rapidly towards me, imprinted a burning kiss on her lips; then, frightened at my audacity, hastened from the house.

As the crisp snow flew scattered by my angry tread, I reflected with rage upon the misery, as I thought it, of my position. A man in years as heart, the penuriousness of my uncle held me like a schoolboy. Money I might have, but not freedom. Northumberland must be my home, as his. Though my wings were strong, I must not fly from the parent nest.

"Better had he flung me forth to starve," I ejaculated, fiercely; "better if he had given me some profession, where I could have fought my own way in the world, and wedded whom I pleased."

It yet was not too late, and I determined to see and put the suggestion to him at once, for the Hall was insupportable parted from Florence.

On entering, I encountered Susie Mayfield, an orphan and *protégée* of Squire Orton's. Rumour whispered that she was the only child of the only woman he ever loved. I believe it was so. Pretty, ever-gentle Susie, I regarded as a sister. Indeed, after Florence, I adored her. She and I seemed one. Though two years her elder, it was to her I had ever carried my boyish troubles; and many a time, in that innocent period of our lives, had wept out my angry passions on her breast.

Once I had been on the point of death from fever—a malignant one—when Susie, despite all remonstrance, had never quitted my couch. On an effort being made to remove her, stamping her foot in girlish rage, she had exclaimed, "If you take me away, I will catch the fever, I will; but I won't if you let me remain!"

She did remain, and when consciousness returned, it was a blessed thing, after the wild, fevered delirium, to gaze on Susie's affectionate little face, as she flitted with a grave air of importance about the bed. I vowed I would never forget it—that I would love her as a dear, dear sister all my life.

I told her so; she blushed, laughed, said she hoped I would, then abruptly quitted my side, not to return for above an hour.

But men are ungrateful monsters. When I got so well as almost not to remember I had been ill, I fear I had neglected Susie Mayfield, especially when Florence Bradlaw, the belle of the county, engrossed my whole attention.

As we now met, I was passing her unnoticed, when starting, she exclaimed, "Oh, Sydney, you are ill! What has troubled you? Why do you look so angry?"

"Ill! angry!" I repeated, sharply; "I am neither. What prying eyes girls have! Pray attend to your music and sewing, and not to me. Where is the Squire?"

She shrunk away as if struck, then answered, "I did not mean to offend, Sydney. The Squire has gone to Otterlee, and will not return till evening."

The slight tremor in her voice, as she concluded, recalled me to a sense of my brutality. Quickly I swung round on my heel, to apologize. She was moving rapidly down the corridor, and I fancied her handkerchief was at her eyes.

"What a savage I am!" I muttered. "What harm has *she* ever done, that I should be such a bearish cub to her? Susie!" I called, following.

She seemed, at first, to think of avoiding me; but without she had absolutely run, I must have overtaken her, so she turned and met me. I could have sworn tears were in her eyes, they were so bright; yet her quiet smile made me doubt.

"Susie, dear," I said, taking her small hands in mine, "I was an unmanly brute to speak to you as I did just now; you are the kindest of kind little women. Susie, I believe you are the truest—the best friend I have."

"I should like to be so, Sydney," she rejoined in low tones. "It is but right I should, for are not you so to me?"

"I!" I ejaculated. "Why, Susie, I am an ungrateful wretch! But, Susie, I *am* in trouble—great trouble. Let that, dear, be my excuse. Don't ask what it is; you shall hear soon, only I must see my uncle first." Stooping, I kissed her. It brought a colour to her cheek, although the salutation was ordinary enough; for, raised together from childhood, we naturally acted as brother and sister. Indeed, I noticed that any endearment of the kind apparently gave singular satisfaction to Squire Orton.

Had not my brain been so full of Florence Bradlaw, it might have occurred to me that he hoped Susie would be the wife of my selection. As it was, I looked upon her so much as a sister, that Susie and marriage never presented themselves together before me.

Content in having apologized for my rudeness, and seen her smile, I proceeded to my own room, to await my uncle's return. It would be some while yet, but my brain was fevered, and I was too restless to support companionship. My mind was made up to ask him to grant me a regular income, and obtain for me the means of entering some profession.

Sitting and pondering, the fascination Florence exerted over me increased in intensity, and I felt it was utterly impossible for me to renounce her. She had confessed she cared for me; her own lips had said "Wait!" and full of the energy of youth, I thought if *she* only would, she yet should be mine. One sentence of hers rang ever in my ears, while my brain reeled under the recollection of the syren glance of her brilliant eyes.

"If you were master of Orton, Sydney, this hand should be yours at once."

I was too madly in love to dwell on the selfishness of this

remark, as also the poor compliment it was to myself; though it struck me, I accepted it passively, as I did her excuse, that "her affection was truest, because free from the folly of romance." I knew, as well as she, that Florence Bradlaw and poverty could never go happily together. So I sat, these words haunting me, till the early winter sunlight changed into night, and the moon rose up, bringing in her train piles of threatening cloud.

The wind, too, began to rise; a drear chill was in the atmosphere or in myself; and stirring the fire to a scorching blaze, I leaned back in my chair, my eyes creating pictures in the glowing coals. "It is eight o'clock," I exclaimed at last, starting from my reverie; "and the squire not returned. He always walks from Otterlee; it is late for that."

Leaving my chair, and approaching the window, I looked out. The land was white with snow, but the clouds were of a dull, leaden hue.

"Suppose I go and meet him?" I thought. "He cannot prevent the interview then, as he might here."

While getting my hat, a hesitation seized me. Should I go? My will seemed divided into two: one said "Yes;" the other appeared to utter a warning "No." I decided for the former, and left the house unseen, by a side-door.

"I will walk to the cross-roads," I reflected, "and wait his coming; he would never take the short cut over the mine-land to-night."

What was it that yet made me long to turn back every step I took forward? What was it that made me *not* turn back, but go on? I have since given those two sensations names—those of Susie and Florence. Florence, here as everywhere then, was the strongest, and I proceeded.

On reaching the cross-roads, I halted. It was a rather elevated spot, and on one side I could see the road that led dipping down to Ivy Lodge. My eyes naturally fixed themselves in that direction, and, consequently, could not fail to perceive a horseman who, at a smart pace, proceeded along it. I recognised him as Colonel Harrison, a devoted admirer of Florence Bradlaw, to whose presence I knew he was bound.

He was handsome in appearance, and the rival from whom

I felt I had most to fear. Clenching my teeth, I struck my foot fiercely in the snow, as I cursed my dependence on another. I cursed, and mentally vowed to free myself from the bondage.

"And be a beggar," whispered an inner voice; "destroying all chance of the future!"

"But, Florence Bradlaw!" added the other. "Ah! if only you were the master of Orton, these troubles would cease; the happiness you crave would be yours for the asking. You might laugh at rivals—even at handsome Colonel Harrison."

Similar ideas were yet haunting me, when a sharp, loud, sudden cry of pain caught my ear. It came from the direction of the mine-land.

Starting, I looked towards it; the cry was distant, and a clump of trees between me and the mines hid my view. Should I go? Yes.

The power which had previously dominated over my actions, urged me now: and, leaping the hedge, noiselessly across the snow, and in the shadow through the trees, I advanced.

Emerging from the latter on to a clear, open space, I beheld before me a man resting on the ground, his back towards me. It was Squire Orton. He had taken the short cut, and, slipping, had evidently come violently down, for he held his knee, and groaned, in pain.

My first impulse was to spring to his aid. The second made me hesitate; a strong hand appeared to draw me back, while the evil counsellor again whispered, "You master of the Hall, and this hand shall be yours."

I stooped. How was it that that huge, jagged stone came so readily into my hand? Others must answer; I know not. It was there; and creeping forward, with all my force I hurled it down on the head of the writhing man, my uncle.

A frightful yell of agony, that froze my blood, escaped his lips. He first bowed his stricken head to the snow; then, by an effort, turned and faced me. Oh, mercy! the horror of that glance.

For a second we gazed at each other—the murdered man and I. In that instant, he had read my every thought. I stood convicted, trembling, helpless before him, till, with a strange, almost exultant cry, leaping up, he caught me round the throat with his long arms, and bent his aged, wrinkled face to mine.

For a moment, I was paralyzed; the thin features, full of fierce vindictiveness, chilled me. The lips moved, but ages seemed to roll over my brain before they spoke. At last the words came gasping forth, "Murderer! Your hands are red with my blood! I guess the reason. The Hall—the money—are yours, and Florence Bradlaw. But my retribution shall be terrible. I curse you; and my curse shall render every moment of your evil life a torture. Never will I be absent from you; as your shadow, shall you ever find me by your side. Sleeping, waking, day as night, the murderer and his victim shall be together. One—one other only shall see me besides yourself; and she—she——"

The voice failed; the jaw dropped; the dews of death stood on the forehead; the rigidly clasped arms weighed me down. It was no longer a man, but a corpse, that clung to me. Terror—abhorrence aroused me to exertion. Making a violent effort, I flung it off: with a heavy, sickening thud, it fell to a heap upon the ground, and I hastened to quit the fearful spot.

But not three steps had I gone, before that strong instinct, inherent in man, self-safety came over me, and I reflected. I must conceal the body.

I looked anxiously round. The locality was familiar to me; and I knew, within fifty paces, was the Fellbrig Pit—one that had been exhausted and disused years ago, its black interior being surrendered to fire-damp and other nauseous, poisonous gases.

What better hiding-place than that?

To approach the body now was necessity; my life, my hope to escape a disgraceful death, depended on it; and giddy, sick with fear, I advanced. The blow had produced blood, and the murdered man lying on his face, it had oozed forth, meandering down the white hair to the whiter snow. With a shivering fright, I glanced at my dress and hands. Had they any condemnatory marks of my crime upon them? No. How my heavily-beating heart rejoiced!

Raising the body, already stiffening, and avoiding any possible contact with the crimson stream, I stamped out its traces on the snow into the earth, then, with my burden, strode rapidly to the pit's mouth. I had no fear of being seen; the place was deserted, and the night dark—so dark that as I drew near, I had to go cautiously, lest, by a false stop, I might find myself over the brink of the yawning chasm, that, laying unprotected, seemed waiting expressly to engulf the unwary traveller.

I found it at last, and kneeling by the edge, placed the body on the ground, then—*rolled it over!*

Oh, heaven! the horror of that moment—the maddening agony with which each dull reverberating thud beat upon my frenzied brain! I could have sworn, too, that a shriek arose from those awful depths.

After a space, when all was still, an impulse urged me to look over. Lying flat, clutching convulsively at the sides, I did so. All was black, impenetrable; till, from the darkness, hundreds of eyes appeared to rise and glare at me; while in the midst was Squire Orton's white face, with a jeering smile upon it.

Shaking in every limb, I crept away; then falling on my knees, covered my face with my hands, and wept, as men in direst agony alone can weep.

Merciful heaven, what would I not have given to have recalled that deed? Impossible! What was done, could never be undone; and finally, dreading to glance right or left, I fled.

Reaching the Hall, I found the entrance by which I had left it still unfastened, and, unseen, regained my own room, locking the door. I lighted the lamp, then replaced my wet clothes by dressing gown and slippers, for I feared showing anything peculiar in my appearance to create suspicion.

Scarcely had I done so, than a footman knocked to know if I would not descend to supper. I excused myself, saying I was busy, and would take supper in my own apartment.

Then I forced my shaking lips to ask if my uncle had returned.

"No," was the reply. "Miss Mayfield thought it very singular, and felt uneasy, but supposed he must have stopped at Otterlee, divining the heavy rain which had come on."

I acquiesced in this readily, for he had done so on past occasions. I even found courage—if that can be termed courage which is the creation of excessive fear—to see and comfort Susie, advising her not to sit up, but leaving the footman to do so, in case Squire Orton returned (how devotedly I wished he could!), retire to rest, saying I felt certain he had stayed at Otterlee.

When I went back to my own room, putting out the lamp, I flung myself on the bed, to bear my agony alone.

Scarcely had I done so, than I leaped up again—every separate root of hair thrilled with alarm—for there, seated in the arm-chair I had just left, was Squire Orton. His face was as it had been in life, only the ghastly wound was visible among the matted gray hair. I tried to think it a delusion of an over-taxed brain. I rubbed my eyes, shut them, opened them; there still the figure sat, placidly gazing at the fire. It was so very still, that it drove me to madness. If it had moved, I could have better borne it. At last, mustering sufficient nerve, I crept from the bed, the farthest side from the figure, and, not looking at it, but stealing round, quickly raked out the fire.

When all was darkness, I turned, to find my position worse. The spirit was still there, but the life-glow of the blazing coals gone; it was now of a cold, grayish transparency. The look it turned upon me showed the fruitlessless of my efforts. With his dying breath he had sworn to haunt me like my shadow, and he was keeping his word.

I stole to bed, and turning my back, covered my eyes with the clothes. It was no good—it was unbearable. The *knowing* it was there was worse than seeing it.

How the next hour passed it would be difficult to describe. A hundred deaths were preferable to the agony I endured. It seemed a lifetime. I knew by the clock that it was but an hour.

As the last beat reverberated through the silent house—twelve—my ghostly visitant rose. My eyes were fixed on him. Anxiously I watched his movements. Gliding to the window, for the first time, he turned and gazed at me; the cruel, vindic-tive smile still distorted its features. Then, floating through the window, he was gone. Thank heaven! But where?

Leaping to the floor, darting across the room, I drew aside the curtain, and looked forth; then, with a cry, recoiled. The night was twilight. Despite the rain, the moon at its greatest power gave to the darkness a dim twilight. Thus I could see the mine-land, which was visible from the Hall, and Fellbrig Pit. It was the latter which caused my terror; for over it, illumined by a halo of bright floating vapour, was Squire Orton's ghost.

I had believed the place where his body had been hid could not be found. He had resolved otherwise.

"My crime *must* come to light," I thought. "He wills it so. His retribution has risen from the grave."

Already I felt the hangman's hands upon me, and worn out by terror and weariness, I fell insensible on the bed.

With morning, rest and daylight brought renewed strength and courage. The vindictiveness of the spirit began to create an antagonistic feeling in myself, while came the assurance that even if the body were found, it would be utterly impossible to bring the crime home to me. Consoled by that, I resolved to play my part in the world as usual, and by a superhuman effort, keep my torturing misery to myself.

The non-return of the Squire next day caused first surprise, then alarm, and it was my suggestion—*mine*—that a groom should ride over to Otterlee, and make inquiries. I knew before he started the message he would bring back—that the Squire had set out to return home at about eight the previous evening. But he brought this additional information, which filled my guilty soul with an exquisite joy. Squire Orton had drank rather too freely, and his friends had tried to persuade him to remain at Otterlee all night, fearing any accident happening him.

This news necessitated a careful search, which gave me an excuse for not visiting Florence Bradlaw. My whole being shrunk from doing so. Not only was she fearfully blended with the crime I had committed, but the murdered man had declared another— a woman—also should see his spirit as I. I believed he meant Florence, and thus avoided her; for my punishment was ever beside me—sitting, walking, sleeping, regulating each silent step and movement by mine, save at midnight, when, for a certain period, it hovered over the gloomy mouth of Fellbrig Pit.

The roads—the fields—the mine-land—were traversed; rewards for any intelligence offered. Need I say in vain? The rain had removed every mark of the dead man's footsteps, by which otherwise he might have been traced; and the whole affair was enveloped in mystery—save to me. The hope of finding him was given up, the surmise being that he had *fallen* into one of the disused shafts. He did not appear, and I was master of Orton Hall.

Even yet I had not seen Florence Bradlaw—I had not the courage. The fact that she was the real cause of the murder clung about my soul; while the constant, horrible presence of the murdered man at my elbow dominated over all other sensations, even my love. It needed the fatal witchery of her eyes to again set it aflame.

I remained much within doors, consoling Susie Mayfield, whose grief for the loss of a protector who had ever been kind to her was great. How my heart sickened and rebelled against the false words I forced myself to utter! How I would, if possible, have shunned her pure presence; but in her sorrow she seemed to lean more upon me, and I feared by any change of manner to arouse suspicion. Crime truly makes cowards of the bravest.

It was some short while after the murder, that, as I was strolling moodily through the lanes, a light step sounded on the frozen ground, and a hand was laid on my arm, as a musical voice, in low accents, said, "Good morning, Sydney; why have I not seen you before? Did you think that *I* had no sympathy to give in your trouble? It is scarcely kind to treat me thus!"

Instinctively I shrunk away from the speaker, I had begun so to fear her. It was Florence Bradlaw. Recovering myself, however, I raised my eyes, and, like one under the influence of the basilisk, fell again her victim. Those beautiful features had always a singular power over me; now, as they smiled as they had never smiled before, I—thrilled with a sudden ecstacy—yielded once more a willing slave. I asked to join her in her walk—I saw her home. I then returned to the Hall, its master, and Florence Bradlaw's future husband.

As I entered, a footman met me. His face was white and scared.

"Oh, Mr. Orton, have you heard the news?" he exclaimed.

"News! What news?" I demanded, irritably.

"That every night the poor Squire's ghost is to be seen floatin' over the mouth of Fellbrig Pit."

The start I gave—the sudden lots of colour—the man conceived but natural to one hearing such intelligence. Also, in his eyes, it accounted for my husky voice, when I asked who had said so.

It appeared that a miner, by chance late abroad, had seen the figure; and flying in mortal terror, spread the news. The next night, several agreed to watch. They, too, saw it; and the rumour getting over the country—the many giving courage to the few— every night the vicinity of the pit's mouth was thronged.

"Pshaw!" I managed to exclaim, contemptuously, though my eyes turned timidly to the figure ever by my side. "What country clods, to believe such absurdities!"

In the dining-room I found Susie. She was seated, sewing busily; but looked up on hearing my step. I expected, as usual, to meet her ever welcome smile; but this time, in its place, an expression of unspeakable horror and alarm spread over her features. Trembling violently, she arose and retreated from me; her lips pallid, her soft eyes dilated, her finger extended, as she exclaimed, "Merciful heaven, Sydney, look there!—there, beside you! Who is he? What—what does he want?"

"He! What, Susie?" I articulated, hoarsely. "Girl, are you mad? What do you mean?"

"He standing by you, Sydney, his hand on your shoulder, is Squire Orton, risen from the dead!"

I opened my lips to deny it; I could not—my tongue was paralyzed. She, Susie, then, was the other to whom my uncle was to make himself visible. I felt the guilty, accusing blood rush to my face. My eyes dropped before the clear, inquiring ones of my gentle companion. I stood a criminal confessed. My crime was discovered, and *to her.* I had no power to refute it.

Swiftly Susie moved forward, caught my hand, and gasped, "Sydney!"

It was a simple word, but the tone in which it was uttered was all eloquent of horror, of interrogation. I made an effort; I lifted my eyes; but rapidly averting them, covered my quivering face from sight.

"Oh, my God!" I heard her ejaculate, as she fell prostrate on the floor.

In an instant I was kneeling by her.

"This—this," I cried, enraged, addressing the spirit, "is *your* work, and you said you loved her!"

It smiled, and fixed its eyes tauntingly upon me. I turned away, and, summoning aid, had Susie conveyed to her room. No sooner had I done so, than an awful fear took possession of me. Supposing, in the moment of recovery, words should escape her lips which would proclaim my guilt to others? The idea had come too late. I could not prevent it now. What did it matter? I began to feel the end must come; what difference, then, if soon or late?

In a dull, lethargic stupor, I waited news of Susie. Each step approaching shook me like a reed.

At last, the door opened, and Susie's own maid entered. As indifferently as I could, I took the note the girl brought, and, dismissing her, eagerly tore off the envelope. The contents ran:—

"Sydney Orton, your secret is safe with me. Heaven forgive you! I hope—I *believe* you must have had some great cause for what you have done; or, rather, that it was occasioned by maddened anger, or accident, for which repentance may atone; but we two must never meet again. By *his* desire, expressed in his will, the Hall is to be my home till I marry. I would fulfil this desire. Heaven knows, I would not fail to do so *now* for worlds! Hence, as no longer I can mix with the household, may I ask permission to keep my present suite of rooms? Illness will be a real excuse, for the blow I have received I shall never recover. Farewell!"

I seized a pen, and, with dim eyes and grateful heart, wrote:—

"Heaven bless you, Susie Mayfield! Each wish of yours shall be complied with. Bless you a thousand times for not quitting this ill-fated house, which your sweet presence alone can purify. Pray for me—save me! One day you shall know all."

After this, I was conscious of a great relief, but also an equally great misery. The Hall was no longer the Hall with Susie away. The report of my possible marriage had got whispered about, and many attributed her seclusion to the fact that she loved me, and her indisposition and retirement were occasioned by the thought of my union with another.

As to that union, I no longer desired it. It tortured me; I seemed to recoil from Florence's brilliant talk and careless laughter. The selfishness of her disposition, which could not sympathize with mine, I began at last to comprehend; and instead, I craved, like a starving man, for Susie's sweet, consoling presence.

But I had gone too far to draw back. I was Squire Orton now; and Florence, as her father, urged on the wedding; so, after a quiet marriage and brief honeymoon, I brought home my bride to the Hall.

Susie, to avoid remarks, occasionally consented to join us in the drawing-room; but the exceeding pallor of her complexion, her wasted features, and depressed manner, were fitting causes for her seclusion. I felt I had murdered her also.

Never once had we two met alone. One day I had encountered her in the corridor, but, with a low, affrighted cry, she had fled from me.

Her aversion, coupled with the ever constant presence of my dead victim, could not fail soon to break down my constitution, and affect my disposition. I grow gloomy—morose.

I had first tried what constant change of society and excitement would do, thereby delighting Florence; but it would not answer—it only made the nights worse, and I adopted seclusion. My wife complained, persuaded, was angry. Each was equally futile. That haunting figure, the remembrance of Susie, and the eager longing for her presence, had made my wife's influence naught. "The longing for her presence?" Yes, too late, I found I loved Susie, with that deep, calm love which never dies.

Florence did not guess *my* secret, but she knew my affection had gone from her; *hers* I had never possessed. She had wished to be mistress of Orton Hall, and she was finding the fruit so coveted, bitter—bitter at the core.

Suddenly a change took place in her—she no longer pleaded nor complained. The expression of her handsome face was stony impassibility. She regarded me curiously, sometimes timidly, and rather avoided my company. I readily fell into her humour, for it suited me.

One morning, on awakening, I found her absent from my side. I looked round, no one was there except my awful attendant.

Since my crime, when sleep, long courted, once quitted me, it never again returned till night; so, rising, I dressed quietly. My wife did not appear, and, gently, I opened the door of her dressing-room. She was there, attired in her customary morning toilette, and writing hurriedly. On becoming aware of my presence, hurriedly she slipped the paper beneath some others, and coldly asked what I wanted.

"Merely to see where you were," I rejoined, turning away.

Shortly after, I heard her bell ring for her maid. Then, in a few moments, the quick beat of a horse's hoofs on the gravel drive attracted me to the window. It was a groom riding from the hall at full speed.

The indifference between Florence and me had reached such a height, that one never interfered in the other's concerns; so I went back to my reading till the hour for breakfast, during which Florence was unusually silent, and I could not fail to perceive was nervously anxious about something; but, occupied with the morning papers, I paid little heed to her.

The meal had nearly concluded, when the footman brought in a card. At the same moment the footman ushered in a Mr. Midhurst—a county magistrate—and two men. Before we could exchange the ordinary salutations, Florence approaching between us, said, in a quick, hurried tone, "Mr. Midhurst, I wrote you this morning that it was in my power to surrender to justice a criminal now at large. I do so. I order—I command the arrest of that man, my husband, for the murder of Squire Orton, whose body you will find in Fellbrig Pit."

I had leaped to my feet, and now stood confounded—aghast.

"Madam!" I cried; "are you aware of what you state?"

"Perfectly, sir!" she answered, frigidly. "What, waking, you deny; sleeping, you have confessed. Night after night," she proceeded, in a kind of triumph, "I have listened, trembling, to the wild sentences uttered in slumber. I have watched the nightmares which have tortured you, till the whole occurrence has been confided to my ear. Yes, the meeting—the cruel blow—the concealment of the body—the ever-haunting presence—*everything*. Murderers, sir, should not marry! Mr. Midhurst, I swear to you, yonder is Squire Orton's assassin! You know whether to arrest him or not."

There must have been that in my quivering face which confirmed her words, for the magistrate, making a sign to the constables, they approached me. I retreated, casting my eyes round for a means of escape. None offered; the windows were locked. So, seizing a chair, I resolved they should not take me easily.

The men had recoiled a step before my threatening attitude, when, abruptly, the door was thrown open, and, as white as death—her lips hueless, her large eyes bright and glistening— Susie Mayfield glided in. Passing by them all, advancing, she threw her arms about me.

"Back!" she then exclaimed, authoritatively, addressing the men. "That woman lies! Sydney Orton is innocent of this deed, and you shall not harm him. If yonder faithless wife denounces him, I say he is guiltless. My word is equal to hers. You have no proofs—none. You shall not take him."

Florence laughed mockingly.

"Certainly it is right that *you* should be his shield and champion, Miss Mayfield," she said—"the assassin of your best friend. Mr. Midhurst, I have done *my* duty; do yours, as you please or not."

"Mr. Orton," remarked the magistrate, gravely, "I am deeply sorry for this; but after the accusation has been made in *such* a manner, I cannot pass it over. Men, arrest Mr. Sydney Orton."

As they drew near, Susie's arms tightened about me. Her sweet, scared face was raised to mine; her eyes beamed affection as alarm; while her trembling lips sought vainly to be firm, as she whispered, assuringly, "Do not fear, Sydney; they *dare* not hurt you. I alone know the truth, and they shall kill me before I confess it—they shall, they shall!"

But at the touch of the constables' hands, her courage gave way, and, shrieking, she resisted their efforts to remove her. I imagined they were handling her roughly, and my love took fire, to the forgetting of my own safety; and, like a tiger, I flew upon them. A scuffle ensued; but I was weak in their grasp. They flung me down. My chest heaved with painful gasps. A moment, I lost consciousness. Then the scene had changed. Feeble, languid, I was lying on a sofa, my coat off, a tight bandage about my arm, the lassitude of illness upon me; and, wearily, I raised my heavy lids.

I was yet at the Hall; and on the hearth-rug, by the fire, stood Susie, talking earnestly with my ghostly companion, whose shape was far more solid and defined, while his expression was irritable rather than angry.

"Dear guardian," Susie was saying—she always called him thus—"I beseech you yield to his desire. The trouble, the disappointment may kill him. Oh, consent to his marrying her! She is handsome——"

"Handsome, Susie!" interrupted the spirit, sharply. "Yes, so are you. But you are the good, the kindest, the best; while she is a heartless flirt, I tell you, whose brainless head is full of only her splendid self. She would but marry yonder foolish lad to be mistress of this old place; and I will not, by yielding, have *him* ruined and my money squandered. He is not the first this girl has wilfully driven to despair. She wouldn't look at him if he were penniless; and I took care to let old Bradlaw know to-day that he will never be otherwise, unless I approve his selection of a wife."

"But, guardian, if he love her?" pleaded Susie.

"He does *not* love her; he is only fascinated as a child might be with the brilliant hues of a snake."

"Oh, guardian! Yet, think; she may be all you say; yet the heart is powerful. Love may change her; she may be different to poor Sydney."

"Susie, you are a darling, brave, noble, generous girl, thus to plead this coquette's cause," said the spirit, taking his *protégée's* face fondly between his hands, and gazing into the brown eyes. "Noble, indeed, when you are aware that you yourself have given your heart and warm affection to my worthless nephew!"

Susie uttered a little cry, and quickly covered her crimson face with her fingers; then, pleadingly looking up, she said, "Dear guardian, who have been to me as a father, why should I conceal the truth from you? But, oh! please, never—never tell him."

"My child, if he has not the eyes to discover the rich gem he might call his, do not think I would debase you by informing the idiot of his blunder. No, let him take his course; I shall take mine. There, do not fret; all danger is passed now; he'll soon be better, since Doctor Gruge has bled him. It was merely a fit."

As he ended, he left the apartment.

Left it, and *my side also*. What! was he not a spirit, after all? Doctor Gruge, and bleeding! Had I been ill? I directed my eyes to my arm; it was bandaged. Had all which had passed been a dream—the visions of delirium? It must be so; in which case, Squire Orton was alive, I was *not* a murderer, neither was I married to Florence Bradlaw.

The inexpressible delight I experienced at these facts was too much for me, and I fainted. When I came to, the lamp had been lowered. Through the withdrawn window curtains, I saw the moonbeams without glittered on vast tracks of snow, while the rich fire-light illumined the apartment within, its red mellow tint throwing out in clear relief Susie's graceful figure as she sat pondering over it. Her face was sad, and I was sure she was weeping. How beautiful, how good she looked! Uncle Orton had said correctly. If with my own eyes I could not discover the priceless gem which might be mine, I deserved none to point it out to my dull brain.

Yes, the delirium had passed, leaving me a wiser man. Of all that had occurred, two events alone were real. First, that Florence Bradlaw had refused me, *because* I was not master of the Hall. Secondly, that Susie Mayfield loved me with her entire heart.

"Dear Susie!" I murmured.

In an instant, a bright smile on her lip, thinking I needed aid, she was by my side. Somehow, I got her hand in mine, and would not let it go. Her bent, averted face showed my touch had at once told my meaning; nevertheless, my lips speedily removed all doubt.

Half an hour after, the entrance of Squire Orton startled Susie away from the sofa. The expression of his features was singular; they displayed satisfaction, blended with a dash of pity. Heightening the lamp, after congratulating me on my recovery, he said, not looking at me, "I have some startling news; I wonder if you can bear it, Syd?"

"Indeed! What is it, uncle?" I asked.

He glanced keenly at me, then added, "Miss Florence Bradlaw eloped this evening with Colonel Harrison."

"Really!" I rejoined, so quietly that it was he who started, not I. "May she be happy."

My wish was not realized, as a case two years later, in the Divorce Court, proved.

Squire Orton regarded me in amaze, which yet further increased, as I added, "Uncle, I am resolved to get married; I trust you will approve of the wife I have selected. Susie, my darling, come to me."

The Squire looked from my extended palm to Susie's blushing cheeks; then striding forward, and clasping my hand as he never yet had clasped it, he exclaimed, "Heaven bless the boy, he has come to his senses at last! Syd, that fit we found you in, lying before a perfectly roasting fire, has saved your life. This shall be a happy Christmas to all of us, my dear, dear lad!"

Need I say it was so? We three saw it in, seated about the glowing logs, my arm around Susie's waist, and listening to the merrily clashing bells, bearing tidings of joy to all hearts, as I told my listeners the story of Squire Orton's Ghost.